MORE TO THIS LIFE

This novel is inspired by true events and real people. While certain names, characters, places, and incidents are products of the author's imagination or have been adapted for dramatic purposes, the story draws from historical record and the enduring legacy of those who served.

More to This Life: The Story of the Boys Across the Pond
Published by Making My Marks Press
makingmymarks.com

Paperback: 979-8-9934630-0-1
Hardcover: 979-8-9934630-2-5
Ebook: 979-8-9934630-1-8

Cover design by Damonza
Author photo by P. J. Marks
Printed in the United States of America
1 2 3 4 5 6 7 8 9 10 25

For the boys across the pond—

And those who helped me find them.

MORE TO THIS LIFE

P. J. MARKS

PROLOGUE

June, 1945
Dolgellau, Wales

THE SHEEP'S BLEATING echoed across the Welsh mountainside as twenty-one-year-old Robert Lloyd checked on his flock while searching for a bull that had gone missing. Then came the drone of aircraft engines, distant at first, but growing thunderously close and low. Nothing like the routine flights to and from Anglesey. Beyond the cloud-filled sky, the engines roared, seizing his attention and paralyzing him with a sense of foreboding.

Robert knew the plane couldn't possibly avoid the looming mountains, but the horror of what followed was no less gut-wrenching. The hulking bomber broke through the fog, hurtling toward the summit as if it might clear the mountain by sheer will alone. Robert's pulse pounded as he watched the plane's desperate climb. It wasn't far—close enough for him to see the glint of cockpit windows, close enough to feel the ground tremble beneath his feet when it struck.

The impact was explosive, tearing through the mountainside near the Mawddach Estuary. The aircraft skidded three hundred feet before its catastrophic demise. Fire engulfed the wreckage, spilling down the slopes in molten streams. The sheep scattered in terror, their bleating lost to the chaos.

Robert's legs felt like lead, but he scrambled up the mountain, unsure of what he hoped to find—perhaps a survivor or some way to help. His eyes stung and teared as the sharp tang of burning fuel filled his lungs, and the futility of it all gripped him. He wasn't a rescuer or a soldier, just a shepherd powerless to offer aid other than summoning help. The plane was twisted and blackened, and there was nothing—no one—left to save.

Hours passed in a haze as Robert struggled to process the enormity of what had happened. When the Americans finally arrived, their grim efficiency as they retrieved the uniformed bodies brought a strange sense of order to the chaos.

The policemen on the scene urged him to leave the area, telling him there was nothing to see, but he couldn't bring himself to wander very far. The bodies were covered, though the row of boots lined up on the wing would forever linger in his mind, a stark reminder of the lives lost. Gaily wrapped packages lay scattered and torn on the periphery, remnants of happily anticipated reunions in the States that would never happen.

Army personnel took on the grisly task of transporting the bodies back to Polebrook Air Base. Several days later, they carried out the burial of the twenty men in Cambridge Cemetery in England, a bleak conclusion to what should have been a joyful trip homeward.

Over time, Robert often found himself wondering about the soldiers' identities. The European war had just ended, and their families must have been waiting for them, relieved that they had lived through the worst. It felt unbearably cruel to have survived the war, only to perish on the journey home.

Who were these men, and what hopes and dreams had they carried with them, only to be snuffed out on the mountainside?

CHAPTER ONE

June 14, 1944
Polebrook Air Force Base, England

SANTO CARUSO CROUCHED in the belly of the plane, his twenty-year-old frame wedged between two .50-caliber machine guns. Cold metal pressed against his skin—a reminder of their deadly purpose and his own fragility. The engines roared, yet his worries whispered louder: would he ever see his family again? He could still remember his mother at the train station, waving goodbye, her smile faltering just before he turned away.

Joining the US Army Air Forces had charted this course, a choice born of duty and a chance for independence, though he couldn't have fully grasped where it would lead. But now, wedged between steel and sky, the weight of it bore down on him, and he wondered if the cost of that choice would be his life. After over a year of training, here he was, a ball turret gunner in the 351st Bomb Group. His job had an impressive title, but he was just a gunner like the rest of them, stationed in the most cramped and life-threatening seat on the B-17, in a glass dome mounted beneath the belly of the plane.

Even at only five foot six, Caruso had to fold himself like a pretzel into the fishbowl that was his station, looking out from underneath the bomber, protecting the entire underside of the aircraft. Despite the fetal position, his was no child's job. And it wasn't for the claustrophobic.

Their first bombing mission was to Le Bourget Airfield, near Paris. The enemy was bound to be out in droves, defending the capital. Sweat pooled inside Caruso's flight gloves, turning his grip on the machine guns slippery and uncertain. Every heartbeat thudded in his ears, each bead of perspiration evidencing the terror he felt but couldn't voice. A fleeting warmth penetrated the cold of the turret as his fingers traced the outline of the small crucifix in his chest pocket. His mom had given it to him right after Pop passed away, confiding that it had been his father's shield against tough times. As Caruso braced himself behind the guns, the memory of his father's unshakable faith stood in sharp contrast to the tremor in his own hands.

As they entered France, black puffs of smoke surrounded them, signifying anti-aircraft fire. Caruso's gunnery instructor's warning echoed in his mind: *Always be on the lookout for flak. Those little black smudges look harmless, but they explode at altitude, sending jagged metal shards through anything—or anyone—nearby. Don't underestimate them!*

He hadn't fully understood the warning until he'd seen the consequences up close shortly after arriving at their base in Polebrook, England. A B-17, riddled with holes, its insides torn apart as if a bomb had exploded, had limped back from a mission. Planes with injured always landed first. Medics had scrambled aboard as a disheveled airman stumbled off, his face pale, eyes hollow.

"What happened?" Caruso had asked in a hushed voice.

The gunner's reply was clipped. "Flak." Tears rolled down his cheeks as he muffled his words. "We lost our radio operator." Hesitating before pulling back the sheet as the body passed by, he gently touched the deceased airman's shoulder before the medics carried him away. Caruso's mouth had fallen open as the deadliness of the air barrage struck him with full force. The top of the crewman's head was completely gone, cruelly underscoring the brutality of war.

That moment had stripped away any illusions Caruso might have had. He now understood the grim reality: he and his comrades were merely replacements for another crew that hadn't made it back. Their only consolation was the hope that their disciplined training would keep them safe. Still, he wasn't alone in relying on more than military indoctrination; nearly every airman, no matter his religious beliefs, clung to prayers and talismans, like the crucifix in his chest pocket, hoping somehow to secure his safe return.

The aircraft shuddered violently, jerking Caruso back to the present. Each jolt squeezed his chest tighter until the reality of his situation crashed over him: he might not make it home. The thought of never seeing his family again, never feeling his mother's embrace or seeing his little sister's impish grin, pierced him more sharply than the bitter cold.

His eyes were drawn to one of the B-17s just ahead as it burst into pieces without warning, disintegrating into smoke and debris, leaving a haunting void where it had been flying just a minute before. Caruso stared, dumbfounded, searching for the little black dots signifying men bailing from the plane in parachutes.

Not a single one.

Sweat trickled beneath his flight suit, even though they were flying at a frigid minus fifty degrees. Death was all around them. It was only a matter of time.

He swiveled the turret, locking onto enemy aircraft diving close—close enough to see the gunners' faces. His heart pounded as he pulled the trigger, ears ringing from the gunfire, the bitter sting of gunpowder filling his nose. Bile rose in his throat as he realized the stakes. Each shot could mean life or death—his or theirs.

They continued toward the target when Stanowick's stammering voice broke through the intercom. "Tail gunner to pilot. One of our planes at our six is hit—they… they're going down!"

Panic swept through Caruso; his hands shook, mouth dry as dust. How long before they would get hit, too? Would he lose consciousness immediately if the turret were struck? With no room in his cramped station, his parachute lay in the fuselage, out of easy reach. Would he have time to put it on?

His tangled thoughts were abruptly cut short as the target loomed ahead. The enormity of their mission slammed into him, and Caruso felt as if he were teetering on the edge of a precipice.

The intercom crackled. "Radio operator to bombardier. Bomb bay doors open." The announcement signaled the time for the bombardier to release the bomb load.

"Bombardier to pilot. I can't get the bombs to drop!" Lieutenant Stevens' voice broke through, taut with frustration.

"What's the problem?" Lieutenant Johnston snapped.

"Bomb bay mechanism's jammed solid, sir. Nothing's working!" A tense silence fell momentarily as he continued to wrestle with the controls, the weight of their failed mission hanging heavy in the cabin, unspoken but undeniable.

"Just close the doors," the pilot said finally, his voice tight. The upper echelon would surely frown upon returning to base with a full bomb load. Someone was bound to be raked over the coals for that one.

The strained mood from the failed bomb drop was interrupted when the plane lurched, and Stanowick's anxious voice crackled over the intercom. "Tail gunner hit!"

Caruso's pulse kicked hard as he wiped his dripping forehead, desperately scanning the skies from his cramped vantage point. Their first mission, and they'd already been struck?

Almost immediately, Stanowick's voice returned, this time tinged with relief. "I'm okay, false alarm. Some flak smashed through my window, but it didn't hit me."

The near miss shook Caruso as if it were his own. He wiped his goggles, smeared with sweat, taking deep breaths to steady his racing heart.

As they veered away from the target, the sky erupted in an explosion that swallowed the B-17 ahead in an instant. Caruso froze, his throat tightening. One moment, the plane had been there—a steady companion in the formation—and the next, it was gone, leaving nothing but fire and debris. No parachutes in sight. He realized bleakly that the parachutes they'd packed were perhaps more to give them a sense of security than for actual use.

What have I gotten myself into? Caruso's fingers found Pop's crucifix in his chest pocket. The 23rd psalm came to his lips—words the priest had made them memorize all those years ago. But never had he prayed with such desperation.

It wasn't until they landed that the iron clutch of fear began to loosen its hold on Caruso's insides, his stomach slowly unclenching from the knot it had been in. His breath escaped in a shaky exhale, one he hadn't realized he'd been holding all this time. Their bird had a broken window and numerous holes in its skin.

They stumbled toward the waiting truck on legs like jelly. The ground felt unnervingly solid and quiet after the continual vibration and noise of the flight.

With each step away from the bomber, Caruso tried to shed the tension that clung to him. But his racing heart followed him like a shadow, a reminder that he had survived when others had not.

Stanowick shattered the heavy silence. "Well… that was a heck of an initiation to the war." Murmurs of agreement rippled through the crew, each man lost in his own reflections. "Wonder what the odds are that we'll make it back home in one piece?"

"I'd rather not consider the odds," Caruso said, forcing a half smile that barely masked the worry on his face. "Let's just concentrate on getting through one sortie at a time."

One down and twenty-nine to go. Each mission felt like they were gambling with death. But he wouldn't voice that—not now. Not when everyone else was already walking on the edge of their nerves.

At the debrief, they were interviewed by Sergeant Teed Smith, whose serious demeanor seemed out of place in their momentary reprieve. The rapid-fire urgency of his interrogation poked sharply at Caruso's weary mind.

"Where did you see anti-aircraft fire? What was the intensity? Did you spot any enemy interceptors? Did you shoot down any enemy planes?"

Caruso blinked at the last question, momentarily stunned. *Shoot down enemy planes?* He'd spent the entire mission praying their own wouldn't fall out of the sky. That kind of precision belonged to gunners who weren't too busy just trying to survive.

Smith didn't wait for an answer before moving on. "Did any of our bombers go down? How many chutes did you see?"

Caruso struggled to focus. At the time, he'd been sure every detail was burned into his mind. Now it was all a blur.

He rubbed the back of his neck with a heavy sigh, feeling the tension in his muscles. "I did see one B-17 explode before us…" His voice faltered, the specifics eluding his grasp. He squeezed his eyes shut, trying to summon the memory. "… and I didn't see any parachutes. Sorry, Sergeant, it's hard to keep it all straight… everything was happening so fast."

Sergeant Smith's gaze softened slightly. "I understand, but every detail you give us can save lives next time. We need to know everything you can remember."

Nodding, Caruso promised to do better next time. The gravity of his role settled heavily into his chest. Inwardly, although he recognized the need for them to collect relevant information, he wondered how he could take note of all the details when his energy and focus were consumed with protecting the aircraft—and just staying alive.

The contrast hit him like a punch: the harrowing chaos of the mission versus the comfort of being home with his mom, stepdad, and sister. Even with the changes at home since Pop died, he longed to sink into their safe, familiar arms. How foolish he'd been to think that joining the military was his ticket to independence, to adulthood. Instead, it had thrust him into a world where survival was anything but certain.

It would take more than luck to come back in one piece.

After the debrief, they were each offered a shot of whiskey, its fiery burn a fleeting distraction from the numbness settling over them. Caruso had never been much of a drinker, but he took his without hesitation.

CHAPTER TWO

June 18, 1944

IT WAS ONE a.m. when Caruso and his crew heard their names called out, alerting them they were flying that day.

Kellogg, the left waist gunner, groaned, pulling his pillow over his head, but Stanowick yanked it away with a grin. "It's our third mission! After today, it'll be three down, twenty-seven to go!" He sounded more like someone with three to go instead of twenty-seven.

As they plodded toward the latrine, Caruso tried to sound casual. "Any guesses where they'll send us today?"

"Who cares?" Kellogg rubbed sleep from his eyes. "Let's just hope it's fast and easy."

Stanowick clapped them both on the back. "Hey, as long as we're together, right?"

Their laughter was brittle, tinged with the unspoken acknowledgment of the risks ahead.

"Come on, slowpoke! It's not a date! Hurry up! We're hungry!" Stanowick was standing by the latrine's exit, waving his arms.

Knowing a close shave ensured a tight mask fit, Caruso gave his face a quick once-over before rushing after the others.

At the chow hall, the crewmen loaded their trays with eggs, bacon, and hotcakes. Caruso stared at his breakfast, but his appetite was gone. He could barely bring himself to pick up his fork.

Across the table, a veteran airman eyed him with amusement, his own plate nearly empty. "First mission?" he asked, crunching into a strip of bacon.

"Third." Caruso picked at his toast, rolling a corner between his fingers.

"Still not eating?" The airman smirked, shaking his head. "Better force some down. You'll need it later."

Caruso's stomach twisted. "I'm fine."

The veteran shrugged, pushing his empty tray aside. "Suit yourself." He took a slow sip of coffee, then leaned forward, his voice dropping. "Just don't toss your cookies in your mask. Ain't no worse way to go than drowning in your own breakfast."

Caruso's hands stiffened around his coffee cup. He forced a swallow, the bitterness sharp against his tongue.

The veteran grinned, grabbing his cap. "Good luck, kid." He clapped Caruso on the shoulder, then strode toward the exit.

Caruso glanced down at his trembling hands and shoved them under the table. His eggs sat untouched, congealing under the mess-hall lights.

After breakfast, Caruso and the others made their way to the briefing room. The space hummed with anxiety, the officer's commanding voice slicing through the tension.

"Today's mission targets the oil refineries in Hamburg," he began, his voice steady and unyielding. "We're carrying eighteen 250-pounders. Expect significant anti-aircraft fire."

A murmur ran through the soldiers, a mixture of resolve and dread. The words "significant anti-aircraft fire" hung over Caruso like a storm cloud, dark and foreboding.

Stanowick raised his hand, a slight smirk on his face. "One question, sir. They serving lunch on this flight?"

Startled laughter broke out. The officer's stern expression softened just slightly. "Humor's fine, Stanowick, but let's stay sharp."

The sobering rebuke lingered like wisps of smoke hanging heavily in the air as the next officer took the stage.

They took off at five twenty a.m., and by nine o'clock, they were over the German coast. The men were on high alert, bracing themselves for battle.

As they approached Hamburg, the intercom crackled with an announcement from Witherspoon, the radio operator. "Throwing chaff." Caruso watched as hundreds of thin metallic strips filled the air and slowly drifted downward. He hoped they'd serve their purpose, sending false blips to the German radar systems and making it harder for their aircraft to be targeted by the Luftwaffe. Still, judging by the number of black puffs hanging above, their efforts didn't seem to offer much help; too many signs of enemy fire dotted the sky.

As they flew over the target, Caruso peered through the window of the ball turret, watching the bombs plummet toward the earth, feeling the aircraft jolt from the rapid release. Sweat slid down beneath his helmet as he scanned the horizon for an imminent attack. Several flak bursts erupted in quick succession, the explosions close enough to shake the plane. Caruso reflexively raised his arms to shield his face as the bomber rocked, shell fragments assaulting them from all directions. One shard pierced the bombardier's window, lodging in the D-ring of Lieutenant Stevens' parachute, missing him by a few inches. Another struck the wall of the tail gunner's station.

A particularly fierce jolt, accompanied by a thunderous boom, sent a shockwave through the plane.

A searing pain ripped through his leg, followed swiftly by a second burst in his arm. His vision tunneled, the world blurring as his body slumped against the turret's cold metal.

The intercom crackled. Distant, distorted voices called out names. Caruso fought to focus, but the words wavered, drowned out by the rush of his own pulse.

"Caruso, respond." A pause. Static hummed. The pilot's tone sharpened, more urgent. "Witherspoon, get him out of the turret. Now. I'm getting us the hell back to base."

❧

With quivering hands, Kellogg retrieved the hand lever and passed it to Witherspoon, who quickly rotated the turret to gain access. Together, they pulled Caruso's unresponsive body from its confines. Witherspoon grabbed the portable oxygen, attaching it to the airman's mask, his face pale but determined.

"He's losing so much blood! Where's it coming from?" Kellogg's voice cracked as his eyes darted over the gunner's crumpled form.

"Here—his leg!" Witherspoon's hands trembled with adrenaline as he yanked back the tattered fabric of Caruso's flight suit. A jagged hole gaped above his thigh, blood pulsing through shredded muscle, soaking the floor beneath him. The air reeked of iron.

"Damn it, he's got shrapnel still in there," Witherspoon muttered, clamping a hand over the wound as he dug in his pocket for a belt. He yanked it tight around Caruso's leg, his fingers slick with blood. "Stay with us, buddy."

A second wound on Caruso's upper arm bled sluggishly, the torn flesh dark and glistening under the cabin lights. Witherspoon secured another tourniquet just above the wound, ignoring the way his own breath came in sharp, uneven gasps.

Despite the chaos, Witherspoon worked with practiced precision: he sprinkled sulfa powder into the wounds, administered a morphine syrette, and clipped the spent tube to Caruso's collar, marking the dose given for the medics. "That's all I can do for now."

Kellogg knelt beside his friend, his expression taut with worry. "Hang in there, Caruso. Just hang in there."

Minutes later, Witherspoon reported the gunner's condition to the pilot.

"Roger." Lieutenant Johnston's response was crisp. "Keep an eye on him while we head back."

Over the intercom, Stanowick's voice broke through. "Tail gunner to crew. I just took down an enemy fighter. That was one for Caruso!" A cheer rippled through the cabin, subdued but heartfelt.

When they finally approached Polebrook, Johnston flew low, near the control tower. Kellogg fired a red flare to signal wounded aboard.

The intercom hissed. "Pilot to crew. The tower says our right wheel's broken. I'll do my best to keep the weight off that side. Brace yourselves; this landing won't be smooth."

The men huddled together, locking into crash positions. Stevens moved from the aircraft's nose back to the navigator's section, whispering a prayer under his breath. "Dear Lord,

I know you're with us. Please protect us as we land. Give Johnston your insight to land this plane safely and give Caruso the strength to pull through."

Johnston slowed the aircraft down as much as he was able until they were just barely above the ground. The plane grazed the runway, screeching, before lurching off course. It bounced onto the grass, skidding and shuddering, and came to a violent halt. The brief hush that followed was eerily deafening.

As they gathered their composure after the tumultuous landing, Johnston's voice pierced the quiet. "Everyone okay?"

Kellogg responded, his voice shaky. "Yes, sir. Thanks to your guts and skill." The others murmured their agreement as they hastily collected their belongings in preoccupied silence.

For a breathless moment, everything was still… until the medics burst aboard. Witherspoon quickly briefed the senior medic, his voice steady despite their ordeal. "Sergeant Santo Caruso, shrapnel wounds to the right thigh and upper arm. Heavy blood loss, but the tourniquets are holding. Morphine administered—one syrette."

The medic knelt beside Caruso, pressing fingers to the pulse point on his neck. "Damn lucky he's still with us." He peeled back the flight suit, grimacing at the soaked bandages beneath. "We need to get him to surgery before infection sets in." He glanced up at Witherspoon. "Good work. We'll take over from here. Thanks." They carefully transported Caruso to the waiting ambulance, which sped away with its precious cargo.

The crew disembarked in silence. Flak holes riddled the wings, fuselage, and turret. The bombardier's shattered window gleamed in the sunlight.

"It's a miracle we survived," Kellogg murmured, his voice thick. His gaze dropped to the streaks of blood on the floor. "I just hope Caruso pulls through."

The men stood in a somber circle, awaiting the truck to take them to the debriefing. Their eyes lingered on the scarred plane—a haunting reminder of how close they'd come to not making it back.

![ornament]

Five days later

A hand lightly touched his shoulder, and a soft voice cut through the haze. "Santo? Can you hear me?" Caruso gradually became aware of his body—then it hit: pain, raw and unrelenting. His right leg pulsed with a deep, grinding throb that drilled into his bones. His arm hung heavy, stiff, and unresponsive, as if not his own. He tried to move his fingers, wincing as the tug of stitches burned through his skin.

As his vision cleared, he saw a petite blonde in white, her hair haloed by the infirmary's stark lights. For a moment, he wondered if he'd been catapulted into the afterlife.

"Well, hello there, soldier. Welcome back." Her radiant smile brightened the sterile room. "My name is Gayle and I'm your nurse. You're in the base hospital. You've had quite a time of it."

"What… what happened?" He spoke haltingly, each word dipped in confusion, his thoughts like balloons floating just out of reach.

"You were shot during an air raid and brought here. I don't know the details, but some mates of yours have been here several times, and they'll be chuffed to bits to hear you're awake!" Her British accent was warm and comforting.

"What… what day is it?"

"It's Friday, and you came in on Sunday. I'm not surprised you don't remember—you lost a considerable amount of blood and were in a lot of pain, so we had to medicate you." Her voice soothed him as she checked the chart with clinical but compassionate efficiency.

A sharp, intense tension seized his leg, squeezing the muscle like a vise. He shifted, just slightly, and a white-hot stab shot up his thigh. A sickening realization crept over him. Something was wrong.

Gayle studied his face briefly and adjusted his blanket. "They got most of the shrapnel out, but there's still a small piece they're watching. The doctors will decide whether it's better to leave it or go back in for another round. How's your pain now?"

He fumbled for words, attempting a quip to lighten the gravity of his predicament. "Well, uh… don't be disappointed, but I don't think I'll be able to take you dancing tonight."

Gayle laughed. "I see you've got your sense of humor, so you must be on the mend. That's good news. You're in for some hard work ahead, so that positive attitude will surely help."

Silent tears traced Caruso's cheeks. He turned away, caught in the chasm between her optimism and the darkness he carried. She couldn't possibly understand how hard it had already been—or how much worse it could still get.

"Oh, Santo, I'm sorry," she said, biting her lip. "I didn't mean to upset you after all you've been through. You're doing brilliantly, really. You'll be out of here before you know it. Listen, the medications make everyone a bit emotional, so don't you worry about that. But now that you're awake, your recovery will gain momentum. Just wait and see." Her eyes locked on his. "You've got a long road ahead, Santo. But I've seen soldiers come back from worse. You've got fight in you—that's what will get you through this. For now, though, you need your rest. I'll be back shortly."

His eyes followed her as she walked into an adjacent room. With his brows furrowed and breathing accelerating, he stared at the closed door until she returned. "Here's something to help you relax." She injected her syringe's contents into his IV.

The cool sting of the medication snaked up his arm, spreading an almost immediate heaviness through his limbs. Relief came first, smoothing the jagged sensations raking his body. Then came the dread, like an unseen current pulling him under. His eyelids sagged and the voices around him blurred, slowly melting away.

The following week, Caruso sat in the chair next to his bunk, dozing intermittently despite whirling thoughts. Who knew that sitting up would be such an ordeal? He remembered the first time Nurse Gayle had helped him out of bed to a chair: she needed two other nurses to help her. With each day, he'd been able to do more, and this morning, they'd accomplished the feat all on their own. How could something as simple as getting out of bed now seem like a forty-mile march?

He was napping when a familiar voice startled him awake. "Caruso! Is this your way of trying to get home faster?" Lieutenant Johnston stood before him, surrounded by the rest of the crew.

The wounded airman grimaced, raising his right hand in a slow, shaky attempt at a salute. The effort sent a ripple of pain through him, but his respect for his superior compelled the gesture, however feeble.

"At ease, buddy. No need to salute here. They say you're doing great. You're going to be moved to the convalescent home tomorrow. Glad to see you alive and well!" His smile was broad.

Caruso gave him a wry grin. "Alive, yes. I'm not so sure about well. But at least I'm not a gold star in my mother's window… yet."

"Not a chance, buddy. We pulled you back from the brink!"

Witherspoon's grin faltered for just a second as he took in Caruso's pale face and trembling salute, but he quickly covered it with a hearty wave. "Hi there, old friend. Good to see you awake and recovering."

"I don't really remember what happened."

Witherspoon nodded in understanding. "It was rough, over Hamburg. We managed to get you out of the ball turret after you were hit. Stanowick even took down a Jerry as we left. We were all sweating it out that we'd get you back in time!"

Podoske, the copilot, stuck his head through the small crowd. "Yeah. Landing was another story—a busted wheel and all. Johnston pulled off quite the stunt bringing us down in one piece." He clapped the pilot on the back appreciatively. "The medics took it from there, got you help fast."

His crew's arrival brought a breath of familiarity, but the reality of his condition held him in painful stillness. Their banter wrapped around him, a blend of solace and sting. Caruso looked at them, one by one. "Thank you all. You saved my life. I don't know what I'll do to repay you."

"No need. You're one of our own. You just keep working to get back with us. We're saving your spot. It's not the same without you, Caruso," Lieutenant Stevens said.

"Thanks, fellas." He let out a big sigh, and the room became quiet. The previously energized atmosphere seemed to deflate as a pronounced sense of exhaustion settled over him, underscoring the long road to recovery that lay ahead.

"You get your rest. We'll visit again soon," Lieutenant Johnston said, giving him a reassuring pat on the shoulder as they turned to leave.

Their voices faded as they departed, and a dull silence settled over him. Their lives would move forward, flying into danger and glory, while his own felt as though it had stalled behind the white walls of the hospital. He'd spend months in rehabilitation while the crew that he'd trained with for the past year kept fighting—without him.

He was going to be left behind.

CHAPTER THREE

June–August, 1944

"WELCOME TO STONELEIGH Park!" The orderly grinned as he opened the door of the truck.

Caruso cringed at the thought of being moved again. His ride to the rehabilitation center in Warwickshire, a little over an hour away from the base at Polebrook, had been jarring—every rut and dip in the road a fresh jolt of pain.

"My name's Thomas," the orderly said, wheeling Caruso through the building. "Hope that lorry ride wasn't too rough. Our roads aren't exactly smooth."

Caruso forced a smile while the gurney rattled over the facility's uneven tiles, trying to focus on anything but the ache in his body. "How long do soldiers usually stay here?"

"Oh, it's variable. They'll place you into a program that suits your specific needs. Your nurse will fill you in on the details. It may seem a bit overwhelming at first. But steady on, you'll adjust to the routine in no time and make great progress."

The pervasive scent of antiseptic filled the air, yanking Caruso back to his childhood tonsillectomy. The metallic bite of the ether anesthesia clung to his memory as if it had happened yesterday. It was remarkable how certain smells could trigger such vivid memories.

They arrived at a large room divided by curtains into cubicles, and Thomas settled him into bed and draped an extra blanket over him. The warmth was immediate, but so was the exhaustion. "Here you go. It was very nice to meet you, Santo. You must be a bit knackered after your journey. Get some rest, and someone will be in to see you in short order."

A soft British female voice roused Caruso from his slumber. "Santo, are you awake?"

He chuckled wryly and opened his eyes. "I am now. Hello." Slowly, his vision adjusted in the dimly lit room.

A beautiful woman, her dark wavy hair arranged loosely in a bun beneath a nursing cap, stood at the foot of his bunk, eyes sparkling. She wore a pristine white uniform. "Just popping in to say hello. I'm Helen, your primary nurse here at Stoneleigh Park. I wanted to stop by this evening and tell you what to expect. The schedule of training here will be intensive. Thomas probably told you about the different levels of trainees. We're starting you in Grade D, and we'll advance you as you're able to do more."

Caruso nodded. "Can you tell me a little about what's involved in the different stages?" he asked.

"In general, the basic program for Grade D is higher in educational pursuits and lower in physical training, because you require more rest periods. As you gain more strength and make more progress, each level will become higher in physical training and proportionately lower in education. The program is designed to improve strength and resistance gradually so you can return to full duty safely once you're discharged. For tonight, just relax and sleep. Your training will start at eight o'clock, so I'll see you tomorrow at six thirty. Good night, Santo."

"You can call me Sandy. Thank you, Helen." *After all I've been through in this war, rehab should be a breeze*, he thought.

Should be.

&

The following morning, the lights went on promptly at six thirty. "Good morning, Sandy!" Helen greeted him with a smile, balancing a small tub of water on her arm. "Hope you slept well. Time to tidy up before breakfast. This is all part of your therapy—you've got to stretch those muscles to get stronger.

"Wash what you can, and I'll be back soon to help you with the rest." She reached over to the bedside cabinet and handed him a small bar of soap and a towel, closed the curtain, and left the room.

Caruso hadn't expected something as simple as washing up to feel like a battle. His right arm trembled under its own weight, the muscles stiff and uncooperative. Every stretch sent a sharp ache through his body. By the time he finished, his limbs were leaden, his breath uneven. How long would it take to get back in the air? His stamina was just a trickle of what it had been before the injury. Would it ever return?

A short while later, Helen parted the curtain and peeked in. "Well, soldier, how did you do?"

Caruso's face lit up with a half smile. "My back is the only thing that still needs to be washed."

"Smashing!" With a wink, Helen picked up the washcloth and washed his back. Afterward, she helped him into his clothing. "I knew you could do it! You are a plucky sort!"

Caruso still wasn't quite used to all the British colloquialisms, but he enjoyed listening to her voice and accent, and trying to figure out the meaning of the unfamiliar expressions. It was as if he'd been dropped into a separate world—so different from the United States. He regarded Helen thoughtfully. Maybe it was that calm, polished ease of hers that made him feel so comforted, even in his broken state.

He looked up as a young girl entered, carrying a tray laden with eggs, toast, juice, and coffee. Caruso's lingering gaze on the breakfast offerings caught Helen's attention, eliciting a chuckle. "Not exactly a fry-up, is it?"

Caruso raised a questioning eyebrow. "A fry-up?"

"Oh, it's just what we call a proper breakfast—eggs, sausages, beans, the lot. We'll get you one when you're a bit more chipper—if the cooks can scrounge it up."

He was starving, for some reason. After Helen departed, he picked up his fork with his left hand and tasted the eggs. The smell of the powdered concoction was nauseating. He was surprised that he missed the rich smell of freshly cooked eggs that they served on mission days. The food had been better at the base—but at least he wasn't wondering if it would be his last meal. As he drained his coffee, Helen returned, and the day began.

Helen wheeled him to the first program, an orientation to the facility that would be presented in a large open auditorium. "This will give you more understanding of what lies ahead. It's always easier to adjust to an unfamiliar environment when everything's not a total surprise," she said. Glancing down at him, she placed her hand lightly on his arm. "You'll often hear us refer to patients as 'trainees' here—it's because we see all of you as learners on the path back to full duty. I'll leave you to it, then, to absorb it on your own. I'll be back when it's over, to take you to the next program."

"Thanks for all your help, Helen." For a brief moment, warmth lingered where she'd touched his arm. Was he imagining it?

While waiting for the presentation to begin, Caruso stared at his hands, clenched in his lap. He'd spent the last year proving himself in the air, feeling invincible, and now here he was—barely able to lift his legs without help. He looked around the room. Some walked in unassisted, while others entered in wheelchairs or on crutches. As a man stepped to the front, the murmuring voices and the shuffling of feet gradually ceased.

"I want to welcome you to Stoneleigh," he said. "My name is Tony Krayer, and I'm the administrator. Since you are all new trainees, we created a motion picture outlining our entire program so you can see what we offer." The lights dimmed, and a photo showing a large group of smiling staff standing at the doorway to the facility was projected.

The video narration began. "We're glad you're with us. Our goal is to restore you to your pre-injured condition and get you back to active duty as quickly as possible."

The motion picture began with an overview of the four grades of trainees, explaining how the soldiers were placed in each based on their condition and capabilities. The camera panned to soldiers from all categories, at various stages of their recovery, working on their assignments. "Our medical officer will evaluate each of you periodically. Your activities will be prescribed based on your rate of recovery and your Military Occupational Specialty. Regardless of the level you start in, our program aims to advance you quickly to the next highest grade. This strategy is successful because it provides facilities and resources to hasten your return to good health and fighting efficiency. It's not enough to cure you of your disease or injury: our treatment must cover the entire period until you are physically and mentally fit to return to your unit."

The camera took viewers on a tour of the facility, highlighting therapy areas, recreational spaces, arts and crafts rooms, and the grounds. It ended by demonstrating what trainees in Grade A could do in their final stages of preparation for discharge. As the film showed men boxing, scaling fences, and navigating barbed wire tunnels, Caruso's stomach tightened. For a moment, he wanted to look away. The men in the film moved like they'd never been broken. It was too much, too far. He couldn't even stand without shaking. How was he supposed to climb fences and scale walls? The memory of his own unsteady steps was fresh in his mind. But then his fists clenched again. He didn't know how long it would take, but he had to get there. He had to.

The film ended, and the administrator walked to the front of the room. "I hope this has given you a taste of what's in store for each of you. It will be a challenging adventure, but I trust you will face it with the same valor that you've exhibited so far in your tour of duty. Remember, each soldier who returns to battle helps preserve the strength of our forces. We stand behind you all the way and look forward to working with you!"

Helen approached him as soon as the presentation was over. "Well, what do you think?"

"I think it's going to be a long journey back. I can't imagine doing some of those things I saw in the movie. Even if I had the energy, at this point I don't have the muscle."

Putting a hand on either side of his wheelchair, Helen bent down to Caruso's level, her eyes steady and kind. Caruso shifted in his chair, uncomfortable under her gaze. But there was no pity there, only conviction. "That's absolute tosh. You wouldn't have made it this far if you didn't have the stamina to persevere. Promise me you won't allow these negative thoughts to take up residence in your mind. You'll make progress every day—even when it doesn't feel like it. Do you trust me?"

Caruso looked at her, his eyes softening as he took in her face. "Actually, I do, Helen."

"Good. Then let's hear no more of that rubbish." She wheeled him to the therapy gymnasium, a sprawling room filled with waist-high bars, weights, and strange contraptions Caruso didn't recognize. "Your next program is physical therapy exercise."

Nearby, a man with a heavily bandaged leg gritted his teeth as he hoisted himself up on crutches.

Another soldier balanced precariously on a wobbling platform. Caruso's eyes lingered on them, wondering how long it would take him to reach that level.

Helen paused, seeing Caruso's look of doubt. "You're doing brilliantly," she said, adjusting the watch pinned to her uniform, its face scratched and worn. "This belonged to my brother. He always said, 'Progress is progress, no matter how slow.' And he was right."

She gestured to a young girl standing by the doorway who didn't look more than fifteen. "Santo, meet Elizabeth. Don't be put off by her youthful face; she's older than she looks. She's going to test your abilities and then assign you exercises for both here and in your room. I'll be back when you're finished."

Elizabeth grinned, her quick movements and bright eyes giving her the air of someone who was constantly in motion. "Let's see what you can do, soldier," she said, her tone both cheerful and determined. "Stand up when you're ready, and I'll be right here to support you if needed."

Caruso followed her directions.

"Excellent!" She pointed to a black piece of tape on the floor and said, "Now, could you walk to that mark and come back?" He did as he was told.

"Perfect! Now, I want you to try an arm movement exercise—it helps with balance and muscle control. Raise your arms to chest height… and bend your elbows like this."

She observed him replicating the movement. "Good. Now let's repeat that motion—outward and back in. Your coordination is top-notch."

At a set of waist-high bars, Elizabeth guided him. "Try lifting your leg while holding on for balance." Caruso managed about thirty degrees. "Can you go higher?" Encouraged, he reached ninety degrees. "Excellent! Now the other side."

The stretch sent a sharp stab through his side, like a knife twisting deep in the muscle. His breath hitched. Suddenly, he was back in the ball turret—trapped, bleeding. He could feel the hot, sticky blood on his hands, hear the roar of the engines and the desperate shouting of his crew. His pulse pounded, faster, harder—

No.

He wrenched himself back. *Focus on lifting the leg. Once more. Just once more.*

They continued with more exercises until Helen arrived. "How is he getting on?" Helen asked her colleague.

"Brilliant. I think he has more in him than he thinks, and I'm eager to see that come out next time we meet." Elizabeth turned to Caruso with an approving look. "What's next is up to you. The more you practice, the quicker you'll progress to the next level, and the sooner you'll be back at your base. At this rate, you'll be climbing fences in no time."

"Sure," Caruso said, breathless. "Maybe I'll run to London for tea after this."

Elizabeth didn't miss a beat. "I want you to work on all the exercises we did, every chance you get. Your balance seems good, but for the leg lifts, you can hold on to the back of a chair so you don't fall. Before you know it, you'll be managing even higher leg lifts outside with no support." She grinned. "And Helen is going to make sure you follow through."

"Thank you, Elizabeth. I won't let you down."

After lunch and a brief break, the afternoon activities began. Caruso participated in various seemingly unrelated exercises: assembling radio sets from obsolete aircraft receivers, taking part in a group exercise that involved tossing a medicine ball while seated, and learning to use a loom in an arts and crafts session.

At first, tossing the medicine ball seemed easy—until his arms shook with fatigue, his core straining against the unexpected weight. The loom, on the other hand, felt like a joke, its tiny threads mocking the callouses on his hands. But he couldn't deny that his fingers seemed steadier by the end of the session. It wasn't much, but it was something—a reminder that even the smallest efforts could add up to something bigger.

Following some downtime and dinner at the mess hall, the evening's recreational activities began. Although Caruso joined in a friendly card game with other trainees, he found it lacked the thrill of the games on base, where money was at stake. Midway through the evening, Helen joined him for a game of ping-pong. He won, suspecting that Helen might have been going easy on him. Nevertheless, he enjoyed spending time with her.

By nine p.m., Caruso was spent and sank down on his bed. Helen approached him, her expression curious. "What did you think of your first day?"

Caruso's tone was a blend of skepticism and fatigue. "Seems like there are a lot of basic activities. The physical therapy exercises seemed useful, but making radio sets felt like a waste of time. I can't see how that will make me stronger. And I never imagined I'd be using a loom," he said, shaking his head with a wry smile and rolling his eyes.

Helen laughed, her voice warm and reassuring. "Every activity is tailored for your recovery—even ping-pong and card games. They're designed to improve your balance and hand-eye coordination, and help you socialize."

"If you'd told me three months ago this schedule would wear me out, I'd have laughed. It doesn't seem like much, but I'm exhausted."

"That's because you're doing more than you realize," Helen said. "Remember how you were when you first arrived at the base hospital? You really took a biff during that raid, and you've come a long way. You're pushing both your mind and body all day. It won't be long before you move up a level. As you grow stronger, we'll add walking milestones. You'll be amazed to see how quickly your body regains strength. But for now, get some rest. There's nothing like a good kip after a grueling day. Good night, Sandy."

"Good night, Helen. And thanks again." He had barely formed the sentence when he fell sound asleep.

❧

After his first month at Stoneleigh, Caruso realized he had greatly underestimated the stamina and determination required for his rehabilitation. Despite this, he recognized the significant strides he had made.

A bright spot in his routine was Helen, the striking brunette in her starched nursing cap and crisp white uniform, always ready to assist him. Early on, when his arm was too weak to hold a pen, Helen had written letters home for him. Her cheerful disposition belied her dogged determination about his recovery.

Helen greeted him one afternoon, her eyes sparkling. "If you've finished with your basic courses, we can get started on your physical training." She paused. "I hear no disagreement, so let's see how far you can walk."

Caruso rose easily and began making his way out the door. "Where to today?"

"Yesterday you managed three kilometers, which was just smashing! Let's try the same path and see if we can extend that distance today."

"Yes, ma'am!" He saluted her playfully.

Helen giggled. "That was a brilliant salute! The therapy on your arm is working wonders!"

After a few minutes, Caruso noticed something that surprised him. His legs were sore, sure, but they didn't feel like lead, and he wasn't gasping for air like he had the week before. Each step was steady, almost comfortable. He glanced at Helen, whose reassuring, cheerful encouragement concealed her watchful eye. She saw it too—he could tell by the small, approving smile she gave him every time they turned a corner. *Three kilometers*, he thought. A month ago, he would have laughed at the thought. Now, each step felt steady, controlled. He was getting stronger.

As they walked through the center and out onto the footpath, they engaged in light conversation. Helen had a knack for drawing out Caruso's thoughts on topics he seldom discussed, like his hometown in Philly, and how life in Great Britain during a war was nothing like he'd ever imagined. When he mentioned his dread of being left behind by his crew, she stopped and touched his arm gently until he looked into her eyes.

"You'll get through this with the same determination that's brought you this far. Your crew saved your life, but it was your spirit that kept you going. Never doubt yourself."

Her words hung in the air, quiet but solid, like a promise. He straightened his back, a smile crossing his face. She was right. He'd come a long way already. More than he often realized.

They continued walking, passing trainees reclining on lounge chairs. "You know, Sandy, you're fortunate to be doing so well," Helen said, nodding her head toward the men resting outside. "Some here aren't as lucky."

Caruso glanced at a man being gently spoon-fed by a nurse, his head wrapped in gauze. "That soldier looks like he's been through a lot." Caruso felt a pang of guilt for complaining about his own setbacks. At least he could walk, talk, and feed himself. The thought hit him with force—he had been spared.

"Yes, a piece of flak cut through his head. It's been a slow recovery, but he recently started speaking again, which gives us hope. It really makes you jolly grateful for all you've got."

Caruso nodded. "Yes. It could have been so much worse. So, Helen, now that you know so much about me, tell me about yourself."

A shadow fell almost imperceptibly across Helen's face as she brushed back her hair, her smile fading slightly. "Oh, there's not much to say, really. I've lived in England all my life. After my dad passed away, my mum went to live with her ailing sister in Cambridgeshire. Nursing has allowed me to help those fighting for our country."

She sighed. "It's good to be busy," she said, smoothing her uniform. Her voice was light, but something in her eyes had shifted—distant. Caruso saw the flicker in her eyes, the way she seemed to pull back. It was a fleeting moment, gone as quickly as it came, but he recognized the look: a hint of something she'd learned to tuck away. Before Caruso could ask, she turned back with a bright smile, as if to close the door on the subject. Yet the way her hands trembled for the briefest moment made Caruso wonder what she wasn't saying.

"I'm sorry about your father. Mine died when I was fourteen—his heart, they said. My mom remarried a year later, and she had my little sister, Caroline. She was three when I joined the army."

Helen turned to face him. "Oh, Sandy, that's rotten that you lost your father so young. I can't imagine how hard that must have been."

Caruso looked off into the distance. "I love them dearly, but yes, all those family changes were difficult. It was like being caught in the past when the world had moved on. When I left for the army and saw the three of them waving at the train station, it was strange to think that it used to be me standing between my parents. Now there's a new Pop and a new little sister, and I'm halfway around the world. My life changed so much in such a short time."

His sigh helped shake off his melancholy. "It's silly. I know they love me and that we're a family, just a different family than what we started out with."

"It's natural to feel displaced. Anyone would. But the Army seems to have given you a sense of belonging, which is wonderful."

“That’s why it’s hard to imagine going on without my crew. But after seeing what wartime in England is like, I honestly can’t wait to get back home to my family. Being a big brother is a nice change, although I didn’t get much experience before I joined up.” Caruso shrugged deeply. “There’ll be a lot of catching up to do when I get back.” The thought of home tugged at his heart, prompting him to change the subject. “Now, tell me more about you. Is there a special someone that brings you joy?”

Helen’s cheeks reddened slightly. “My dog, Archie, is as faithful as they come. He’s being looked after by my neighbor. His loyalty means the world to me.”

“Dogs are incredible, aren’t they? I miss my Cracker Jack back home.”

Helen smoothed her uniform and looked away briefly with a sigh as they neared the doors to the rehabilitation center. “Four kilometers today! Starting tomorrow, you’ll be in Grade C. You’re making splendid progress!”

Caruso beamed, as proud as if he had earned a medal. “If only a promotion in the Army were that easy! Thank you, Helen.”

It wasn’t just the distance that mattered—it was what it represented. He was moving forward. The thought filled him with a quiet pride, the kind he hadn’t felt in weeks. Maybe he really could get back to the air, back to his crew.

“We’re an excellent team,” Helen said. “And your hard work certainly shows.” She glanced at her watch. “When I come back, we can play for the ping-pong championship.”

“I’ll be the envy of all the men, playing ping-pong with you!” He winked at her, trying to hold on to some part of the moment that he sensed had passed between them, remembering the way she had touched his arm and looked into his eyes.

"Perhaps, but remember, this is all part of your therapy."

As she turned to walk away, he had to have the last word. "For now. But just wait. We'll be dancing before you know it." She glanced backward, shaking her head with a smirk and rolling her eyes.

He was probably breaking some rule about fraternizing with hospital staff, but doubted the Army would begrudge a wounded man a little hope. After all, a fellow needed something to look forward to, didn't he?

CHAPTER FOUR

August–September, 1944
Stoneleigh Rehabilitation Center

ADVANCING TO GRADE C meant longer, tougher training. Group exercises now included foot-high hurdles alongside daily walks. Caruso's legs burned with every leap, his breath steady but strained. It wasn't graceful—more of a hop than a jump—but it was progress.

The focus of the instructional courses also shifted toward preparing for life after Stoneleigh. One morning, as they walked to the auditorium, Helen explained the first order of the day. "Today's lecture will be on the psychological aspects of returning to duty."

Caruso gave a half laugh and shook his head. "Being in battle is what we've been trained for," he said. "It's a tough job, but we all know what to do. I'm not sure how psychology fits into this."

"Just keep an open mind," Helen said with a light tone, her expression understanding yet firm.

Soldiers in various stages of recovery filled the auditorium. Dr. Zorman, who oversaw the rehabilitation program at Stoneleigh, called the room to order. "We're pleased to have Dr. Thomas Macaluso with us today, a flight surgeon from the Eighth Air Force. He's extensively studied the psychology of injured servicemen. His insights will prepare you for your duties after you leave here."

Smiling, Dr. Macaluso approached the podium. "Good afternoon, soldiers. I'm sure that some of you, or maybe all of you, might think psychology is some kind of hocus-pocus." The audience responded with a gentle chuckle. "That's understandable, especially since it's rarely discussed openly. But the psychological effects of war injuries can linger long after the physical wounds have healed. You're not alone, and it's not unusual to struggle emotionally when you return to duty. Everyone does, to some degree."

At first, Caruso dismissed it. Psychology? What did that have to do with war? But as Dr. Macaluso spoke, something shifted. Looking around, he realized the others weren't just listening—they were absorbing every word. *We're all in this together*, he thought. *None of us is as unaffected as we pretend.*

Caruso hadn't thought much about what lay ahead, beyond getting through the next day of rehab. But now, the doctor's remarks stirred something deeper. What would it be like to climb back into a turret after everything that had happened? Could he ever be the same man he was before? Maybe he didn't have to be. Maybe that was the point.

The lecture concluded with a few closing remarks. "For those who won't be returning to their previous roles, life after discharge from Stoneleigh may be less daunting. However, every one of you should expect challenges that will make you question your abilities, and maybe even your sanity. Physical trauma affects more than just the body—it influences your insights, judgments, and reactions, both in and out of combat. Your flight surgeon on base will check in on you regularly. Being open and honest with him is crucial—he's here to help. The US Army Air Forces stand by you—just as you've stood by us. Thank you."

The applause that followed filled the room with a new understanding and respect. As Caruso walked back to his cubicle, he overheard snippets of conversation among the men.

"He's right," said one. "A buddy of mine struggled a lot, adjusting after his injury. He was too embarrassed to say anything at first, but it was obvious to all of us. He had to go to a flak house for a few weeks."

"What's a flak house?" another asked.

"It's a retreat in the countryside—they treat you like royalty and let you relax, away from all the reminders of war."

"Sign me up," said a third, chuckling. "Sounds like something I might want to try."

Helen was waiting when Caruso returned from the lecture.

"Are you ready for your endurance training, Sandy?" She offered him some hand weights as they walked outside.

Caruso grinned. "It's the highlight of my routine!"

"It's nice, isn't it, to get outside and enjoy the fresh air?"

"Yes, the grounds and the walking trails are beautiful," he said, thinking that the real reason it was his favorite part of the day was because he got to spend it with her.

"It makes the work of physical training so much easier," Helen said.

"Yes. And the pleasant conversation is a bonus." He turned to look at her. "So, tell me, what was your life like before the war?"

"Ah…" She exhaled softly and looked away. "It's almost hard to remember life before the war. No rationing, no petrol shortages. No blackout curtains or air-raid drills. You could walk into a shop and buy what you needed—no coupons, no queues. And no Andersons."

"What's an Anderson?"

"It's a home air-raid shelter. They're nothing fancy—just sheets of corrugated steel stuck into the ground—but they keep us safe. I've spent too many nights in ours, wondering if our house would still be standing when we came out."

"I can't imagine living like that. We have shelters on base, but fortunately, we haven't had any direct strikes. Not yet, anyway."

"Things were very different before the war. People weren't so worried about what tomorrow might bring. It seems like a lifetime ago.

"War really changed things, but some positives have come out of it. The British rallied together when everything went to pot." She stopped walking and looked into Caruso's eyes. "And having the Americans join the war definitely improved our lives."

"Meeting you has changed my life as well," Caruso said. "God only knows where I'd be without you."

It wasn't just her care, though that was part of it. It was her belief in him, the way she looked at him like he was whole—even on the days when he felt broken. She made him want to keep going, even when he wasn't sure he could.

Helen's face reddened slightly, and she began walking again, gesturing for him to continue with her. They reached the door of the facility, and she held it open for him. "Enough of this idle chatter. Every day, you're getting closer and closer to your walking endurance goals. So let me tell you what we're working towards in the next level, so you can prepare yourself." She sat down on a bench inside, gesturing for Caruso to do the same.

"The regimen in Grade B is much more vigorous than Grades C and D. It includes running, jumping, and six hours of physical training with calisthenics, drills, marching, and other outdoor activities. All this is to get you back into the physical and mental condition you were in before your injury. There'll also be ward and camp duties, instruction, and tactical training. As before, we'll have a variety of recreational and diversional activities to fill your evenings. It's a long day, but it's intended to build stamina."

Caruso chuckled as they rose and walked the rest of the way to his cubicle. "Just talking about it is draining whatever stamina I have left." His mouth wrinkled into a droll smile.

"I'll be honest with you, Sandy. It will seem like that at the start. But it'll get easier, I promise, if you just stick with it. Everything's difficult in the beginning. Remember how hard everything was at first in your military training, and then it all became second nature. You've already been through this same kind of preparation. You can do it again. I know you can. You'll be good as new, straight away."

Caruso watched Helen's lips curve into a smile, his gaze drifting up to her warm brown eyes. Had he ever noticed how perfectly they matched her chestnut hair? For a fleeting moment, he wondered what it would be like to kiss her. Their eyes met, something unspoken passing between them—until, as if breaking a spell, she turned away, smoothing the bedsheets with deliberate focus.

⁂

September 23, 1944

Caruso was dozing in his chair when his crew arrived—an unexpected sight, given the distance to Stoneleigh. "Hello there, Caruso!" Lieutenant Stevens' eyebrows arched in disbelief as he took him in. "You've come a long way since we last saw you!" The others nodded.

Caruso quickly filled the awkward silence that followed, addressing the unspoken. "It's swell to see all of you! When are you done over here?"

"We finished yesterday. We would have been done sooner, but they raised the required missions from thirty to thirty-five. They gave us a free bonus mission, so we ended up doing thirty-four. We're sure glad it's over! There were so many days we had our doubts we'd make it through," Lieutenant Johnston said.

"Not with you as the pilot," Caruso said. "You've always been the best." He looked at the others. "All of you, really. You saved my life."

"You've done the hard work here, Caruso. And you'll be going home soon, too." Podoske smiled, clapping him on the back. "I hear you're moving up to Grade A shortly. You'll be heading out in no time."

"When do you leave for home?" Caruso asked.

"In a few days. We wanted to come and say goodbye."

Caruso struggled to manage the flood of emotion within him, a mix of joy for their safety and a sharp pang of loneliness at being left behind. "That's great news. I just hope you all get a furlough when you get back to the States."

"Well, we aren't sure of anything yet," Kellogg said. "As usual, the brass doesn't tell you anything until they want you to know. Still, it'll be great to be out of the line of fire and back on safe ground. We're taking a troop ship back to New York, and then they'll let us know what's next."

Caruso nodded. "That's the Army way. Well, best of luck to you all, and I'll see you over there when I get done here."

His gaze lingered on each of them—his crew, his brothers, the men who had pulled him from the wreckage and willed him to live. "I want you to know I'll always be indebted to you." He meant it, every word. And yet, as he forced a smile, he wondered if they could see the truth beneath it—the quiet ache of being left behind.

Shifting gears, he asked, "Say, how did you all get here? It's quite a distance from Polebrook, isn't it?"

Witherspoon chuckled. "We camouflaged ourselves as supplies leaving the base. And we bribed a soldier, a fella they call Zeus, to act as our lorry driver. He's even waiting for us outside. He told the brass he was delivering equipment, so no one asked too many questions. Hope we don't get discovered, or one of the MPs on base is going to get an earful."

"Well, you better get going. Fellas, thanks again for the visit. It really means a lot to me."

Stevens stepped forward and reached out his hand to grasp Caruso's. "We'll see you back home, Caruso. Godspeed."

They all exchanged handshakes that turned into hugs. After they left, Caruso sat in his chair, pondering the uncertainties ahead and how he would keep going without his crew.

The silence in his cubicle suddenly felt heavier. Their presence had filled the space with warmth—now it was just empty air. He could still hear their laughter, feel their handshakes, but those moments were already slipping into memory.

They were moving on. It wasn't their fault—it was just how things were. But knowing that didn't make it any easier to bear.

Then he looked up and there she was, standing in the doorway. Helen. The ache in his chest eased just a little.

And for the first time in a while, the future didn't feel quite so distant.

CHAPTER FIVE

HELEN OPENED HER diary and picked up her pen. It seemed that ever since she had met Sandy, her thoughts had been running in jumbled circles, and sometimes writing helped to sort them out.

I never thought I'd find myself feeling this way for another man. I remember when I first met Roy. I was certain that he'd be my first and last love. But now, several years on, and after being on my own for what feels like donkey's years, I find myself drawn so strongly to Sandy. A patient of all people!

I've always been professional with my patients, and there've been a few soldiers over the years who tried to worm their way past my guard. But I never felt the slightest inclination. Not once. Until now.

Sandy's different. He wears his heart on his sleeve, a tenderness that calls to me. Yet there's a strength in him, too, a quiet resolve I so admire—especially given all he's been through.

The other day, his crew came to visit, with the news that they were headed home. The look on his face when I entered the room was heartbreaking. He looked so utterly on his own, poor love. I wanted nothing more than to go to him, to take him in my arms. But I didn't dare.

Instead, I gave him a smile and told him to pull up his socks (which made him laugh—he finds the way I speak amusing) and reminded him that he'd come through this the same way he's faced everything else: with courage and quiet determination. That's what's kept him going, bless him.

Last night, after all the activities ended, he and I went out for a walk. I probably shouldn't have gone, knowing how I feel about him, and suspecting that he feels the same. Sometimes he looks at me with such intensity, as if he's searching for something he hasn't been able to name. I can feel it. That wanting. But always, he hesitates.

I was glad he did—because I'm not sure I'd have had the strength to resist.

But last night, standing beneath the trees as the breeze rustled softly through the leaves, I shivered… not so much from the cold, but from something else entirely. The way he looked at me, so open, so unguarded. It unraveled me.

He pulled me gently to him, and the warmth of his body was like slipping into an old woollen cloak. So comforting. So… familiar. And yet not. It was something more. I felt… safe. And wanted. And, for the first time in a long time, truly seen. I looked up at him, and, God help me, I kissed him. And it was the most wonderful feeling in the world.

If anyone discovered that I kissed a patient, I'd be sacked without question. I can't afford to lose my position. What would I do with myself?

But it's more than the job. I crossed a line I swore I wouldn't. And here I am—heart full, head spinning, and no clear path forward.

CHAPTER SIX

October, 1944

CARUSO'S HEART FLUTTERED when he saw Helen enter his cubicle. Today was the day. He was leaving Stoneleigh Park. It had been over three months, and it was hard to believe how much his life had changed. He hoped his relationship with Helen would deepen now that he was going home.

"Well, Sandy," she said. "You did it! You're on your way!"

"Yes, it was a long road, but I made it to the other side." Caruso looked into Helen's eyes. "I'm going to miss you."

"Sandy, I know you're nervous about what lies ahead, but I promise you'll do fine." Helen's tone was light.

"I'll miss you not because I'm worried about what's next, but because my days won't be the same without you around."

"Yes, but you'll do it as you've done everything in your life, with courage and commitment."

"No, but I mean…"

"I know what you mean." Helen placed her hand on his arm. "We've made a nice team." Her voice dropped to a whisper. "I… I felt it too."

She glanced away, jaw tightening as if stopping herself from saying more. Her fingers clutched the hem of her sweater, bracing against an unseen force, as she busied herself with gathering his things and placing them into a bag. "But life keeps moving and we have to go on."

Caruso's breath slowed, remembering when he saw his crew for the last time. "Why does this have to be goodbye?"

Helen let out a heavy sigh as she continued collecting his belongings, her gaze averted. "Sandy, my work consumes me. This center isn't just around the corner from Polebrook. And you have a lot of work to do back at the base. Your rehabilitation is far from over. You'll have a temporary assignment while you reacclimate, and they'll probably have you participate in practice missions to start… You're going to be very busy."

Caruso refused to be deterred. "I would never be too busy for you."

Helen turned to face him directly, her tone firm. "Listen to me. The timing is all wrong."

"What do you mean?"

Her cheeks flushed a deep shade of red as she glanced downward, fingers trembling slightly as they pulled at a stray thread on Caruso's blanket. She seemed desperate to avoid his earnest, searching look. "It's… it's just not realistic. You've been living a singularly focused life for three and a half months. And my life here is, by its very nature, one-dimensional. It's the middle of a war, and the focus should be on that. I'm committed to my job… and to all the injured servicemen."

"We could find a way," Caruso said.

"No…" Helen took a breath, her voice cracking. "We can't. Not now. It's just… it's not possible." She looked away, as if fighting for composure. "You must believe me." Anguish lined her forehead. "Sandy, my job is extremely important to me. I've tried very hard to keep things professional between us. Please don't make this any harder."

Confusion clouded Caruso's mind, as if he were trying to see through a thick haze. *Why is she pulling away from me? Didn't the kiss we shared mean anything? Have I misread her all along? Or is she just too scared to let herself hope for something beyond this war?* Caruso had always prided himself on his ability to fight through anything, but for the first time, he wondered if this was a battle he wasn't meant to win.

It seemed like just yesterday they were standing by the ping-pong table, the rhythmic sound of their volley echoing around the rec room as her laughter mingled with the sounds of the game. Her sparkling eyes had lit up her entire face, a vivid memory that felt like a cruel contrast to the distance between them now. He'd sensed she felt something for him, even back then. "I just don't understand why you're so determined that we can't have anything more."

Helen's eyes filled. "Stop tormenting me!" Then, seeing Caruso's expression, her voice softened. "We live in two different worlds. Perhaps if we'd met in another time and place…"

Caruso shook his head, then raised his arms in surrender. The room that had been his refuge, where he had met Helen, now felt cold and sterile. "I won't ruin our last day together by arguing with you. Will you at least tell me you'll write to me?"

Her taut facial expression relaxed. "Of course I will. But will you write back to me?"

"You can count on it," Caruso said. He was silently gazing at her when Thomas, the orderly, entered his cubicle. His broad frame filled the doorway as he flashed a grin that brightened his weathered features, embodying the robust cheer he was known for around Stoneleigh.

His jaw unconsciously dropped as he caught sight of Caruso. "Crikey!" He gave a warm chuckle, quickly softening his voice as he took in the somber looks exchanged between Caruso and Helen. "I say, old chap, you look a lot better than you did when I brought you in a few months ago! It's been quite a journey, hasn't it?"

Caruso turned and smiled, nodding his head at Helen. "I had a lot of help and support. Everything was great."

"Smashing! Your lorry's waiting outside. I'll bet you're eager to get back to your base."

"Actually, I got injured shortly after my arrival on base. My stay here at Stoneleigh has been longer than at Polebrook, so it almost seems like I'm leaving home again."

"Sounds like you've had a rotten time of it since you came over. But you seem like a plucky sort. Keep that positive outlook."

"Yes, yes," Caruso said, as he turned to face his nurse. "Helen…"

Her hug interrupted him. "Godspeed, Sandy. Remember everything I've told you." Her arms wrapped around him with a warmth he wanted to hold on to forever. He felt the faint tremor of her breath against his shoulder, the soft press of her hands on his back. Caruso hesitated a few moments longer than customary, breathing in her scent, trying to memorize it. When she pulled away, her perfume lingered, a ghost of her presence he knew he'd carry long after he left. She turned away, brushing quickly at her cheeks.

"Thank you for everything. I wouldn't have made it without you." Caruso's voice was thick. He hesitated, his eyes on hers, a silent plea. "Don't forget me."

"Impossible." But her smile wavered, her eyes lingering on his as if searching for something she wasn't ready to name, fighting the tide of emotions threatening to break free.

For a fleeting second, Caruso wondered if this was what all soldiers faced—leaving behind a piece of their heart in a place they might never return to. Stoneleigh had been his cocoon, a place to heal and grow, but Helen had been the thread stitching him back together. Could he really move forward without her?

Thomas gave a friendly nod and checked his watch. His loud chuckle filled the cubicle, cutting through the heavy silence like a burst of sunlight through gray skies. "Blimey, it's like a funeral in here! Come on, mate, you're heading off to better things!"

Then, sensing the tension in the room, Thomas placed a reassuring hand on Caruso's shoulder and squeezed gently as he bent down to speak more softly to the soldier. "It's hard to leave good people behind, though, isn't it? But you've got this, mate. It's tough, but you're tougher."

For a brief second, the weight of Thomas's hand anchored him amid the swirl of his inner turmoil. Drawing in a slow, steadying breath, his resolve strengthened. He looked back at Helen one last time, hoping to burn the image of her into his memory—her chestnut hair tucked neatly beneath her cap, her hands clasped tightly at her sides as if to stop herself from reaching for him. She quickly turned away, but not before he felt the anguish of seeing her eyes brimming with tears and not being able to take her into his arms. He wanted to tell her how much she meant to him, but the words stayed locked in his throat.

༄

Polebrook Air Base

Without his friends there, Polebrook felt different, though much remained unchanged. The pungent scent of fuel and metal still clung to the air, mingling with the damp chill that seeped into everything. He'd almost forgotten how the cold settled into his bones until he stepped back onto the base. Captain Monahan, his Commanding Officer, welcomed him back and escorted him to his new barracks to settle in.

The lingering scent of sweat and damp wool hovered in the barracks, a mix that made his stomach churn with an odd blend of nostalgia and unease. When he sat on one of the cots, it creaked beneath him, the three square mattress biscuits shifting awkwardly—a sharp cry from the modest comforts of Stoneleigh. Even the sounds—boots scuffing outside, the distant hum of aircraft—felt unfamiliar, like a song he couldn't quite remember. He surveyed the room, restless.

The only man in the barracks was a tall, lanky soldier with dark, wavy hair, stretched across his bed, writing a letter. He rose from his bunk, smiling kindly. "Hi, I'm Lester Rhein. Welcome. Or should I say welcome back? We heard you were arriving today. Glad to hear your recovery went so well."

Caruso shook his extended hand. "Thanks. I'm Santo Caruso. Just 'Caruso' is fine. Sounds like you're from Philly, too, same as me?"

Lester's eyebrows shot up. "Yes, I am! What are the chances, all the way over here? That's great! We'll have to catch up after you get everything ironed out.

"I arrived about a week ago, so I've only had instructional classes so far," Lester said. "I'm a top turret gunner. What about you?"

"Ball turret gunner. Or at least, that's what I was when I left. I'm meeting with the flight surgeon in a little while. He'll have to give me clearance to fly. I was told I may get assigned a temporary position at first."

Leaning back against his bunk, Lester flashed an easy smile. "Is your crew out flying a mission today?"

Caruso faltered, his duffel feeling suddenly heavier. He managed a polite nod, his response brief. "They're gone. They finished their missions while I was in rehab," he said. "I don't have a crew anymore." The words tasted bitter. The loss settled over him, dense and immovable. They'd been his family in the air, his anchor in battle. Now, the world was too quiet—only echoes of their laughter and the roar of engines remained.

Lester's expression shifted to one of understanding, but Caruso was already turning away slightly, his thoughts drifting to the crew he'd lost, and the distance still left to travel before he could feel at home here—or anywhere.

"That's rough. Well, maybe they'll set you up with a new crew. Captain Gannon'll know what's next."

"Before I got injured, the flight doc was Captain Block," Caruso said. "I guess he left, too. Everything's changed."

"Well, it's all new to me," Lester said, his voice carrying a trace of excitement mingled with a bit of apprehension. He glanced around the sparse barracks, which held only the barest of necessities. A small coke stove to ward off the cold stood in the center of the room. "Guess we're in the same boat." He hesitated, as if unsure how to break through Caruso's silence. "Maybe we can figure it all out together."

"Yeah, maybe." Caruso wasn't sure he was ready to forge new friendships so soon. He held up his duffel bag. "Which bunk should I take?"

Lester pointed to a cot adjacent to his own. "You can take this one. Must be a lucky spot; the fella in it before you just went home yesterday."

Caruso gripped the duffel bag's strap tightly. After a brief hesitation, he tossed it onto the bunk with a forced smile. "Great. I'll take all the luck I can get," he said, his voice a combination of hope and resignation. He glanced around the barracks, the deepening shadows mirroring the somber thoughts that clouded his mind. The coke stove's gentle heat did little to lift the chill that had settled inside him since his return. Home had never felt so far away.

Later that day, Caruso stood in Captain Gannon's office as the flight doctor greeted him with a firm handshake. "Welcome back, Caruso."

"Thank you, sir."

"How does it feel, returning to Polebrook?"

"Well, it's a little strange. I spent more time in the rehabilitation center than I'd spent here before my injury. Frankly, it feels like I'm starting all over." He looked down at the ground. "My crew has gone home."

"Yes, I know. That makes it particularly difficult, but not insurmountable. How are you feeling physically? My report said that you did quite well; better than they had anticipated."

"I feel pretty good. They trained me hard at Stoneleigh. It was like boot camp all over again, especially once I got to Grade B."

Captain Gannon chuckled. "Yes, that's what I'm hearing. But they have excellent results. We have several men who've been able to go back to their regular duties."

"Will I?"

"Would you like to?"

Caruso hesitated, the automatic "yes, sir" catching in his throat. Did he want to fly again? The answer should have been obvious—of course he did. But the thought of stepping back into the ball turret without his crew, of facing those endless skies alone, made a knot in his stomach. Still, what else was there?

"I'd like to get my missions completed and get back to the States like the rest of my crew, sir."

"Good. We'll ease you back into military life gradually. For the first week, our goal is to ensure you can handle a complete duty schedule, but in a non-combat role. For that reason, I'm assigning you to Supply. We have someone out for a week, so you can fill in there. I've spoken with Captain Nichols over there and you'll work with Private Calvert P'Pool."

"Sir…"

"Before you say anything, Sergeant, let me have a word. I know this might not be what you expected, especially after risking your life in the air. However, every position in the Air Forces is vital to defeating the Germans. This assignment will ease you back into combat and show how all operations fit the bigger picture. It will also assure us you can work a full day. I know they gave you heavy training at Stoneleigh, but sometimes things become apparent on base that weren't noted during rehab."

The captain leaned back in his chair, his gaze lingering on Caruso before he continued. "After your time in Supply, we'll have you work as an armorer. When that's completed, you'll take part in practice missions with some new crew, and then, if you feel ready, you'll return to battle. To win this war, we need every soldier we have."

Gannon stood up, signaling the end of the conversation. "We appreciate your service, Sergeant, and your dedication. You're dismissed."

"Yes, sir." Caruso saluted and left the building, his mind a whirlwind as he began walking slowly back to the barracks. *Is this why I fought so hard to recover? To count crates of supplies? How long will it be before I'm flying again?* His heart sank lower as he realized he wouldn't be getting back home anytime soon.

As he walked, Caruso's eyes caught on a patch of wildflowers pushing through a crack in the pavement. Against the gray expanse of the airfield, the flowers stood out—a stubborn splash of color, alive in a sea of monotone.

He knelt, touching a petal, its delicate softness stirring memories of Helen's garden at Stoneleigh. Her voice echoed in his mind, painting vivid images of sunlight and blooms, comforting yet unbearably distant.

He wondered what Helen was doing right now and if she, too, felt the separation between them. Her steady encouragement had been his anchor, her laughter a light breaking through even his darkest days. He could still hear the way she said his name, soft and full of warmth, and without her, everything felt unmoored. Her reluctance to deepen their relationship bothered him, yet he clung to a thread of hope that she might still reconsider. The surrounding quiet increased his sense of isolation, each step reminding him of the life he'd temporarily left behind. But as he reached the barracks, he squared his shoulders and forced his gaze forward. The uncertainty of what lay ahead hung over him like storm clouds, but Caruso straightened his back. He'd faced worse before—and he'd face this, too.

CHAPTER SEVEN

IT WAS NEARING the end of the week, and Caruso's muscles cried out as he trudged into Supply and slumped into a chair. His limbs felt heavy, as though each step drained him further, and his vision blurred with the kind of exhaustion that even sleep couldn't seem to cure. The return to working with minimal breaks had been unexpectedly challenging. Would he ever feel like his old self? He was barely in his twenties, yet he had no energy. If he couldn't even handle this, how was he supposed to get back in the air? Letting out a long breath, he felt the weight of accumulated fatigue.

"You look as worn out as the racehorses right after the Kentucky Derby," Calvert said, his voice teasing. "But don't worry. Recovery takes time. I've seen plenty of other fellas just out of convalescence—it's always slower than they expect."

Caruso's lips pressed into a thin line as he regarded Calvert. Glancing around the room, he took in the stacks of unopened boxes, envisioning the daunting task of sorting and distributing their contents. His shoulders sagged under the burden of just the thought, a silent groan forming in his mind.

Calvert leaned closer, lowering his voice. "In two weeks, if you come back and tell me I was pulling your leg, I'll give you a week's ration of my cigarettes. And believe me, I don't give those away easily."

"I thought I was putting in full days towards the end of my time at Stoneleigh," Caruso said, shaking his head. "Navigating through all those tunnels and climbing six-foot walls—it was tough, physically demanding work. Yet here I am now, lifting a few boxes a day, and I can't believe I'm this beat every night."

Calvert nodded. "I know what you mean. The fellas never realize it, but when you first return to base, it's a continuation of your treatment plan. There's no expectation that you're ready to get back to combat immediately after you leave Stoneleigh."

Caruso considered Calvert's words. He hadn't seen it from that perspective, but the exhaustion he felt every night was undeniable. It was as if his body was betraying him, despite his mind's determination to be ready for action.

Calvert winked, a teasing glint in his eyes. "Not to mention, I daresay that the distance from your lady love may be part of the fatigue problem. It seems men have far more energy when they're in the company of a beautiful woman."

Caruso couldn't help but chuckle, despite himself. The mention of Helen brought a bittersweet pang to his chest. He could almost hear her laugh, see the way her eyes crinkled when she teased him. The memories felt close enough to touch, but the distance between them made him ache. "Maybe you're right," he said, his voice quieter. "Helen always did have a way of making everything seem easier. How did you get so smart?"

Calvert grinned. "I've had my share of women that I've tried to impress."

The sound of heavy footsteps and a loud knock at the door interrupted their conversation. A towering figure filled the doorway, his thick arms cradling a teetering stack of boxes that seemed too precarious for anyone but him to manage. Despite the size of his load, he moved effortlessly, as if he were born to carry the weight of the world. Caruso did a double take at his hulking physique as the brawny soldier carefully set down the boxes.

"Oh, hello, Zeus," Calvert said. "Caruso, this is Morris Lizewski. We all call him Zeus. Among many other duties, he handles the unloading of supplies. Today's delivery day, as you can see."

Caruso's ears perked up at the mention of the name, tugging at a vague memory in the back of his mind. A moment later, a smile of recognition crossed his face. "You smuggled some of my friends in to visit me at Stoneleigh a few weeks ago! They told me how they'd hidden in your truck with the supplies. I really appreciate you helping them out. Hope you didn't get into any trouble for it."

"No trouble," Zeus said, a thick Polish accent coating his broken English. "Happy to help. Nice men."

"Yes, they are. They were my crew. They saved my life." Caruso's words carried a tinge of nostalgia.

Zeus nodded solemnly. "They said was very important meeting."

"It was. We hadn't seen each other in a long time, and they were leaving to go back home. Thank you again."

Lizewski's smile broadened as he handed the supply list to Calvert for review.

"Zeus has been here almost as long as I have," Calvert said. He examined the document with a satisfied smile. "Thank you, Zeus," he said, returning the signed list. "See you next week."

With a nod, Zeus departed.

ൟ

During a quiet moment in the supply room, Caruso sorted through the new shipment. Calvert gestured at the pile and tossed him another package. "They're not letters from sweethearts, but they're all waiting to be opened."

Caruso caught the package mid-flight, then wavered, a half smile crossing his face. He turned the package over in his hands, imagining for a moment that it might hold something personal, something from Helen. But it was just another supply shipment. Easier to face than waiting for letters that never came.

Noting the mood change, Calvert caught Caruso's eye. "Thinking about Helen again?" he asked, a knowing look softening his eyes.

Caruso nodded, the corners of his mouth forming a sad smile. "Yeah, it's hard not to."

Calvert gave his shoulder a light squeeze, his voice earnest. "You'll hear from her, Caruso. And when you do, let her know how much she means to you." With a reassuring smile, he turned back to the task of unpacking boxes, leaving Caruso to his thoughts.

ൟ

The week ended more quickly than Caruso had anticipated. Reflecting on his time since returning to base, he realized he'd not only learned a great deal from Calvert, but had also forged a meaningful connection in a place he least expected. Now, with his stint in Supply drawing to a close, a familiar melancholic ache crept in—the sadness of parting ways with a friend.

He finally understood the wisdom behind his assignment to Calvert's team. Supply had been the ideal sector to ease his transition from rehab back to active duty. It wasn't just about managing resources; it was a complex operation that required keen insight and meticulous planning. Calvert, ever knowledgeable and supportive, had made the introduction to ground operations both insightful and comforting. Caruso couldn't help but feel grateful for the unexpected lessons and bonds formed in this unlikely place.

Caruso noticed that Calvert also seemed to have appreciated their time together, relishing the opportunity to share in the vicarious thrill of an airman's stories.

"When I got drafted, I wanted to be on the flight crew, but a hip injury when I was younger disqualified me," Calvert said. "After hearing about your battle injuries, though, maybe it was for the best." He smiled wistfully. "Still, I have to admit… I've always dreamed of flying in a B-17 and owning one of those flight jackets the crews wear."

"Being in the air really does change your perspective," Caruso said. "But if you ever get the chance, let's hope it's in peacetime so you can enjoy the ride."

Laughing, Calvert shifted topics. "Still, sounds like your convalescence wasn't all bad. Speaking of which, do you think you'll see Helen again?"

Caruso's gaze dropped, a shadow crossing his features. Just the mention of her name made him ache inside. "I don't know; she hasn't written yet. She seems to think the timing of our meeting was wrong, whatever that means." He was still puzzled and pained by her final words to him.

"Well, you never know what'll happen," Calvert said. "I've dated many women in my short life, yet here I am, still searching for my one and only. A base full of men just isn't the best place to find her." His mouth twisted into a wry smile, his eyebrows raised in resignation.

Pausing, his eyes brightened as he shifted in his seat, a spark of enthusiasm igniting his features. "Say, we've got monthly dances with ladies from Oundle and Peterborough. Some of the fellas even put together a band—they're really something. You should come to the next one."

"Sounds like it would be fun," Caruso said, glancing at his watch and noticing the time. "Well, I need to head out. Thanks again, Calvert. Maybe we can grab a pint sometime."

"You'll find me at The Rose & Crown in Oundle—my usual haunt. It'd be great to see how you're doing. Take care of yourself."

As Caruso walked back from Supply, he couldn't help but smile at Calvert's optimism. It was the kind of energy that could only exist far from the front lines. Back at the barracks, though, reality waited.

Lester and one of the other men in his quarters, David Rapoport, both looked up from their card game when he walked in. Lester nodded at a large bag on Caruso's bunk. "Hey, Caruso, did they finally bring back the rest of your stuff?"

Caruso picked up the bag and rummaged around inside, his face lighting up as he pulled out a framed photo of a smiling man who appeared to be in his thirties. "Thank goodness!" He clasped the picture to his chest, lingering for a moment before turning it around to show the men. "This is my pop. He passed away when I was just a kid," Caruso said quietly, his fingers brushing the edge of the frame. "This is all I've got left of him, so this is irreplaceable."

Next, he retrieved a small family photo. "This is my mom, my stepdad, and my little sister. Boy, I'm sure glad to have these back!"

Then he reached in and pulled out a large, black, rumpled article of clothing. Shaking it free, he recognized his leather flight jacket, mostly intact except for a rip in the arm where he'd been injured. The sight of his own dried blood on the dark leather caught him off guard, a visceral reminder of how close he'd come to not making it back. He held it to his chest like an old friend. The weight in his hands felt heavier than it should, thick with the memories of his crew and the missions they'd flown together.

"Yeah, I think most of it's here…" He held up his leather jacket for the two men to see. "…although this one's a little worse for wear. Damn, I really loved this jacket. I still remember when my crew and I got our flight jackets. We were so proud!"

"Well, this is your chance. Better take it," Rapoport said. "Put in a req for replacement of anything missing or damaged. And in the meantime, get them to repair the old one. It'll probably take 'em forever, but it'll get done. Hell, it's the least they can do for all you've been through with this damn war."

"You're right… might as well. Can't hurt." Caruso gently folded the jacket, setting it aside with care—a gesture of respect to his past and acceptance of the future. "Thanks. I'll take care of that now."

CHAPTER EIGHT

THE FOLLOWING DAY, Caruso reported to the Ordnance Section for his next assignment. A tall fellow with a medium build and a strong New York accent introduced himself as Sheldon Coons, inviting Caruso to call him Shel. With his round glasses and crisp uniform, Shel carried himself with a quiet confidence that seemed older than his twenty-three years.

"This kind of work should suit you perfectly," Shel said. "And it'll get you one step closer to the big birds. Here, we do the regular maintenance on armament that you've trained for." He glanced at Caruso, a shared understanding passing between them. They'd both come a long way from the blindfolded drills of gun assembly, each step forward a reflection of their dedication to their unit. The real test now lay in the hands-on work, where every action carried weight.

"Our duties with the actual bombs, bomb racks, and bomb release mechanisms will probably be new to you, though."

Caruso nodded. "In my first mission, the bombardier couldn't get the bombs to drop. The ground crew didn't find anything wrong with the bomb release mechanism, but it was a tense moment."

Shel pushed the frames of his glasses up the bridge of his nose, looking deep in thought. "High altitude can change things. The bitter cold at altitude can freeze mechanisms that work fine on the ground. Despite thorough checks, the true test comes in actual combat. We rely heavily on the aircrew's reports to guide us. Ensuring everything works perfectly is our top priority."

"And we appreciate it," Caruso said. "Knowing you're all doing your best gives us the confidence we need up there."

Switching subjects, Shel went on: "So, about the bombs themselves, let me first show you the igloo."

Caruso's brow furrowed as he tilted his head, puzzled.

Sheldon wore the slightest trace of a smile, as if enjoying Caruso's confusion, but didn't elaborate. They drove by jeep to a large building that Caruso had never noticed before. They stepped into the shadowy quiet of the igloo, and Caruso immediately felt a chill—not just from the colder air. The dim light inside made the bombs look even larger, their smooth metal shells reflecting just enough glow to seem alive, as if the bombs themselves were holding their breath. Silent now, but brimming with destructive potential, they seemed to hum with a latent energy that made the hairs on his arms stand on end.

The pungent smell of metal and faint traces of oil filled his nostrils, a symbol of the mechanical and destructive nature of the war. Their footsteps echoed in the room, the eerie reverberations underscoring the significance of its contents. "Gee, I hope there's never an explosion in here. That would be a disaster in this kind of storage facility."

"Funny you should say that," Shel said. "Just a few months ago, there was a huge bomb explosion at Metfield Air Force Base, only a few hours from here. It really brings home the importance—and the risks—of this work."

"What happened?"

Shel pushed his glasses further up on his nose as his voice took on a somber tone. "Back in July, while the hoist operators were on break, a few trucks loaded with bombs arrived at the base. The drivers got impatient and unloaded the bombs themselves without waiting for a crane. What they didn't know was that these bombs contained a more explosive compound than usual. One bomb dropped, hit the ground, and the next thing you know, it set off a chain reaction. The explosion killed several men and destroyed multiple aircraft, shutting down the base temporarily."

Shel paused, letting the gravity of the incident sink in. "It's a powerful reminder of why we adhere so strictly to protocols."

The story of the Metfield explosion lingered, a grim reminder of how quickly things could go wrong, even far from the skies. Yet, in the methodical work of the Ordnance Section, Caruso sensed something he hadn't in months: the chance to regain control. Here, precision mattered. Here, he could ensure that everything functioned perfectly—not just for himself, but for the aircrews who depended on it. Still, for someone barely in his twenties, it was a heavy burden to bear. Caruso exhaled slowly. "Hard to forget something like that."

"You're not kidding. One thousand two hundred tons of bombs exploded, shaking the countryside for several miles," Shel said, his tone grave. "I've been telling that story to every new soldier who comes here. A real-life example sticks with them better than just a warning."

They reached a secluded area where technicians prepared bomb fuzes—precise, deliberate, aware that one mistake could be fatal. "This job can be monotonous, but its importance to our missions makes it worthwhile," Shel said, almost echoing Caruso's thoughts. "It's all about believing in our cause."

Caruso was thinking of their conscientious bombardier, Lieutenant Stevens. The paradox of Stevens' gentle nature and the deadly tasks he performed was clear, yet his belief in their purpose reconciled him with the harsh realities of war.

As Caruso walked back to the barracks, the cool English air reminded him how wide the gulf was between the ideals they fought for and the tasks they carried out to defend them.

In the muted light of the barracks, Caruso's thoughts shifted between his dual desires: returning to the skies and maintaining the fragile link with Helen. As he settled onto his bunk each night, his yearning to fly again blended with the pull of his longing to hear from her. She was a constant presence in his mind, and he eagerly awaited mail call at the end of each day.

Finally, an envelope arrived with a Warwickshire postmark, the handwriting unmistakably feminine. His heart skipped a beat, and with trembling hands, he tore it open, eager to rekindle their connection. It was the first letter, and he was desperate for any sign of her feelings.

Dear Sandy,

I'm sorry for the delay in writing. I hope you know it's not because I haven't been thinking of you. Quite the opposite.

I've been wondering how you're settling in back at the base, surely eager to return to your missions. Trust me, the right time will come. Everything happens for a reason.

I've been missing having you around Stoneleigh. It's not the same without you. You may be surprised to know that you were an exception to my usual reserve with the other trainees!

I hope you're settling in well, even without the familiar faces. No worries, in short order, you'll have a whole collection of new friends.

Let me know how you're doing.

Fondly, Helen

In his excitement at hearing from her, Caruso had barely skimmed the letter, searching for something that reflected that his feelings for her were mutual. He reread it more slowly, finding her words both soothing and frustrating. "'Fondly,'" he muttered under his breath, rolling his eyes. It felt so formal, almost distant. But as the barracks grew darker and quieter, memories of their time together softened the sharp edges of his doubt. The laughter, the teasing, the kindness—they all seemed to linger in the words she'd written.

"She misses me," he said softly, a smile creeping onto his face. The ache of loneliness softened, like a knot beginning to unspool.

Sitting down with pen and paper, Caruso began to write back. He wasn't sure what he'd say, but he knew he had to try. Whatever lay ahead—on the ground or in the air—Helen's letter gave him something to hold on to, a reason to keep going.

CHAPTER NINE

November, 1944

THE BARRACKS WERE steeped in icy darkness when a flashlight's beam cut through, stabbing at Caruso's closed eyes. "Rise and shine, Caruso! The bombs await!" The voice grated against the fragile boundaries of his sleep. Groaning, he shielded his face and swung his legs over the edge of his bunk, the cold floor jolting him as sharply as the light. It was only midnight.

Work in Ordnance went beyond gunnery duties and assembling bomb fuzes. The department also managed the delivery of bombs to aircraft and their final preparations, tasks performed in the dead hours of early morning, long before the aircrews were roused.

The icy air stung his cheeks as he trudged to the latrine, the silence replacing the usual morning banter. It reminded him of his solitary first days after he was injured. Only when he reached the bustling squadron headquarters, where others were already gathering equipment, did he feel a semblance of camaraderie in their shared commitment to the day's early start.

Caruso heaved the equipment into the truck and clambered aboard. As the vehicle lurched forward, he grabbed the side, steadying himself as they headed to the bomb dump. He shivered, both from the chill and the anticipation of his new duties.

The drive along the gravel road under the starry sky brought back memories of tracing constellations with his father. Those moments, especially their last shared gaze the night before Pop's sudden passing, wove a bittersweet thread linking past to present. Remembering his father's approving nods brought a comfort that countered the cold, blurring his vision with the impact of his recollections.

The truck's abrupt halt at the bomb dump snapped Caruso back to the present. They set to work under the scant starlight. Caruso chuckled as he noticed a bomb marked "SPECIAL DELIVERY FOR ADOLPH." He leaned over to a colleague as his fingers brushed the icy metal. "Hope this one hits its mark." Memories of the Metfield disaster—a harsh reminder of what could go wrong—gripped him. "Let's handle these carefully," he said under his breath, tension lining his words.

The repetitive, backbreaking rhythm of loading bombs pushed Caruso's limits, his muscles screaming as he heaved the cold, unforgiving metal into place. Still rebuilding his strength, every motion—from fuzing to final checks—felt like a battle against his own body. As he neared the end of the shift, cold had seeped through his gloves, turning his fingers stiff and uncooperative. His arms trembled, each movement a battle against fatigue.

When they'd completed their last delivery and the sky hinted at dawn, Caruso felt the exertion of the night's work. His stomach growled. The ride to the mess hall was quiet, each man lost in his own thoughts of their necessary but grueling work. For Caruso, the night had stretched on interminably, but he was at least a step closer to returning to the skies.

❧

The week flew by, each day blurring into the next. On days with no missions, Caruso switched to gunnery repairs, a welcome respite from the physical exertion of bomb loading.

While he was servicing one of the guns, Kenny Craumer, the gunnery instructor known for his robust build and thick dark curly hair, approached him. What began as a conversation about technical tasks turned to memories of combat, with Kenny disclosing that air sickness had rerouted his military course from the skies to the ground.

"I never thought I'd trade clouds for solid earth," Kenny said, a hint of nostalgia in his voice as Caruso assisted him with the firearms. "But you know, there's a clarity you gain down here that you don't always see in the air. Sometimes, the change you resist most offers exactly what you need. I fought tooth and nail against being reassigned. Thought it'd feel like failure. But now I see it's just another way of serving—and surviving."

Caruso had already begun to see his ground duties in a new light, but hearing Kenny voice it aloud gave the idea a kind of validation: he wasn't the only one learning to serve differently.

❧

Later that day, as Caruso tramped back to the barracks, his thoughts turned to flying and to Helen. Her silence gnawed at him, the unanswered letter a growing weight in his chest. He could almost hear her voice, warm and steady, telling him everything happened for a reason. But instead of comfort, the memory of her words only deepened the ache, an echo of something that now felt too far away. He wondered if she thought of him at all or if, in her busy world at Stoneleigh, she was already moving on. Maybe he should, too. But first, he needed to fly again. It was the one thing he still had a say in.

Absorbed in his thoughts, Caruso opened the door to his barracks and was unexpectedly doused with a bucket of cold water that had been precariously balanced on top—a well-known prank from Bob Smith, the infamous joker of the base.

The shock and absurdity momentarily sliced through his spiraling thoughts, prompting a reluctant grin. "You got me," Caruso said, catching the towels his comrades, howling with laughter, threw at him. As he swiped at his hair, the lighthearted break from the relentless routine of military life momentarily eased his tension.

Refreshed and now somewhat amused, Caruso mentally prepared to meet with the flight surgeon, Captain Gannon. This wasn't just any routine check-in. It was the bridge back to the place where his skills and training were fully utilized—up in a B-17. For months, he'd fought for this moment. But what if Gannon didn't clear him? What if he was stuck on the ground, hauling bombs while other men flew missions? The thought twisted in his gut. He took a steadying breath, straightened his shoulders, and kept walking, his resolve firm. This was his moment to prove he belonged back in the air.

Each step forward signified his eagerness to fill the void left by his crew. His life had hit a stagnant phase, sidelining him from his purpose.

He mulled over what he wanted to say, how to put into words not just his physical readiness but his commitment to rejoining the fight from the air. He aimed to reconnect with his identity as a flier, to close the emotional and professional gap that had widened during his recovery.

Finding Captain Gannon available, a mixture of relief and determination settled over him. He paused at the door to collect his thoughts. Now was the moment to make his case.

"Hello, Sergeant," the captain said. "I was going to find you later today, but you've beaten me to the punch."

Caruso sat a little straighter, his voice steady with resolve. "Sir, I appreciate your seeing me. I've worked in Supply and Ordnance, gaining perspective. But I belong in the sky. That's where I can make the most difference."

Gannon nodded, folding his hands on the desk. "I understand your eagerness, Caruso. But tell me, how have you been handling the pressure? It's not just about physical readiness; mental readiness is just as important. The last thing we need is someone up there who's not totally prepared."

A flush of frustration swept through Caruso; his hands clenched briefly, though his expression remained composed. "Sir, I've managed everything fine—from waking up for the bomb deliveries to handling the tasks at hand. I've been sleeping well, no issues. I'm not just ready to return; I need to," he said, his insistence evident in his face.

For a long moment, Gannon regarded him in silence, his eyes narrowing as if measuring the sincerity of Caruso's words. Finally, he sighed softly. "Alright." Gannon leaned back in his chair, folding his hands as he studied Caruso for another beat. "You've worked hard since returning. I've heard good things about your time in Supply and Ordnance. Take a few days off, and then we'll start you on some practice flights. We need to make sure you're fully functional in the air again. The turrets are cramped, and your physical limits will be tested. I'll be watching closely to see how you handle it."

"Yes, sir. I'm confident I'll be fine. Thank you," Caruso said, a guarded relief washing over him as he saluted and left the office. He'd learned in the Army that when you get the answer you want, it's best to thank the person and exit quickly before they have a chance to change their mind.

But as he stepped into the cold corridor, Caruso knew the practice flights would test him—not just his body, but his will to face battle again without the safety net of his old crew. For now, though, he clung to the hope that this was his first step back to the place where he truly belonged.

The skies weren't just his calling—they were where everything else faded. The roar of the engines, the pulse of the mission—it was the only place that made sense. Even Helen's silence couldn't follow him there.

The war couldn't wait, and neither could he.

CHAPTER TEN

ON THE MORNING of his first practice mission since his injury, Caruso joined Bob and Lester at an old, scarred table in the corner of the bustling mess hall. The air was thick with the smell of overcooked eggs and burnt toast, mingling with the bitter tang of coffee that had been left too long on the burner—a harsh, almost sickening reminder of each day's unrelenting pace. Men shuffled in and out to a collage of laughter, clinking utensils, and the occasional tired sigh.

Lester was talking to another airman, and Bob was sitting quietly, staring into space with a queasy look on his face. "Hey, Bob, what's the matter?" Caruso asked.

Bob's gaze fixed on the untouched food on his tray as he turned slowly toward Caruso, his eyes unfocused and distant. His jaw tightened, his words barely audible in the din. "I'm okay, just… not feelin' so good."

As Caruso glanced around the crowded room, a flicker of memory surfaced—his own jittery nerves during those initial flights over England, not so different from Bob's current unease. He remembered his crew's anxiety, wondering how different flying over England's skies would be from what they'd rehearsed back in the US. The difference this time around was that Caruso had been on some missions and had a better idea of what to expect.

Caruso slid a piece of toast toward Bob. "Eat up; it'll clear the fog—out there in the sky and in here," he said, tapping his chest lightly. "Think of today like a practice run on familiar ground: no flak, no fighters—just us and the clouds. Like riding a bike, you know? We've got experienced officers on deck, too. It'll be a milk run, Bob. Promise."

Bob let out a long, slow sigh. "It's not about their experience. It's just…" He stopped, looking as if he was about to be sick.

"What is it?"

Finally, Bob spoke, his eyes shrouded in emotion. "It's the takeoff that gets me. What if we crash and burn?" Bob's fingers traced the rim of his coffee cup, his grip tightening with every word. "Back in the States… one of our instructors got fed up with us messing up a drill and decided to take the controls himself. It happened so fast—I barely remember the exact moment it went wrong. He couldn't get altitude. The plane tilted hard to one side and slammed into a storage facility. It went up in flames instantly, like a match to gasoline. He never made it out. I can't get that image out of my head—the fireball, the smoke… It's almost burned into my brain." Bob dropped his gaze to the table.

"I just keep thinking, if it could happen to him, it could happen to anyone. Once I'm in the air, I'm fine. But beforehand, I just can't shake that vision. And it takes over. I can't think of anything else."

Caruso paused. He knew that fear, had felt its cold grip—yet now wasn't the time to share his own battles. Instead, he placed a steady hand on Bob's shoulder, giving a gentle squeeze. Just then, a sudden clatter from the kitchen made him flinch, the sound oddly reminiscent of artillery fire. For a fleeting moment, the thunder of past air combat burned in his mind. Caruso quickly covered his reaction, refocusing on Bob, ensuring his face showed no sign of the momentary distraction.

"I know it's hard to shake a memory like that. But you're not alone in this. We'll tackle this step by step. For now, let's start with something simple—eat that egg and toast." Bob did as he asked. "Good. Now let's go. We'll get through just fine." With a final nod to Bob, Caruso stood, leading the way out of the dining area, the clamor dimming behind them.

At the briefing area, they were introduced to the men who would be on their crew. Although most were new to Polebrook, as Caruso had predicted, three experienced officers would oversee the others. Second Lieutenant Howard Hibbard was to assume command of the aircraft this morning, with Captain Joe Robinson as the copilot. Both looked knowledgeable and had calm demeanors. The navigator was Captain Joe Glover, a tall, gangly, no-nonsense-looking man whose somber visage easily evaporated into a warm smile, transforming his appearance entirely.

They took their seats in the room. After the training officer had given them details about their upcoming flight, the meteorologist, First Lieutenant Richard Higley, stepped forward. "Visibility is currently inadequate, but we project improvement in the next thirty minutes. If the weather doesn't lift, it will require an instrument takeoff," the weatherman said.

Hibbard glanced at Robinson, eyebrows raised—an unspoken understanding of the challenge ahead. Caruso turned and glimpsed Bob wiping his sweaty hands on his pants.

As the reporting continued, the radio officer outlined the day's radio procedures with methodical precision. Next, the group navigator outlined the takeoff order, and the formation positions each plane would assume once they converged at the designated buncher—a low-powered radio beacon that served as a rallying point for navigation before forming up. "This may be a practice mission, but treat it as a valuable opportunity to practice your formation flying skills. Remember, accuracy is key: too spread out, and we're vulnerable; too close, and the risks of collision rise. Stay alert and communicate any irregularities to your pilot immediately."

As the briefing concluded, the crew's focus shifted to the flight ahead. Stepping out into the brisk air, the navigator's words lingered in their minds, each man mentally preparing for the precise demands of formation flying. Caruso and his crew piled into the back of the truck, cramming themselves tightly together. Bob stared straight ahead, unspeaking, as they jostled about while heading to the hardstand where their plane was waiting.

As Caruso was preparing to board, he recognized John Montgomery, the crew chief, walking with a clipboard in hand, chewing gum as usual while reviewing the recent repairs that had been made to each aircraft. Montgomery, known on base as "Gummy" for his constant gum-chewing habit, looked up as Caruso approached.

"Morning, Gummy," Caruso said. "Any concerns about our bird today?"

"Nope!" Montgomery pushed the gum to the side of his mouth while he nodded toward Boyd Dobbs and John Leasure, two of the plane mechanics. "Dobbs and Leasure made a few minor repairs last night, nothing major. She would've flown today's mission, but I wanted them to go over her again from top to bottom this morning just to be sure. Now I'm confident she's good to go."

"You're a good man," Caruso said with a wink, clapping him on the shoulder. "Where would we be without your attention to detail?"

As they approached the plane, Caruso touched Bob's shoulder and leaned in. "Just focus on the first few minutes during takeoff. Remember, it's just a brief part. You've managed it countless times before. Hold fast to that." Bob nodded mechanically, his expression still tense and wary. His hands flexed and released, over and over, as if he were trying to shake off the fear.

The crew hoisted themselves into the aircraft one by one. Caruso winced as he pulled himself up to board, his recovering limbs still rebelling from the strain. He completed his pre-flight checks and looked over to see Bob meticulously performing his own, though he seemed more robotic than engaged. Then, head bent downward and lips moving, he folded his hands in prayer. Caruso hoped Bob was right, that this would all pass once they got airborne.

The first flare fired, and they started their engines, running through another pre-flight check. Finally, the flare for takeoff was fired, and the last of the planes began their roll. Fortunately, the weather had lifted to afford decent visibility for their departure. Caruso sat near Bob at the waist, taking in his grim demeanor. He felt sorry for the poor fella.

Once they were off the ground and stabilized, Bob was a different person, relaxed but absorbed in his tasks. The greenish tinge to his face had disappeared. *Funny what a difference a few minutes and a change of scenery can make*, Caruso thought as he made his way over to the entrance to the ball turret.

As he began to step inside, his foot hovered in midair, refusing to move. The usual clank of metal reverberated through him, but this time, it felt sharper, heavier—like an iron gate slamming shut. His hand tightened on the cold steel of the turret entry, but it didn't feel solid—it felt like it might crumble beneath him. The hum of the engines vibrated through his boots, growing louder, echoing in his ears like distant flak. A shiver ran through him, spreading out like a crack in ice. His pulse kicked up a notch, his breath coming faster as his fingers hovered over the turret's frame. He blinked, trying to dispel the sudden cloud of memories that fogged his vision—flashes of chaos, noise, pain.

"Caruso?" Bob's voice seemed distant.

"I'm… I'm going in. I'm fine," Caruso said, his voice distracted and hardly convincing. He forced himself down into the turret, his movements stiff, as if someone else were controlling his limbs.

It took all his mental strength to step down further and position himself in the glass sphere. *His legs cramped as he settled in, muscles stiff from months of disuse. Even though rehab had strengthened them, they still protested the confined area.* As he gazed at the airspace around him, he felt a sense of unease. He closed the turret door, the click echoing too loudly. His heart pounded, a tacit reminder that no amount of practice could erase the scars of actual battle.

"Deep breaths," he said to himself, his voice a whisper. His hands trembled, and a buzzing started in his ears. The sound seemed to swallow everything else, like he was trapped in a vacuum. As his vision blurred, he wondered if he was going to pass out. Bending his head down, he tried to get blood flow to his brain.

Somehow, by sheer will, he stayed in his crouched position. The humming in his ears was deafening, and he could barely hear the intercom when it sounded. He suddenly realized exactly how Bob had been feeling.

Sweat trickled beneath his helmet, and he feverishly tried to wipe it away.

He forced himself to look outside, trying to reason with himself that he wasn't in a war zone, and wasn't going to be hit. The planes around him were all from his squadron, yet his body's physical response was as if the Luftwaffe was right there beside him, taunting him, ready to take him down.

The intercom crackled, the voice sounding miles away. "Copilot to ball turret. How are you doing in there?"

He stared at his hands—quivering, useless—and forced them to grip the controls. The microphone felt too close, his breathing too loud inside his mask. If he hesitated too long, they'd know. He swallowed hard, steadying his voice before keying the mic.

"Ball turret okay. Everything's fine."

He was panicked inside. For months, he'd been eager to be back in the turret, and now he was dumbfounded at his body's reaction. He hadn't expected this at all, and wondered what the hell he was going to do to get past it.

For the entire flight, it was all Caruso could do to stay in his position until the pilot announced they were headed back to base. The trip was a blur. It felt as if he'd been unable to catch his breath the whole time, despite having put on the oxygen mask before it was even needed. Spinning the crank to open the door, he peeled himself out.

After they landed, Bob looked over at him. "Your face is beet red, Caruso. Are you okay? You didn't talk much when you came out."

Caruso's heartbeat still thundered in his ears, and his muscles were stiff from holding himself together for so long. He needed space, needed air—but Bob's concern pressed on him like a burden he couldn't shrug off.

"Of course I'm okay! You're a fine one to ask!" Caruso could feel the heat rising up his neck. "I just got hot in there. How'd you like to be all curled up in that tiny space with all these clothes on?"

"Relax, Caruso. I was just concerned."

"You have no idea what it's like in there." Caruso jumped out of the plane, breathing a heavy sigh as he trudged ahead of the others, his clothes soaked through.

His thoughts tumbled over one another like pennies in a can as he marched ahead, sweat dripping from his brow despite the chill in the air. This had only been a practice run, no flak, no enemy fighters, and still, he'd barely been able to stay in the ball turret. What would happen on a real mission? He'd thought he was ready, that the months of rehab had toughened him up again. But the panic in the turret told a different story. He was hardly the one to have given a pep talk to Bob that morning when he could barely function himself. At least Bob's problems were only on takeoff—his own problem was much worse. *What if I can't defend us against the enemy in a real mission? What if we all go down because I freeze?*

He thought back to Stoneleigh, to the psychologist's quiet warnings about the hidden scars of battle. Back then, Helen had been there every day, her voice reassuring, pulling him back from the brink. *You've got more fight in you than you know, Sandy*, she'd said once, her eyes holding a quiet conviction that had kept him moving forward. Now he was alone, with twenty-seven missions standing between him and home. The distance to the finish line felt insurmountable.

For the first time, Caruso wasn't sure he'd make it.

And that fear was more suffocating than anything he'd faced in combat.

CHAPTER ELEVEN

IT HAD TAKEN all his resolve, but Caruso had forced himself into the ball turret for each of his last four practice missions. Unlike Bob, who agonized before each flight but was fine once they'd taken off, Caruso's demons came when he got into his position. He regretted not paying more attention during the psychological support presentations at Stoneleigh, but he'd been so sure back then that their words didn't apply to him.

Practice flights were constantly monitored, a measure to ensure everyone could do their job. He had made it a point to appear calm and relaxed, especially under the watchful eyes of observers. Yet the complete opposite was true: he was a bundle of nerves. The panic simmered just under the surface, showing no signs of abating.

His sense of foreboding had deepened just the day before, after several bunkmates were shot down and presumed dead. Their stripped bunks upon his return served as a harsh reminder of war's swift toll. He was drowning, and the only thing keeping him afloat was the hope that finishing his missions would finally set him free.

This morning, hopefully his last practice mission, Caruso opened the hatch and stepped down into the ball turret, drawing a deep breath and steadying himself. Although he'd managed to keep up appearances, each mission had been a private war.

He kept his voice level on the intercom, responded to oxygen checks without delay, and masked every trace of the panic that still simmered beneath the surface. No one had suspected a thing—and that was the point. Falling behind meant scrutiny, and scrutiny could mean grounding.

From his view in the turret, the formation looked tight, the crew moving like clockwork. He didn't dare hope he was getting better, but he hadn't fallen apart either. Maybe he could hold on long enough to make it home.

En route back to the base, Caruso crawled from the turret, his muscles stiff and his body soaked in sweat. He made small talk with the crew, even forced a smile or two. No one seemed to notice the way his hands still trembled.

The next day, Caruso was lying on his bunk reading when a tall, spindly man with wavy brown hair entered, followed by several others, all with the telltale bewildered faces of new airmen on the base. "Hi, I'm Max Marksheid," the soldier said. "Radio operator. And these are my buddies." He gestured to the men behind him.

"This is Anthony Del Percio, better known as Perch. He's our tail gunner. And Francis Pisman—we call him Frankie—he's our ball turret gunner." Pointing to the others, Max introduced them one by one.

"I'm Caruso." The arrival of the new recruits sent his already-low spirits spiraling further downward. As he watched them, he couldn't help but see the shadow of his own crew in their fresh faces. He could still hear Stanowick cracking jokes to hide his nerves, the easy banter between Kellogg and Witherspoon, and Stevens' steady voice rallying them all as they walked back across the base for the first time. The smell of fresh duffels, the scrape of boots on the floor—it all came rushing back. They'd been full of nervous laughter and hopeful dreams of glory. He'd believed in them, in their invincibility. And now? Now, he was the one left behind, staring at empty bunks and wondering if these new boys had any idea what lay ahead. The irony of their naïve optimism pressed down on him, darkening his mood.

Max looked around, his expression uncertain. "Which bunks should we take?"

"You can take this one," Caruso said, nodding to an empty bunk adjacent to his own, his eyes barely lifting from the *Stars and Stripes* paper he was reading. "Or that one." His gesture toward a nearby bunk was dismissive. "Or one of those three," he said, his tone curt as he barely moved his head to indicate the group of bunks across the room. "None of those boys are coming back." The unspoken fate of the prior occupants hung in the air, unaddressed.

Max swallowed hard, licking his lips, the implication of Caruso's words hitting him like a slap. "Thanks," he said weakly, cocking his head at his crew and raising his eyebrows, his face quizzical as he shrugged his shoulders. He turned back to Caruso. "The Commanding Officer told us the mess hall is open. We're pretty hungry. We'll just put our gear down and be on our way."

Caruso nodded, his eyes focused on his paper. From the corner of his vision, he watched the newcomers settle in, their easy movements highlighting just how out of place he still felt.

As they left, their banter was still audible despite the diminishing sound of their footsteps. Once alone, Caruso stared at the closed barracks door, wondering what would become of the new crew.

This group had stirred a vague memory, elusive at first, then slowly crystallizing painfully clear. The man they called Perch reminded him of Stanowick, with his twinkling eyes, always seeming to be on the verge of finding the humor in something. Caruso's thoughts tiptoed over each crewman that he'd felt such a kinship with; these men who had worked so hard to get him back on safe ground. Suddenly, everything that had happened over the past several months came rushing back. He sank into his pillow, letting the solitude of the room magnify the emptiness he felt inside.

Later that day, Caruso was summoned to meet with Captain Gannon to report on his progress.

"Well, Sergeant, tell me how it's been going," the flight surgeon asked.

Caruso lied smoothly, his face a blank slate. "Everything's swell. No problems." The office walls seemed to echo the tightening grip of his own confining emotions.

"How are you feeling in the turret—physically and mentally? Any lingering pain or issues?" Gannon's gaze was steady, probing.

Caruso forced a grin, his heart thudding in his chest. "None at all, sir. The rehabilitation worked wonders." He kept his voice light, casual, as if the thought of stepping into the turret didn't twist his stomach into knots every time. He couldn't afford to give the captain even a sliver of doubt. Not now.

"That's great news. I'm glad to hear it. Not everyone is as fortunate. Still, I'd like to continue meeting with you periodically to make sure there are no issues. Sometimes problems take a while to reveal themselves."

"I'll be happy to report to you as often as you require," Caruso said. "Returning to regular missions as soon as possible is a priority for me. I'm sure you need all your men in the planes."

"Yes, that's true. Okay, then, I'll put you back in circulation for missions."

"Thank you, sir. Will I have an assigned crew?"

"For now, you'll be classed as replacement crew, so you won't be assigned a specific team. When we need a ball turret gunner, we'll call you in. At times, you'll be flying with men you've flown with before, but at other times you'll likely see new faces."

"Thank you. I don't mind working as a replacement, as long as I'm getting more trips under my belt."

"Your willingness to continue missions is commendable, especially considering your recent injury." The captain smiled briefly, shifting topics. "By the way, we'll be standing down this weekend, and since it's the last Saturday of the month, we're having a dance with some ladies from Oundle and Peterborough. It might be a nice opportunity for you to enjoy yourself after all the hard work you've put in these past few months. The men always seem to have a great time." He winked. "As do, of course, the ladies."

"Thank you, sir. I've heard about the dances." Caruso hesitated, the thought of mingling with strangers both tempting and exhausting. What was the point? He couldn't shake the image of Helen's smile, her absence still fresh. But then, maybe a little noise and company would drown out the hollow ache that haunted him wherever he went. "Maybe I'll stop by."

"Hope to see you there, Sergeant."

As Caruso left the flight surgeon's office, a cool breeze whipped through the airfield, stinging his cheeks. The captain's words echoed in his mind: *We'll be standing down this weekend. Maybe you should enjoy yourself.* But the idea of actually enjoying anything felt oddly out of reach.

His boots crunched over the icy ground as he passed a delivery truck unloading crates of Thanksgiving supplies. The sight triggered a swell of homesickness, memories of warm kitchens and crowded tables flashing through his mind.

And then there was Helen. Her voice rose unprompted in his thoughts. He envisioned her smile, the way it softened her features, bringing with it a flicker of warmth. Her laugh when she teased him over a game of ping-pong, or the way her hair caught the sunlight when they walked outside, echoed in his thoughts. Her kiss. For the briefest moment, the memory of her presence dulled the ache of loneliness, like a match struck in the dark. Yet just as quickly, the awareness returned of the daunting reality of the holiday ahead without any of his loved ones.

November 23, 1944: Thanksgiving

Caruso was awake before dawn, the barracks around him still quiet. As he lay there, staring at the ceiling, the images of Thanksgivings at home came flooding back: his mother bustling at the stove, his little sister's giggles as she dipped her finger into the mashed potatoes. Even the clatter of plates and his stepfather's endless storytelling, things that once grated on his nerves, now felt like treasures lost to another world. Rising, he dressed slowly, bracing himself for the day ahead, full of forced smiles and memories that would squeeze his heart.

ණ

Returning from a walk, he took in the holiday chatter of the other men.

"I sure miss my mother's cooking, more on Thanksgiving than on any other holiday," Rapoport said. "It'll sure be hard to be away from them this year."

"Yeah, I know what you mean," Max said. "It's been four years since my family's been together for any holiday. Before I shipped out, my brother Harry was in the Navy, so he was gone for a few years."

"Two of you from one family in the war? Isn't there some rule against that?" Rapoport asked, incredulous.

"Not if you enlist. After Harry got back, I re-upped, so it wasn't like I didn't volunteer for this. And there are a lot of children in our family. I have another brother, Guly, and two sisters, Betty and Gussie, so I don't think my parents could claim a hardship even with both of us gone."

"Man, Max, your mother must have been busy all week preparing for Thanksgiving to feed all those mouths!"

"She sure did! Luckily, she knew how to cook; she could make something special out of nothing at all! And my family had a farm, so we were fortunate to always have something to eat."

The men's banter swirled around Caruso like smoke, choking him with memories of the family he longed for but couldn't reach. Every laugh, every shared memory pulled at the threads of his tightly woven façade, threatening to unravel him. He didn't begrudge them their joy—he even envied it. But the warmth of their camaraderie only reminded him of how far away he felt from everyone, including himself. His yearning was so fierce it was almost physical. Tears brimmed his eyes, threatening to overflow. Caruso blinked rapidly and buried his head in a magazine, hoping they would leave him alone.

ᯉ

Later in the day, despite the strict rationing that was so prevalent throughout the country, the 351st managed to serve turkey with all the trimmings.

Chaplain Tom Richards rose to address everyone before the meal began, his calm voice carrying over the clatter of trays and silverware.

"I want to thank all of you for your sacrifice and your selfless service. We have much to be thankful for. Let us now all bow our heads for a moment of prayer, to ask God's blessings on this food, our families, and each other." His words were weighted with a conviction Caruso couldn't quite muster. His lips moved silently, but his heart wasn't in it. He wished he could believe, as the chaplain seemed to, that progress in the war was something to celebrate. But all he could think of were the empty bunks, the letters left unanswered, and the faces he would never see again.

As the prayer ended, the men eagerly dug into their feast of turkey, mashed potatoes, cranberry sauce, and various pies. For a short time, the mess hall almost felt like a family gathering. Stories of past holidays flowed, mingling with wistful plans for future Thanksgivings with loved ones.

When Caruso returned from chow, he sat down and wrote a letter to his mother and stepdad. Even though they wouldn't read it for at least two weeks, they'd know he'd been with them in spirit.

Dear Mom and Pop,

It's Thanksgiving and I have so many memories of home. I was thinking about the last Thanksgiving together. I miss you so much. It's been far too long.

We had turkey with all the trimmings today, and for a little while, we pushed away thoughts of combat as everyone celebrated the holiday. With the strides we've made in the war, there's sure a lot to be thankful for. I hope we can be together next year.

I am well, so don't worry about anything.

Love, Sandy

He reread the letter twice before placing it in the envelope, lingering over the words as if they might somehow bridge the gap between here and home. Although he'd masked the depth of his struggles, he saw no point in burdening his family with the harsh truth. They'd be heartsick with worry. Better to just keep things light and upbeat.

As he sealed the envelope, the sound of men's laughter outside wrenched his heart. He remembered when he and his old crew had shared stories that ended in chuckles, just like the ones he heard outside. His vision blurred as he wondered what they were doing, wherever they were. He couldn't believe how much had changed in a few short months. Where he'd once been smack in the middle of a core of great fellas, now he was completely isolated.

He shifted in his seat as he traced his fingers over the letter to his family. He needed to keep facing forward and set aside all the fears that plagued him.

He'd been on the fence about attending the dance on base, unsure if he could summon the energy to handle the forced cheer and the company of strangers. But then a flicker of determination took hold. He thought of his mother, always finding joy in the smallest things, and of Helen, who had somehow made him feel stronger just by being herself. The war wouldn't pause, and neither would the loneliness—but perhaps for one night, he could set it aside. He'd go to the dance. Not because everything was fine, but because for a few hours, he could pretend it was.

CHAPTER TWELVE

BUTTERFLIES SWIRLED IN Helen's chest, a nervous energy she couldn't remember feeling this intensely before. Facing the closet, she surveyed the selection. Everything seemed so shabby. New clothes hadn't been an option since the beginning of the war, and everyone was making do with what they had. Helen rifled through her dresses, her hands pausing at her favorite. Pulling it out, she held it up against herself, looking in the mirror. She'd always received compliments when wearing it, with people commenting how well it brought out the auburn highlights in her hair. Though several years old, it would have to do.

After carefully spraying perfume on both wrists, Helen rubbed them on her neck. A smile crossed her lips. Perfume was the one extravagance she refused to give up. The spicy floral scent of Chantilly always lifted her mood, making her feel dressed up, even when she wasn't. A childhood memory surfaced of trying on her mother's various perfumes, Mum smiling from the doorway as Helen pretended she was going out with some tall, dark, and handsome man.

She slipped the dress over her head, zipped it up, and turned around in front of the mirror, smoothing her hands over her body. At least the dress still fit perfectly.

Taking a seat at the dressing table, Helen applied some light makeup. She aimed to look smart enough to turn an eye, but was cautious about not going overboard. After all, this wasn't an actual date. Picking up her lipstick, Helen paused, staring into the mirror. It had been so long since she'd gone out; was this the right decision?

Slowly, she painted her pale lips with a color that went with the dress. Her hand wavered slightly. Mum had always advised moderation in everything, a chuckle hidden in the warning. It was a lesson easier said than practiced, especially on nights like this.

Yet, given the uncertainty of these times, who knew what tomorrow would bring? There was nothing wrong with wanting an enjoyable evening and a little harmless companionship. These past few years had been painfully lonely, with work providing a mere diversion from her isolation. But no one benefited from living such an austere life. Everyone deserved a holiday from the day-to-day drudgeries now and then.

Tonight was about shaking off the endless routine of work and solitude. At least, that's what she told herself. Yet the small, excited flutter in her chest refused to listen, hinting that this night might be about more than a simple change of scenery.

The pearl necklace and earrings she'd received from Mum for her twenty-first birthday accentuated the dress beautifully. They were usually reserved for special occasions, but tonight felt significant enough to wear them. With a war on, one couldn't predict when the next opportunity for celebration might come. Just getting out was a special occasion in itself.

Helen's reflection in the mirror seemed to question her motivations. Were her intentions for the evening really as innocent as she insisted? What was she hoping for? A nice conversation? A moment to forget the war? Or something else entirely—something she wasn't quite ready to admit to herself? Maybe tonight was about proving she wasn't invisible, not to herself and not to anyone else.

Would her friends think she was mad if they knew of her plans?

She almost laughed out loud. Some of them had landed themselves in situations that made this seem like small potatoes in comparison. They wouldn't bat an eye. But her best friend, Christine, would undoubtedly raise an eyebrow and ask if she was sure she knew what she was getting into. They'd discuss every possible scenario that might unfold and what Helen would do in each case. They laughingly called these preparations "scripts," a ritual they indulged in regularly.

Glancing at the clock, Helen quickly fetched her things and locked the door. The destination was merely a block and a half away, but the brisk night air urged a quick pace. She clutched her coat close. A small crowd had already formed. She joined the short queue, rubbing her gloved hands together vigorously. Pulling her hat down further, she saw the lumbering vehicle arriving. She was on her way.

The bus was only about half full, but the passengers were jostling right and left as it traversed the pitted pavement. With all that was going on in the world, the roads had fallen into horrendous disrepair. Not only were there no supplies, but there were no men to do repair work. Most everyone's tires were well past their prime, but with rationing, everyone had to muddle through. She had often seen posters with pictures of military jeeps, admonishing: "They've got more important places to go than you! SAVE RUBBER!" At least there was still some transportation available most of the time.

The vehicle lurched forward, each stop stretching the night thinner. Helen's gaze flitted to the window, watching the lamplights flicker in the dark like erratic heartbeats. With every stop, a new batch of unfamiliar faces boarded, each one a reminder of how far she was from her familiar world. Every jerk of the bus knotted her stomach tighter. The evening wind seemed to whisper doubts, causing her to question every decision. "What am I doing?" she asked herself, her voice barely audible above the groan of the aging engine.

As the bus crept through the darkened streets, her lips went dry, and her heart pounded. It was just like when she was a teenager, attending her first dance with Bobby Appleby. She closed her eyes and took a few deep breaths to calm her nerves.

At last, the bus halted, thrusting her from her contemplative state. Gathering her belongings, she buttoned her coat and thanked the driver as she stepped off. The cold air snapped at her cheeks, and each footfall echoed on the pavement, a lonely sound that seemed too loud in the empty street. There wasn't a soul in sight, but the faint glow of The Hand & Heart beckoned, a warm spot of light in the chilly night. Her feet moved swiftly, almost of their own accord, eager to close the distance to the pub.

She hesitated at the door, fingers hovering over the cold metal. She drew in a steady breath. The undertone of voices inside suggested a hiatus from her thoughts, a plunge into anonymity. Pushing the door open, she slipped into the room, her eyes taking a moment to adjust.

Inside, the clink of glasses and low laughter filled the air. Three men at the bar turned at the sound of the door opening.

Avoiding their eyes, she scanned the room, spotted a sign for the loo, and made a beeline for it. The loo was always a good place to gather one's nerve.

Helen went in and glanced in the mirror, her confidence wavering. But it would be daft to turn back now. Smoothing her hair and reapplying lipstick, she hoped that looking smart would make it easier to get a lift.

She exited the loo with her head high, looking straight ahead. As her vision readjusted to the faint lighting, she scanned the faces quickly, bypassing those at the bar and spotting a solitary figure in the corner, finishing a pint. The parallel silver bars on his US Army uniform glistened in the hazy light. Her heart raced—a mix of excitement and a twinge of guilt nipping at her conscience as she moved through the pub. Determined, she walked toward him, her eyes gleaming as she caught his eye.

He rose and smiled as she approached his table. The three at the bar looked on, frowning and shaking their heads as they watched the man and woman speak briefly to each other. The officer nodded, his eyes beaming, and paid his tab. The two of them walked toward the door, deep in conversation.

"Look at that—barely a word exchanged, and she's off with him," said the first man at the bar, his tone dripping with envy. "Doesn't even need to try, does he?"

"It's the brass, innit?" the second man grumbled as he thumbed his flat cap back, a wry smile playing on his lips. "Lucky sod. Just once, I'd like to be the one getting a dish like that."

The third man, a burly fellow with a bold grin, raised his pint like it was a trophy. "Eh, cheer up, mates. Maybe next time she'll pick a bloke without all the shiny medals."

They burst into laughter, toasting their misfortune as the pub door swung shut, sealing Helen's night into fate's hands.

CHAPTER THIRTEEN

That same evening
Polebrook Air Base

CARUSO ADJUSTED HIS tie in the mirror, his reflection staring back with vacant eyes. Why was he even bothering? The only woman he wanted to see was miles away—if she even wanted to see him anymore. He couldn't stop wondering why Helen had pulled away, despite everything they'd shared. He ran a hand through his hair, sighing. Maybe she'd grown tired of writing to a broken man. Or maybe she saw through his attempts to act like everything was fine. After all, how could she understand what he didn't even understand himself?

"Well, no use thinking about it," he said under his breath, squaring his shoulders. *Too bad Helen can't see me now. I've changed—stronger, more confident. Well, except when doing the job I was sent here to do.* His eyes shifted away from his reflection. *If Bob can get through his fear of flying, so can I. After all, it's only nerves. No one ever died from the jitters.*

He sighed, trying to push it all from his mind and focus on the upcoming dance. If nothing else, it would be nice to hear some live music for a change. The fellas on base had been practicing with their band, and they were pretty good.

Lester's exasperated voice broke in on his thoughts. "Come on, Caruso, stop admiring yourself! At this rate, all the beer will be gone by the time we get there! And if you get any more handsome, none of the gals will be interested in the rest of us!"

Rapoport shifted his weight rapidly from left to right. "Yeah, let's get going before everyone pairs up!" He grabbed his jacket and headed for the door, the others quickly following into the crisp night air.

The Army had worked its magic, transforming the plain room into an enchanting dance hall, complete with beautifully decorated posters and captivating pictures. The band was going strong. "I haven't seen so many women in one place since arriving in England!" Lester said, beaming, as he took in the room. "Isn't this something? Wow, what a crowd!"

"Looks like there are a few left for us!" Rapoport said, eyes mischievous as he rubbed his hands together.

A pretty blonde smiled at Caruso from across the room, eyebrows raised in a hint of suggestion. *Too bad I'm not interested in any of them*, he thought miserably. He couldn't get Helen out of his mind. Still, he had to admit: the atmosphere was festive, lively. Maybe, just for a little while, he could set everything aside and just enjoy the night.

"Caruso!" A hand tapped him on the shoulder from behind. He turned and found himself face-to-face with Calvert. Caruso's eyes widened as he glanced at the two chevrons on his friend's uniform.

"You were promoted! You're a corporal now? Congratulations!"

"It's been a long road to get here." Calvert explained his past frustrations after being turned down for a promotion due to his lack of combat experience, a decision he had found bitterly unfair. "I was furious with the entire Army," he said. But just the week before, his fortunes had changed when he'd been made a corporal. More thrilling still, a temporary opening in Intelligence had emerged, and the captain had requested him by name to serve as his assistant. Calvert's eyes sparkled with enthusiasm and pride. "Captain Nichols said it's a great opportunity—and it might even become permanent!"

Caruso smiled at his friend's exuberance. "That's swell, Calvert. You deserve it. Tonight, you have every reason to celebrate!"

"Yes, and I plan to! See you later!" Calvert turned and headed off into the crowd.

Glancing around the room at the impressive spread of food and drink, surrounded by happily smiling men with one or two girls on each arm, Caruso couldn't help but feel out of place. Once, he had been the one people gravitated toward, but tonight, he just wanted to disappear into the background.

He sank into a nearby couch, focusing on the band playing a lively tune. They were a good-sized group of talented musicians. He recognized John Leasure, one of the plane mechanics, looking right at home playing his guitar. It was fascinating to see a different side of these men, many of whom he had worked with side by side. Caruso noticed that both Lester and Rapoport were already dancing with some attractive women on the crowded dance floor. Neither of them had quite mastered the Lindy Hop, but they were having a good time. Max and his friends were there, too, but kept a distance, wandering around the room and mingling with the others.

The music shifted, and Caruso recognized "I Get Along Without You Very Well (Except Sometimes)." *They're playing my song*, he thought to himself dryly. Not wanting to watch all the couples slow dancing, he got up and went over to the food and drinks to occupy his mind.

A voice came up behind him. "I thought you liked to dance, Sandy."

Caruso spun around, his breath catching. His heart slammed against his ribs. He blinked once, then again. Was this real? But there she stood, radiant and breathtaking. That burgundy dress, the way it hugged her frame, the soft curl of her hair—it was like a dream he hadn't dared to hope for.

Helen. Here.

"Helen…" His voice came out as a whisper, filled with awe and disbelief. He grabbed both of her hands, feeling their warmth as if to reassure himself she wasn't a dream. He inhaled deeply, her familiar scent enveloping him like a warm hug. "My goodness! Look at you! You're beautiful! What are you doing here? How did you…? When did you get here? I was just thinking about you!"

Helen's eyes twinkled, her laugh soft and nervous. "A colleague at Stoneleigh told me about the dance and said that all ladies were welcome. I didn't skive off from work; I had the night off and nothing else to do…" She smiled, looking up at him shyly. "A bus brought me to Peterborough, then a kind soul took pity on me and gave me a lift the rest of the way. That's why I'm a little late.

"I wanted to see how you're getting on." Her face flushed pink as she said the words, her eyes glimmering with both joy and something he couldn't quite name. "You're looking very smart, by the way."

"I'm over the moon now! Gee, Helen, it's really swell to see you." Caruso found it difficult to erase his grin.

Helen giggled. "You should see your face! You're gob-smacked! Just the reaction I was hoping for!"

"I still can't believe my eyes! Wow, you're really here! What a surprise! I didn't know if I'd ever see you again. I never heard from you after my last letter… I thought I might have scared you off!"

Helen looked down, then back into his face, her eyes glistening. "I just didn't know what to say."

"That's silly. We've never been at a loss for words!"

"Well, anyway, it's nice to see you." Just at that moment, the band started playing Duke Ellington's "In a Sentimental Mood." Helen grinned impishly. "And… I think you owe me a dance."

"May I have this one?" Caruso asked, bowing deeply before taking her hand and leading her to the dance floor.

As they swayed to the mellow rhythm, Caruso couldn't remember feeling happier than he did right then. He wanted to hold her forever. "I missed you, Helen… so much." He whispered the words into her hair and caressed her back. Sighing contentedly, he inhaled the perfume he remembered from Stoneleigh, stirring something deep inside, pulling him closer. Helen didn't answer, but her head rested lightly against his shoulder, her silence saying everything.

When the band switched to Benny Goodman's "Sing, Sing, Sing," she leaned back slightly, her eyes sparkling with mischief.

"Come on, Helen," Caruso said, grinning. "Let's show them how it's done."

They moved across the floor with a rhythm that felt natural, almost instinctive. The crowd watched as they spun and swung, their movements fluid and in sync. The lively songs continued, and everyone joined in with the merriment. When Glenn Miller's "In the Mood" began, the dancers once again stepped aside, admiring Helen and Caruso as they did the Lindy Hop. Caruso's grin widened as Helen laughed, her cheeks rosy from all the excitement. For the first time in months, Caruso felt like himself again.

As the music transitioned from lively rhythms to a slower melody, the group dispersed, some seeking refreshments, others a break from the energetic activity. Caruso and Helen, still catching their breath from the spirited moves, made their way to the less crowded edge of the room where the drinks were laid out. The relative quiet contrasted with the still audible hum of the main dance floor, providing a semblance of privacy amid the ongoing celebration.

They stepped away, still breathless, Caruso gently guiding her toward a small bench in the corner. "We stole the show," he said, grinning, brushing a curl from her cheek.

"Only because I had such a good lead," she teased, but her voice softened. "Sandy… I missed this. I missed *you*."

He reached for her hand. "I've missed *everything* about you. Even your fussing over my posture."

She laughed, then looked down. "It's easier when I'm with you. Being here tonight makes it feel like everything could just… work."

Caruso's voice caught in his throat. "Maybe it *can*."

"Gee, Caruso, you didn't tell me you were such a good dancer!" Calvert's voice broke through their momentary solitude as he approached, his face alight with amusement and a trace of surprise.

Caruso laughed softly, his gaze lingering on Helen with unspoken admiration. "I haven't done the Lindy Hop in quite some time, but my mother always made sure I knew how to keep up on the dance floor. And tonight, I have a great partner," he said. "This is Helen, my inspiration."

Helen's glance met Caruso's fleetingly—a quiet nod to their deeper connection. "He's too kind," she said, her voice light and cheerful.

"This is Helen?" Calvert's tone warmed with recognition. "From Stoneleigh?"

Caruso nodded, eyes sparkling. "Yes, that's right. Helen, this is Corporal Calvert P'Pool."

"Pleased to meet you, Corporal." Helen smiled, extending her hand to Calvert. They exchanged a few pleasantries, and Calvert left the two of them alone to catch up.

Caruso poured them each a glass of punch, and they stood side by side, sipping from waxy cups.

"Still better than hospital tea," she said, wrinkling her nose.

"Barely." He smiled. "But I'll take it. With you here, even this tastes different."

When the music shifted again—slow, lilting, mournful—Caruso didn't hesitate. "Another?"

Helen didn't answer, but her hand slipped into his, and they returned to the floor.

This time, she was quiet. Resting her head against his chest, her fingers gently clasped behind his neck, she swayed with him like they were the only two people left in the world.

He wanted to freeze time. To bottle this moment.

They stayed on the dance floor all night, the music a perfect parallel to their deep connection. But somewhere in the quiet rhythm, he felt her start to pull away.

For him, the evening seemed to pass in an instant, but as Helen glanced at her watch, the glow in her eyes dimmed. "I must get on, Sandy."

Caruso paused, the music and laughter around them suddenly feeling distant. He watched her, the joy of their dance fading into a confusing mix of emotions. "That's it?" Caruso's voice cracked slightly, and he cursed himself for sounding so raw. "After everything we shared, can you really just walk away?"

Helen hesitated, her fingers fumbling with the clasp of her coat. "Sandy, this night was… perfect. But it can't change what needs to be. I told you before, I—" She broke off, her gaze dropping to the floor. "If I don't leave, I'll miss my bus."

"I'll find someone to give you a ride back later," Caruso said quickly, his voice low and urgent. "Or tomorrow. Please, Helen. Don't leave it like this."

Her eyes brimmed, but she avoided his gaze, blinking hard. "Tonight was lovely, but some things are better left as beautiful memories." Her mouth opened as if to say more, but then a shadow passed across her face. "Sandy, I—" But she stopped herself, exhaling sharply, and turned away, hands trembling as she finished buttoning her coat.

Caruso looked at her, his voice barely above a whisper, his bewilderment slowly turning into realization. "You don't mean that. I thought tonight meant… Are we just supposed to forget all this?"

His hands gripped hers, desperate for her to stay. "I know you have feelings for me. Why can't you explain?"

Her voice faltered, barely audible. "I've tried, Sandy. I have. But some things… they don't fit into words." She inhaled sharply, blinking fast. "You're a good man."

Helen collected her belongings and walked out the door toward a waiting truck that the Army was filling with ladies destined for Peterborough. Caruso kept pace beside her. "A good man, but not good enough to continue to see? I don't understand!"

"I-I'm sorry. I have to go. It was wrong to come, I see that now. Thank you for a lovely evening. Goodnight, Sandy." She leaned over to kiss him on the cheek, but he quickly shifted his head, bringing their lips together, and she didn't pull away. He wrapped his arms around her and held her tight.

As she slowly disengaged herself, cheeks flushed and eyes glistening, a wave of emptiness crashed over him. He watched her walk away, head down, every step seeming to widen the chasm that had suddenly sprung up between them. She quickly boarded with the other ladies just before the truck began pulling away, not looking up as they left.

He followed the taillights with his eyes until they were out of sight, fading into the darkness like a puff of smoke. He stood frozen, long after the last glimmer of the vehicle was gone, staring into the blackness. The ache in his chest was unbearable—a reminder of everything and everyone he had lost. Another name added to the long list of goodbyes he never wanted to say. His fists clenched, and his voice was barely a whisper against the cold wind. "I won't give up, Helen. Don't you give up, either."

He felt like he was murmuring into the void, his words swallowed by the night. They hung there, unanswered, as he turned back toward the dance hall. The music and laughter inside felt like they belonged to someone else, in another world. For Caruso, the night had ended, leaving only the quiet weight of what might have been.

CHAPTER FOURTEEN

A few days later

CARUSO PACED THE empty barracks, the sound echoing off the walls, a bleak reminder of his aloneness. Helen had put him off once again, leaving him frustrated and yearning for connection. At the same time, he was eager to return to battle, yet forced to mask his turmoil within the confines of the ball turret. The strain of handling it all alone was becoming unbearable.

His thoughts kept turning over, falling on top of each other like the colored glass in the kaleidoscope he had as a kid. Hoping a walk would quiet his mind, he stepped outside. The cold seeped into every gap in his coat, as pervasive as the doubts plaguing his mind. A lone, crumpled leaf skittered across the path, aimless and at the mercy of the biting wind.

Will I ever be able to function in the turret like I used to? Helen had always told him to take one mission at a time and not look too far ahead. He certainly wasn't the only man to return after injury, but the thought of stepping into a room full of strangers, their eyes weighing him, churned his stomach. Could he trust men he hardly knew? Now, survival might hinge more on luck than skill.

He threw his cigarette on the ground and crushed it under his boot. He'd never smoked before coming to England. Now, it was becoming a habit, despite the nausea it brought and the way it tightened the pit in his stomach.

The next morning, Caruso reported for his first real mission since his injury. He went through the motions—breakfast, briefing, checklists—each step a ritual that scarcely kept his anxiety at bay. The target was Misberg's oil refinery. The CO's words barely registered. Flak expected. Stay in formation. The lead ship would guide them in.

He sat through it all, nodding at the right times, gripping the crucifix in his chest pocket. When they finally took off, the cold of altitude seeped through his boots, his gloves, his bones. The ball turret was as confining as ever. He clenched his jaw, forcing his breathing steady.

When the bombs dropped, something went wrong. Their lead ship released too early, and the rest followed. "Bombs fell short," the radioman said. Caruso cursed under his breath.

Back at base, the landing was smooth. But Caruso was seething.

"What in blazes happened with our bombs?" he snapped.

"Lead goofed up the drop," the radioman mumbled.

"Do they even bother training these guys anymore?"

The radioman flinched, his shoulders stiffening. "Hey, it wasn't me." His voice was low but defensive.

Lester stepped between them, a hand on Caruso's shoulder. "Take it easy, Caruso. We all made it back, didn't we? That's more than some can say."

Caruso bit back a retort, his jaw tight.

⁂

Caruso lingered in the debrief room after the others had cleared out, collecting any still-full glasses left behind. The burn in his throat was preferable to the fury in his chest. He thought of Albert, a gunner from another crew who'd died that day. Oxygen failure. One mission. One mistake.

There was no logic to it. Good men died. Bad ones, too. It didn't matter. Caruso stared into the bottom of his glass and thought of all the telegrams still to come. Mothers who'd wake to find their sons gone.

He was deep in thought as he walked back to the barracks, and the distant clamor of voices gradually pierced his reflections, a vivid contrast to the silence he'd just left behind. The call for mail broke his thoughts. He almost turned away.

"Caruso!" The sudden call jolted him to attention, a surge of unexpected emotion tightening his chest. The envelope was in his hand before he even realized he'd moved. The handwriting was unmistakable.

Helen's letter felt like a lifeline, each word dissolving a fraction of the distance and despair that had wedged within him. He tore open the envelope, a rush of warmth flooding his chest.

Dear Sandy,

I wanted to write to you all that I couldn't find a way to say when I came to the dance. I had such a lovely time with you.

Please forgive my quick departure that night. It was so tempting to stay longer. My coming to the dance was a spur-of-the-moment decision and in retrospect, although I know I left you with more questions, I don't regret coming.

We didn't discuss how you were readjusting to being back on base. I do want to tell you I've never met any man who has the resolve and stamina you do, and that is what will get you through. Don't let your nerves get to you. You've been well trained, and I'm confident that you know what to do.

You've already been through the worst of the worst. Just take everything day by day and focus on the blessings we spoke of at Stoneleigh. You survived your injury for a reason. Don't look too far ahead—hold on to the strength that carried you this far and let it see you through your tour. Each day may seem endless, but you are building resilience. It's the hope in our hearts and our unyielding spirit that makes a path through the darkest of times, just as they did back at Stoneleigh. (Remember when you didn't think you'd ever get out of there?)

Know that I hold you tight in my heart and I look forward to whenever we might meet again.

Stay strong and well, Sandy. Have faith in yourself. I have faith in you.

Love,

Helen

Memories of their time together at the dance flashed into his mind: the way her laughter had cut through the noise of the crowded hall, how her eyes had sparkled under the lights. He reread Helen's letter, its words slicing through the day's gloom. Her voice seemed to fill the spaces around him, a thread of hope and a semblance of peace weaving through the turmoil.

Helen had been right about Stoneleigh. At the time, every morning felt like a defeat waiting to happen. But somehow, step by step, he'd pulled through. Maybe today was no different—just another step.

He also remembered the evenings they'd spent just talking, her British manner and colloquialisms adding a sweet charm to their conversations. At a time when the war was claiming every piece of stability, her support buoyed him, reminding him of the strength he carried within.

Pressing the letter against his chest, warmth seeped through the cold walls he'd built around his heart. The smile it drew felt like the rediscovery of joy, the texture of the paper under his fingertips contrasting with the gentle words written on it. The weight of the day's events and the ongoing toll of the war seemed momentarily lighter, as if Helen's faith in him had bolstered his own belief in himself. It was a thought that carried him into sleep, a rare calm in the storm. Maybe Helen was right. Even now, there were still flickers of light, if you remembered to look. Helen always knew just the thing to say.

CHAPTER FIFTEEN

The next day

CARUSO PERCHED ON the edge of his chair, his fingers dancing with anticipation as he reached for the pen. The ink flowed as if drawn by something deeper than excitement—a pulse of hope rising in him like steam from a kettle.

Reaching automatically toward the cigarette carton, his fingers met only air. He frowned, scanning the desk. Empty. The bottle beside it had less in it than he remembered, too. He stared at both for a moment, then looked away.

Helen's letter still lay open beside him, the words folding around his doubt like a warm blanket. He needed to see her again. Saying what he felt in person—*that* would be real. But the logistics seemed daunting. Then it struck him: he knew exactly who could help.

~

"I really appreciate your taking me, Zeus." Zeus had pulled off this kind of thing before—he'd smuggled Caruso's crew in for a visit months ago. To him, sneaking off base for a quick trip wasn't a big deal. He'd cover by saying he was delivering something, and no one would ask too many questions.

"No problem. You visit friend?" Lizewski's English might be broken, but his warmth always shone through.

"You could say that. It's a nurse that I met when I was in there."

"Ahh." He nodded, a twinkle of mischief in his eyes. "Perhaps more than friend?"

Caruso's grin widened. "I'm hoping so. We'll see." The lorry crawled through the streets toward Stoneleigh, each turn agonizingly slow. She'd be just as surprised to see him as he'd been to see her at the dance. *Gobsmacked*, she'd said. The word lingered in his mind, drawing a slow, fond smile. The lilt of her voice and the British turns of phrase never failed to captivate him.

The journey seemed endless. When they finally arrived, the familiar walkways of Stoneleigh now felt different as Caruso approached the building. The cold winter air bit at his cheeks, and each footstep resonated like a drumbeat in his ears as he reached the entrance and hurried inside the place that had been home to him for months.

A new face greeted him at the nurse's desk. "Excuse me…" he said, hesitant to interrupt.

"Hello there, soldier. How can I be of help?"

"I'm looking for a nurse named Helen."

The woman's smile brightened. "Oh yes! I know Helen well. Unfortunately, she's not here right now. Took some unexpected leave."

A crease of concern formed on Caruso's brow. "Is she okay?"

"Oh, absolutely. Sorry to alarm you. Everything's fine." The nurse paused, her smile faltering as she searched through some papers on her desk. "She mentioned something about her husband."

Caruso's heart skipped a beat as the room spun subtly. "Her husband?" The word "husband" landed like a direct hit, the kind that leaves you stunned before the pain sets in. His breath hitched. He blinked, certain he'd misheard. He paused, inhaling deeply to steady himself.

The room seemed to tilt, the nurse's voice blurring as if coming from a distance, her words muffled through the haze of his shock. "Yes, he's in the RAF. Went missing for a bit; he only just got back. They're sorting things out."

Caruso felt the ground shift beneath him. For a moment, he was lost, adrift in the news. Then, as he leaned against the cool wall of the corridor, the reality began to seep in, cold and unwelcome.

"Quite romantic, don't you think? Can you imagine—" Caruso saw her glance up, taking in his knuckles, taut and white against the counter. The walls of the corridor seemed to close in. He struggled for air, desperate for space to understand the stunning revelation.

He stumbled into the hallway, vision swimming as his memory reeled. *Her quick subject changes. Her hesitation at the dance. The way she looked at me like she wanted to say something but never did. Has she been trying to tell me all along? Have I been too blind—or too hopeful—to see it?*

The air turned sharp and thin, like there wasn't enough of it to go around. The nurse's voice faded into a dull hum behind him as if she were speaking from underwater. Struggling to process the news, he barely noticed the nurse's softer, pitying tone as she murmured to her colleague, unaware that Caruso could hear her. "Poor chap looked like he'd seen a ghost. This war, it's tearing them apart inside and out." The reply was lost to him as he lurched to a railing. The flutter of butterflies swirling in his chest collapsed into a nauseating heap; his thoughts tripped over each other. *She's married?*

The news struck Caruso like shrapnel, shredding defenses he hadn't known he possessed. This was a war zone he'd never trained for. The halls echoed with the distant noise of hospital activity and muffled voices, each sound evidence of the world moving on around him, oblivious to his crumbling reality. Cold sweat clung to him as he burst toward the exit, gasping for air. The open door beckoned like a bail-out into uncertain territory. The frosty cold stung his lungs as he sprinted toward Lizewski's lorry, the door slamming shut with a finality mirroring his turmoil.

"That was fast," Zeus said, his eyes reflecting a mix of concern and curiosity. "How things go?"

"She wasn't there." Caruso's tone was flat, his mind a whirlwind of confusion and disbelief.

"Sorry for that. You leave message?" Zeus's voice was gentle, an attempt to comfort the palpable misery radiating from Caruso.

"What?" Caruso blinked slowly, pulled from his thoughts. "Oh, no, I didn't. It doesn't matter."

"No worry. It work out." Zeus's smile was reassuring.

The words resonated, unearthing a distant memory. "My mother used to say that when I was upset. I never believed her."

"Mama always know best," Zeus said.

Caruso managed a half smile. "That's what she said, too. But I didn't want to hear it at the time."

The rest of the ride was filled with Zeus's attempts at conversation, but Caruso remained deep in thought, his mind spinning. Upon reaching the base, he mumbled his thanks and began the solitary walk to the barracks, his legs dragging under the burden of his discovery.

Their shared smiles and touches, once sources of tingling anticipation, now felt like the sting of disloyalty. Anger bubbled within him, heat flushing his cheeks as he wrestled with confusion and hurt. His boots struck hard against the cold ground, every step a blow against the questions spiraling in his head. Why had she maintained this charade? Every letter, every moment they'd shared—it had all felt real. *Has she been leading me on? Did she just not know how to tell me? Did she mean any of it? And if she didn't… what the hell was she thinking?*

The intensity of it all chased him away from the barracks. He couldn't go back, not yet. He needed space to clear his head and work through the betrayal. Turning, his eyes landed on a stray bike propped up against a building. Men on base had a habit of renting bikes from the store in Oundle and never returning them. Without a second thought, he mounted the bike and pedaled away.

Despite the tumult of his thoughts, riding through the crisp air offered a welcome respite, the rhythmic pedaling helping to calm his nerves. Almost without realizing it, he found himself covering the three miles to Oundle, eventually coming to a stop at The Rose & Crown. Leaving the bike leaning nonchalantly against the wall outside, he stepped inside, seeking consolation in the pub's familiar embrace.

Under the muted lights, his gaze settled on Calvert, who sat cradling the remains of a pint at the bar. Caruso felt a wave of relief at the sight of his friend and made his way over, the smell of ale and wood polish wafting up to his nostrils as he approached.

"Hello, Calvert, we meet again. I haven't had the best of days, so seeing a friendly face is a welcome change," Caruso greeted him, trying to muster a smile.

Calvert turned in his seat, surprise lighting up his features. "Caruso! Gee, I haven't seen you since the dance! You and Helen looked so happy together." Then, taking in Caruso's long face, he tilted his head in concern. "Say, what's got you so down?"

Caruso sighed heavily, his hand sweeping across his face as he looked up at Calvert, his newfound knowledge nearly suffocating. "Honestly, I'm not even sure where to start. It feels like I just got hit with a bomb. But let's grab some pints. I've got a story that might take a while.

"I went AWOL to see Helen at Stoneleigh," Caruso said, his tone heavy. "Thought it might help steady my nerves—being in the turret's got me all twisted up. Didn't expect to find she's got a husband back from the RAF, on R & R."

"You're kidding me!" Calvert's brows shot up, his eyes widening.

"I wish I were. Apparently, he wanted to surprise her. Well, Calvert, I don't know about her, but I was surprised as hell. Felt like a Jerry bomb dropped on me. And here I'd been thinking we might have something. I've been a yo-yo, bouncing between her ever-changing emotions. One minute she seems to be interested, and the next, she's pushing me away."

Calvert listened, his own experiences with disappointment echoing Caruso's feelings of betrayal. "It's natural to feel that way. But maybe there's more to the story. It's too soon to make any decisions. Give it time."

Caruso's strained voice evidenced his frustration. "There's no point in talking to her now. It's all too late."

Calvert nodded, his response measured. "You're in a tough spot, Caruso, I'll give you that. Back home, facing the difficulties of running a store taught me something important: troubles aren't permanent unless you decide they are. Understanding Helen's actions won't change the past, but it could change how you face what's next."

"Calvert," Caruso said, his voice tight, "I don't think your store's struggle and this betrayal are even close to the same thing." *If there was a reason for her actions, she surely could have told me*, he thought. *Instead, she side-stepped the truth. She came to see me only to then say we couldn't have anything more. Later, she wrote that she looked forward to seeing me again. She pushed me away, then pulled me toward her. How could her words be true when she's married?*

And what kind of a person is she, that her husband was missing in action, and she didn't stay completely faithful? Granted, we only shared a kiss or two, but she was the one who came all that distance to see me. What did that say about her?

Calvert placed his hand on Caruso's arm. "Back home, we say that even the darkest cloud might water your field. It's hard to see that now. Maybe there's a reason things happened this way. You're caught in a storm, but storms always pass. Give it some time. I agree that it's too soon to talk to Helen now; everything is too raw. But maybe in time. When the dust settles, things might become clearer. You ever think maybe she came to the dance to find clarity for herself, too? War makes a mess of things—it's not always about loyalty or disloyalty. Sometimes it's just survival." Calvert looked at Caruso earnestly. "And about your trouble on missions, have you talked to the flight surgeon?"

"No, and I'm not going to! Look, the only way I'll get home is by finishing my thirty-five flights. If I tell them I'm having problems, they'll delay my missions. I'm not willing to risk that. I'm already behind! The crew I trained with is already back in the States!"

"If you're willing to continue missions despite the strain, that's your choice. But remember, your decisions affect more than just you—they affect your whole crew, and maybe others, too. You have to decide what you can live with.

"I know I'm not up there dodging flak and facing Jerry, but I've seen enough to know you carry a heavy load back to the ground. Those flight docs are here to lighten that, not just for you, but for everyone counting on you. Just don't completely close the door on seeking help." He glanced at his watch. "I have to get back. Think about it, will you? Your well-being affects everyone around you."

Caruso gave a half smile and shook his friend's hand. "Thanks, Calvert. I'll try to give it some time. Maybe my nerves will settle, and if Helen contacts me again, I'll hear her out."

He turned back to the bar, his thoughts still swirling, and ordered a double whiskey. When the bartender brought it, he stared into space, fingering it thoughtfully. Then he downed it all at once, paid the tab, and left.

Caruso returned to the barracks to find Max and his crew in animated conversation that ceased abruptly as he entered, leaving an uneasy silence.

"Am I interrupting something?" he asked, a hint of irritation in his voice.

Max reassured him quickly, sensing his mood. "No, not at all. Just sharing some nerves about tomorrow's mission. It'll be our first time up against the Jerries. What was your first time up there like?"

He leaned against the doorframe, and a tight, humorless smile crossed his face. "First time up? It's like stepping into another world. In training, you're just getting your wings wet. But on a real mission? It's no man's land. Nothing can prepare you for that reality. Every sortie after… it's a roll of the dice. Your head's on a swivel, watching for bandits and praying your bird doesn't take a direct hit."

"Sounds intense," Max said, casting uncertain glances at his crewmates. "How do you handle it?"

"You stick to your training, keep your crew close, and hope Lady Luck's in your formation that day. And with each safe landing, you wonder how you cheated the odds yet again.

"And when you're not up there, you find ways to forget you ever have to go back," Caruso said quietly. He thought about how he'd started lingering after the debrief, collecting any leftovers of bourbon that had been set out for the airmen after battle. The haze of smoke from endless cigarettes clung to him, as did the isolation he wore like a shield against the memories. Numbing the fear with alcohol, losing himself in the dulling of his senses, was easier than confronting the nightmares that followed him on the ground.

As he turned away, he reflected on his earlier conversation with Calvert. His friend's advice about facing hardships resonated more than he expected. Maybe dealing with Helen wasn't so different from handling his duties in the air. Both required facing fears, making tough decisions, and sometimes, just putting one foot in front of the other to get through. He wondered if mastering one battle could help him navigate the other.

The next day, following a harrowing flight, Caruso and his crew burst into the mess hall for dinner, their voices loud and slurred with adrenaline, exhaustion, and alcohol. Caruso's gaze fell on Max, whose crew had their first flight that morning and had been assigned as spares. They'd returned to base after formation, not having been needed for the mission.

"Hope you boys enjoyed your little practice run today," Caruso said with a sneer. "Don't think the Army always does it this way. My first day was hell! I saw a plane go down right before my eyes—a direct hit. Just fell straight down. No one got out. Miracle we made it back in one piece. That kind of thing is an initiation, you know what I mean? At least we were broken in right. Don't expect every day to be like this one."

Max's gaze flicked to his crewmates, who all looked away in awkward silence. The sting of Caruso's words hung in the air, heavy and suffocating. Max led his men to a far corner, where their laughter faded to a murmur, leaving Caruso alone with his bitterness.

As the mess hall commotion enveloped him, Caruso felt a surprising pang of sudden regret. His words had only isolated him further, driving a wedge between himself and the others. He realized, in a rare moment of reflection, that his anger wasn't directed at Max or the others but at himself and the situation he was powerless to change.

He sat alone, his untouched food growing cold. The adrenaline had burned off, leaving nothing but exhaustion and the bitter taste of his own words. He'd lashed out, but at what cost? He was pushing them away—all of them. And the worst part? He knew it. He toyed with the idea of apologizing to Max, a gesture to bridge the gap he'd created, not just with Max but with all the men. Yet, reaching out and admitting weakness felt as daunting as facing enemy fire. For now, he stayed seated, lost in thought, the isolation heavy on his shoulders.

Navigating Helen's mixed signals felt like flying blind over enemy territory—every word a potential ambush, every gesture a false sense of security. And just like in the air, there were no guarantees. No way to know if he'd make it through unscathed.

As the sounds around him transformed into a soft drone, Caruso found himself longing for a reprieve, not just from the war, but from his internal battles. The realization that he had fiercely pushed away the camaraderie he yearned for was a bitter pill to swallow. In that moment, Caruso understood the war he was fighting wasn't just in the skies but within himself.

CHAPTER SIXTEEN

HELEN OPENED HER diary carefully, smoothing the pages as she gathered her thoughts. She couldn't believe the predicament she was in. Her mind was spinning. She took a deep breath and sat down to write.

> *I've really mucked everything up. And now it's even worse than it was. Roy came to me a few days ago—surprised me at Stoneleigh. I was gobsmacked. I hadn't seen him in so long—I didn't even know if he was dead or alive. He looked well, but thinner.*
>
> *I didn't know how to react. All these months—years, really—barely hearing from him… I just felt so disconnected from him. Which, in part, may explain why I fell so hard for Sandy. And then felt so guilty for it.*
>
> *Roy looked nervous when he saw me, and now that I know the truth, it all makes sense. He's fallen in love with someone else. And she's expecting their baby. He came home only to ask me for a divorce so he could marry her and give the baby his name.*

I should be relieved. Once we're divorced, my heart can be free to love again.

Instead, a tangle of emotions overwhelms me. Unexpectedly, I'm hurt. But why should I be? He and I both fell in love with others, it seems. War turns everything topsy-turvy, doesn't it?

I feel ashamed. I've torn Sandy's heart asunder, I know it. Jean, my colleague at work, told me a man had stopped by to see me while I was away with Roy. It had to be Sandy. She said that when she mentioned I had taken some time off with my husband, his face turned pale, and he turned and walked away. Without a word.

I'm heartsick with worry, but I don't dare contact Sandy. Not yet. It's not right. I must finish this marriage with Roy, and if there's anything left with Sandy after that, we'll have to sort it out.

My heart is breaking, knowing how betrayed Sandy must feel. And of course he feels that way. What he must think of me.

But I know what I need to do first. I'll set things right. And when the dust finally settles, maybe Sandy will find it in his heart to forgive me.

CHAPTER SEVENTEEN

December, 1944

CARUSO FOLDED HIS laundry in silence, methodically placing each piece into his trunk. With everyone either on a mission or out for training, Caruso found himself alone in his quarters. He'd briefly flirted with the idea of going to London on pass but decided to stay on base and sift through his thoughts.

But no matter how he tried, his thoughts kept circling back to Helen.

He ran his fingers over the frayed edges of a worn shirt. The stillness of the empty barracks unnerved him, contrasting sharply with the rhythmic, almost hypnotic droning of the B-17's engines. Those vibrations had lulled him into a false sense of security, right before the sky erupted into a sea of flak. His grip tightened around the fabric, white-knuckled, as if bracing for impact, as vivid, loud memories pulsed through him. He paused, hands trembling slightly, struggling to push the flashbacks away.

Caruso shook off his melancholy and sank into a chair, pulling a small, pressed flower from the pages of his notebook. The petals felt brittle under his fingertips, a delicate reminder of something that had once felt so vibrant. He wondered if she still thought of him, or if the memory of that evening walk at Stoneleigh had faded for her as much as it lingered for him. As he began a letter to her, his words stumbled, tangled with emotions too complex to convey. Crumpling the paper, he began again, setting aside both the flower and his unresolved feelings to write to his parents instead. He forced a cheerful tone into his letter, pausing every few sentences to second-guess his words. If his mother and stepdad knew the truth about his well-being, they'd be sick with worry. He pressed the pen harder against the paper, determined to shield them from that.

Dear Mom and Pop,

I'm doing fine so you don't have to worry. I'm back to my regular duties and feeling as good as new. Your prayers for me have surely been answered.

How are things back home? I bet Caroline is growing up so fast. Please send me a recent photo, or I won't recognize her when I return! Hope everything is going well at the barber shop. Wish I could be there to give you a hand.

I miss you all so much. If you happen to see any of my friends, please give them my best regards and tell them to write! Getting mail is the highlight of our days.

Love,

Sandy

A memory of his father flashed through his mind. He had died so young, at thirty, only nine years older than Caruso was now. Caruso's life had shifted drastically after Pop passed, and even more so in the war. Thinking about it prompted his emotions to swell within him like a wave.

Sealing the letter, he stood up, wiping his forehead. Remembering Helen's words, he resolved to keep moving forward, despite whatever obstacles fell into his path.

The quickest way out of this war was to keep doing his missions. He'd told himself time and time again that fear doesn't kill you. Pop used to tell him to keep his eye on the goal. Back then, he was talking about sports, but it applied to wartime, too, Caruso was certain.

Tucking the letter into his pocket, he pulled on his jacket and stepped outside, picking up one of the abandoned bikes lying nearby.

A voice called out behind him. "Sergeant Caruso?" Turning, he saw an Army private holding out a bag.

"Yes, that's me."

"I have your replacement order."

Caruso looked at him quizzically.

"For your crew jacket."

Caruso brightened. "Thank you very much." He took the bag and headed back to the barracks to try on the new jacket. It fit perfectly, but felt stiff and unfamiliar. His original jacket had molded to him over time, and despite the blood stains on the interior and the stitches from the repair, it was like an old friend. After a moment's contemplation, he folded the new one into his knapsack and attached it to the bike waiting outside.

He pedaled quickly, the brisk motion warming his legs as he wove through the base toward the mailbox. Each turn of the wheels pressed the letter tighter to his side—a reminder of the half-truths he'd written home. He wondered when the war would end—but more than that, he wondered who he'd be when it did. Would there be anything remaining of the man who left home? Or would he be nothing more than the sum of his missions, the weight of his losses? After slipping the letter into the mailbox, he pushed on, the rush of cool air across his face offering a small escape, a brief respite he hoped the warmth of the pub would extend.

~

Tom, the bartender, greeted him warmly as Caruso entered the softly lit pub in Oundle.

"Hi, Tom, how's everything?" Caruso ordered a double whiskey and lit a cigarette.

"A bit quiet today, but it's still early. How are you doing?"

Caruso frowned. "Well, I could be better… but given that it's wartime, I could be a hell of a lot worse."

Tom chuckled. "Is it Army troubles? Or lady troubles?"

Caruso shrugged. "A bit of both, actually."

The door to the pub slammed. Caruso turned to see Calvert, pale and stricken.

"Calvert, what's wrong?" Caruso asked.

Calvert's lips quivered as he looked away. "I just got a telegram." His voice broke. "My mother passed away."

A heavy silence fell between them, laden with unspoken condolences.

"Oh, that's terrible news. I'm so sorry, mate." Tom brought him a whiskey and poured one for himself and Caruso. "On the house, Calvert." He raised his glass. "To your mum. May she rest in peace."

Caruso placed a hand on Calvert's arm, his voice low. "I'm real sorry. Do you want to talk about it?"

"It was her heart. My father was with her, and she died in his arms." Calvert's face crumbled. "It's my fault," Calvert choked out. His fingers dug into the edges of the bar, his body trembling. "She was so worried about my being over here. I told her I was fine, that I wasn't in danger, but she never believed me. And now she's gone. Because of me."

"No, Calvert." Tom's tone was firm. "You can't blame yourself."

Caruso nodded. "Tom's right; she had a bad heart. Just like my pop. He passed away when he was only thirty-eight. I was just fourteen. We had no warning."

Calvert looked up at Caruso, tears streaming down his face. "I didn't know. How did you survive it, Caruso? I don't know how I'm going to go on."

"Day by day. Remembering the good and letting that guide you."

Tom nodded in agreement.

"I can't believe I'll never see her again. And that I missed her funeral and burial. I didn't get to pay my last respects! And when I left to join up, I didn't even say goodbye. Why didn't I hug her and kiss her goodbye? So she'd have had at least that, instead of a silly note?" Calvert's lips trembled and his shoulders slumped.

Caruso's throat tightened as he listened. He knew that feeling—regret settling in his gut like a lead weight. There were no words big enough to fill the chasm of loss, so he simply reached out and placed a hand on Calvert's arm, steadying him like a brace against a collapsing wall. "Calvert, we all do the best we can with what we have. You're a good man. She knew what was in your heart," Caruso said, his voice softening as he took in his friend's grief. There was a brief silence, filled only by the low murmur of the pub and the clinking of glasses as they all sat, immersed in their own thoughts. Caruso paused, taking a slow sip of whiskey. "You honor her by living, Calvert. By being the man she knew you could be."

Caruso glanced down at his knapsack and then back at Calvert. He thought of his own father's death, how the loss had felt like stepping into a world without solid ground. He remembered the emptiness, the way people's words of comfort rang hollow. And yet, somehow, he'd found a way forward. Maybe his idea of this small gesture could offer Calvert a foothold, a thread to cling to when everything else felt like it was unraveling.

"This might not be the right time, but maybe it's the right reason. I brought you something today, not knowing you'd be bearing such heavy news. But maybe it'll lift your spirits a bit." He reached into his bag and carefully pulled out the new crew jacket, extending it toward his friend. He hoped it would provide some comfort, a small token of brotherhood in this harsh reality. "I know you always wanted one. After my accident, I ordered a new one since mine was ripped, but I managed to fix the old one. Looks like this one was meant for you."

Calvert smiled, his face still wet with tears. Sliding off his bar stool, he pulled it on. "Thank you," he said, looking first at Caruso and then at Tom. "Both of you. It means a lot to have friends like you."

"We're all in this together," Tom said. "And that jacket suits you."

"Wear it in good health, my friend," Caruso said, shaking his hand. Then, raising his half-empty glass, he said, "God's blessings to your mother and your family."

Calvert nodded. "I should head back. Thank you, both of you. This… it means more than I can say." His voice was thick with emotion, each word seemingly an effort.

Caruso stood with him, offering a supportive arm on his shoulder. "You're not alone in this, Calvert. We'll get you through this."

Tom, behind the bar, nodded his agreement, acknowledging the shared strain of loss. "Take care, Calvert. And remember, this place is always here for you."

Calvert managed a weak smile, clasping Caruso's hand tightly for a moment before turning toward the door. The gentle jingle of the bell on the pub door echoed a soft farewell as he departed.

Caruso sat at the bar, his mood unexpectedly lighter than when he'd walked in. Calvert's loss made Caruso reflect on his own family and the importance of support during difficult times. He remembered his mother's words when they used to gather donations at church for those in need: *Helping another helps yourself.* Nothing had changed in his own life, but his spirits were paradoxically lifted by offering friendship and solidarity to his comrade.

Caruso exhaled, the whiskey burning his throat but doing nothing to dull the ache inside. He met Tom's gaze, then lifted his glass. "Another round," he said quietly. "For the ones we've loved and lost—and the ones we're still holding on for. Because sometimes that's the only thing that keeps you going."

As Tom poured the drinks, the faint light of the pub gave off a warm glow, a haven in the night for those adrift in memories and loss.

CHAPTER EIGHTEEN

A FEW DAYS later, Caruso mailed some letters home and, before returning to the barracks, stopped by to visit his friend.

Engrossed in his paperwork, Calvert glanced up at the sound of Caruso's footsteps.

"Hi," Caruso said, his smile kind. "Didn't mean to interrupt your work, but I just wanted to see how you're doing."

"Thanks. I'm okay. My work and planning the Christmas party for the kids from Oundle is helping to take my mind off things. And it's good that you stopped in; I could use your help."

"What is it?"

"We need an elf to help with the festivities. Would you do the honors?"

A moment of hesitation gripped him. Could he even fake the joy these kids deserved? Lately, it felt like the war had drained every last drop of warmth from him, leaving nothing but exhaustion and cynicism. But then—unexpectedly—something flickered within him, a forgotten ember of mischief. His lips twitched, a chuckle breaking free before he would stop it. "Well, I've never pictured myself as an elf, but how can I say no to the children?"

A big grin beamed across Calvert's face. "Oh, thank you! With all you have going on, I wasn't sure if you'd be able to. And I know you're still recovering. There won't be anything strenuous."

Calvert's eyes brightened as he laid out the plans. "We'll transform the hangar into something magical—lights, decorations, maybe even a Christmas tree if we can get our hands on one. The kids will arrive all wide-eyed, and the men will escort them to the mess hall for a proper Christmas dinner. And then—Father Christmas." He grinned. "Gifts, carols, the whole works. For one evening, just one, they'll forget about ration books and bomb shelters. They'll just be kids."

Calvert looked at Caruso with renewed interest, cocking his head. "Say, do you, by any chance, play the piano?"

Caruso grinned, raising his eyebrows. They'd had a rickety piano at home, and his father had taught him how to read music. He'd suffered through all the piano drills only because he loved sitting next to Pop, listening to him explain the different tempos and how they could completely transform a piece of music. "Well, I wouldn't say I'm a professional, but Pop taught me to play a bit."

"Would you be willing to lead the Christmas carols?"

"You want me to sing, too?" Caruso's eyes widened in mock disbelief. "Now, that may cost you," he said, winking.

"Once you see how much fun the youngsters are having, that'll be all the payment you'll need. Will you do it?"

Caruso nodded, his eyes shining with delight. "At your service. It's the least I can do, for all you've done for me. And bringing a little Christmas to these children will do the same for us all, I think."

"Definitely. I know it's going to be swell. They've had to give up so much for this war," Calvert said. "I've seen the looks on their faces when I ride over to Oundle. And they're so happy with any small offering. You should see them smile when they get a piece of gum or candy. It's like I'm giving them the world."

"To them it probably is just that. You know, Calvert, it's a real nice thing you're doing."

Calvert grinned, blinking rapidly to clear the sudden moisture in his eyes. "Helping others always makes me feel good, so I guess I have my own selfish reasons.

"Back home, at Christmastime, we'd donate items from our general store to families in need. Their faces when we delivered the donations were unforgettable. I guess this is my way of bringing a bit of home to England during the holidays. It's possible, even with a war on." He paused. "Sometimes, though, I wonder if I'm trying too hard to pretend everything's fine. If I stop moving, even for a second, it all catches up with me."

Caruso nodded. "Yeah, I know the feeling." Then, hesitant to sink back into melancholy, he switched gears. "I'll be happy to help you out. Who's going to be Father Christmas?"

"I haven't gotten that one figured out yet, but I know the perfect person is out there."

"You know what I like about you, Calvert?" Caruso asked, clapping his friend on the shoulder. "No matter what happens, you've got this way of believing things will turn out fine. And somehow… they always do." He hesitated, studying his friend. *How does he do that?* The thought nagged at him. Calvert had lost his mother only days ago, and yet here he was, pouring himself into making Christmas happen for kids who weren't even his own. *Maybe that's the trick,* Caruso mused. *Keep moving, keep giving, and don't let yourself sink.*

Calvert nodded. "My mother always said things have a way of working out. And somehow, she was always right."

"Sounds like our moms were made from the same stock."

The two shook hands, and Caruso began walking back to the barracks, but not before Calvert called out to him, "Don't forget to practice those carols, Sergeant Elf!"

Caruso smiled to himself. "An elf," he said softly, shaking his head in disbelief. "If my family could only see me now, they'd never believe it."

As Caruso continued his walk, his smile waned in the encroaching dusk, the horizon swallowing the last rays of the winter sun. The talk of the planned Christmas party clashed with the somber scene of bombers being readied for battle around him. Thoughts of how the celebration could fill the children with small joys drifted through his mind, contrasting against the cold, metallic undertones of the imminent mission. The air carried the low rumbling of engines, a constant reminder of the delicate balance between the brief, cherished moments of celebration and the ongoing demands of war.

He paused, his eyes following the mechanics moving with a quiet urgency, their heads down, their tools clinking against the cold metal of the bombers. Nearby, a group of officers huddled, their voices low and their faces drawn. One of them glanced in Caruso's direction, his gaze heavy with something unspoken.

The bombers stood in the dimming light like silent sentinels, their hulking frames casting long, jagged shadows across the tarmac. They loomed in the dusk, reminders of missions to come, of men who wouldn't return. A familiar knot tightened in his stomach, a premonition of sorts that tomorrow's mission might be particularly demanding. The brass hadn't spelled it out yet, but he could read the signs: extra mechanics swarming the planes, officers speaking in clipped tones, men moving with that tight-jawed urgency that always preceded bad news. A chill brushed over him. Inhaling deeply, he steadied himself against the uncertainties of the next day, murmuring a prayer for the strength to face whatever challenges lay ahead, and hoping that all his comrades would return to enjoy the small amount of Christmas cheer they would manage to muster.

When Caruso arrived at the barracks, he found Max there, murmuring to a little dog. "Let me get you something to drink." Max filled his helmet with some water. The little dog's fur was matted and dirty, but his eyes were bright, full of curiosity and trust. His tail wagged furiously as he lapped up the water, droplets splashing onto Max's boots. "Are you hungry?" Max pulled out some potatoes scavenged from the mess hall, which the dog devoured eagerly. "I'll have to get the fellas to bring you some of theirs, too," Max crooned.

"What's that you've got there?" Caruso asked gruffly, looking over Max's shoulder. "Where'd he come from?"

Max hesitantly explained the story while Caruso scratched behind the dog's ears, the puppy leaning into his hand, his tiny body quivering with excitement. "I found him out in the woods. I took him to the base hospital, and they x-rayed his leg. It's just a sprain. I named him Snafu."

Caruso looked down at the puppy and smiled despite himself. He could never pass by a dog without thinking of Cracker Jack back home.

Snafu flopped onto his back, paws curled, his tail thumping against the floor in eager anticipation. Caruso chuckled despite himself. "You know, little fella, you've got it all figured out. Just lie back, let someone else do the work." He rubbed the puppy's belly, feeling the soft rise and fall of its tiny chest, the warmth beneath his palm. For a moment, the tension in his own shoulders loosened, as if this small, trusting creature had absorbed some of the weight he carried.

"Hey, Caruso, do you think you can watch him for a while? It's his right back leg that's sprained, so he can't be too active. I've got to go over to the post office to mail a letter."

Caruso laughed. "Yeah, I'll keep an eye on him and make sure he stays calm. We can keep each other company. See you later."

Caruso glanced out the window. The laughter and chatter from outside the barracks' doors reached his ears, reminding him of the camaraderie that felt just out of grasp. He sat down on the floor with Snafu, absently scratching his head. "I have a dog like you back home," he said in a low voice, allowing himself a moment to think about the warmth and sense of belonging that seemed a lifetime ago. The contrast between then and now, and the chasm between him and the others, felt more pronounced lately.

"Hey, little friend, want to take a stroll outside?" he asked, grabbing a rope to use as a leash. Outside, a handful of men tossed a ball back and forth, their banter easy and unburdened. Caruso lingered, watching the ball's effortless arc through the crisp air. For a second, it reminded him of summer evenings at home—of pop flies and outstretched mitts, of voices calling "I got it!" But the memory soured almost as quickly as it surfaced. That was a lifetime ago, another version of himself.

He turned away, the small dog at his side, both of them out of step with the world around them. The laughter trailed behind him, thin and distant, like a song he used to know but couldn't quite remember.

CHAPTER NINETEEN

A HEAVY, GRAY dawn loomed over the airfield as Caruso climbed aboard the bomber, the wind carrying the metallic scent of fuel and frost. The engines roared to life, louder today—angrier, almost, as if forewarning them of the mission's weight. Caruso exhaled sharply, pressing his palm against the cold metal of the turret. Today felt different. The weight in his gut told him so. He braced himself in the cold, hard reality of the aircraft's interior as the bird began its lumbering journey.

The bomber groaned under the weight of six 1,000-pound bombs, its engines straining as it tore down the runway. Caruso held his breath, the end of the tarmac rushing toward them, until the pilot finally lifted them into the air at the last moment. A beat passed before the aircraft steadied, and only then did he exhale, his breath fogging the icy glass.

The weather was merciless, as predicted at the briefing. Flying through dense cloud always made Caruso nervous; the disorientation of losing sight of sky and ground made him fear they might collide with another of their own. The pilots relied on instruments that Caruso prayed would all work.

Breaking through at fourteen thousand feet, they emerged into sunlight and assembled over the rendezvous point, searching for their flight group's flares so they could get into formation. It always seemed miraculous to Caruso when they were successful.

They flew out over the Channel, heading to Ludwigshafen in southwest Germany, their target a chemical plant. They'd been warned to expect a strong defense, and Caruso prepared himself for the worst.

He hadn't flown with any of this crew before, and his heart raced with the unknowns of what the day would bring. Caruso felt sure this was going to be a tough mission, and he focused on the thought that each one completed was another step closer to going home.

Flying above twenty-five thousand feet, dark thunderheads swirled menacingly around their aircraft. Caruso offered a quick prayer for protection from harm, each word a desperate plea. From his cramped position in the ball turret, the clouds passed by in chaotic streaks of motion, casting the sky in a shifting curtain of shadow. Swallowing hard, he concentrated on his task, adjusting his gear and double-checking all his equipment one last time. Sweat trickled down his back, each drop a reminder of his vulnerability. Alone in his bubble, the isolation and inability to see was unnerving.

As he searched the skies for threats, his father came to mind. Caruso knew that if Pop had lived, he'd still be as proud of him as ever. He'd be bragging to all his friends that his son was "beating those Jerries" and "doing his bit" for the war effort. He'd carry one of his son's military pictures in his billfold, opening it wide, proudly, for anyone who would take the time to look.

Suddenly, the sky exploded in black plumes, flak shattering the air around them. Caruso's pulse hammered. He clutched Pop's crucifix, whispering the 23rd psalm, his breath fogging the turret glass. Then—a glint.

Messerschmitts. Stalking them like wolves in the snow. A flash of silver and then, suddenly, one of them was there—so close Caruso could see the faces inside—locking onto them with lethal precision.

Heart pounding, he barely felt his fingers tighten around the triggers before the twin .50-calibers erupted to life, spitting fire into the freezing sky. The bullets tore through the enemy plane's wing, sending it plunging below. The others quickly scattered, the hunters becoming the hunted.

The assaults continued around them, each blast jolting the plane with bone-rattling force, causing the turret to shudder. Caruso couldn't help but think of the stories he'd heard—turrets jammed mid-flight, gunners trapped as the planes spiraled down. Shaking the thought away, he focused on the skies, scanning for threats.

His hands quivered, the cold creeping into his cramped space and heightening his tremors. But it wasn't just the frigid temperature: a primal fear seized him, clawing at his insides with every explosion. Amid the roar of the engines and the staccato of gunfire, the world outside morphed into a blur of gray and black.

It was in this moment between the overwhelming noise and terror that he saw him.

Pop.

Standing as clear as day, his face was warm and familiar, untouched by time. He clutched something in his hands—a small photograph he used to keep in his wallet. Father and son frozen in a sunlit past, grinning side by side. Caruso could almost hear his father's voice, wrapping around him like a steadying hand: *You've got this, Sandy. You're stronger than you know.*

For a fleeting second, it felt like time itself had paused, the noise and terror suspended in the calm, steady voice of his father. Then it dissipated, replaced by the crack and roar of the world around him. He blinked rapidly, not just to clear the sweat that stung his eyes, but also to try to recapture the vision—but it was already gone.

As the battle raged on, Caruso was left with an ache in his heart where his father's image had been. The encounter, brief as it had been, lingered with him, stirring both longing and determination. In the seclusion of his turret, surrounded by the realities of war, Pop served as a lamppost, guiding him through the dark skies.

The intercom crackled. "Bombardier to crew. Bombs away." The aircraft lurched with the sudden loss of weight, and the pilot banked left to escape the enemy air fire.

"Pilot to crew. Everyone check in with me one at a time. I want to make sure no one's been hit."

One by one, voices crackled through the intercom. Each affirmative eased the knot in Caruso's gut.

Then—a pause.

Too long.

The pilot's voice returned, lower now. "Walsh is hit." He directed the radioman to bring oxygen and belt tourniquets to try to stop the bleeding, and ordered the bombardier and navigator to move the injured copilot to an area where he could lie down.

"He seemed okay at first, but… now he's out cold."

Caruso listened with dread to what sounded like a replay of his own injury. His heart raced, and his stomach was balled into a knot. He winced as he overheard the radioman murmuring reassurances, his voice taut with strain. Caruso prayed Walsh would make it and that they'd all get back to base safely.

As the plane left the target area, Caruso gratefully raised the ball turret, his hands still shaking. The sky, dark with thunderheads, mirrored the tumult inside him. He frowned, hoping that the pilot could manage to get them home despite the distraction of his injured comrade.

"How's Walsh doing?" Caruso asked the radioman.

"He's awake again and has some abdominal pain. His leg is numb, and he's worried he may be paralyzed."

Caruso grimaced. And he'd thought his own injuries had been bad. There was always something that could be worse.

Descending to eight thousand feet, they removed their oxygen masks. Walsh was holding his own as they made their way back to base.

Paris stretched below them, a city in shambles. Its streets were a patchwork of craters and broken foundations, scars on a land that would take generations to heal. Whole neighborhoods erased. The Eiffel Tower still stood, a lone survivor.

Caruso swallowed hard. He'd always understood war in terms of enemy targets and survival. But below, the sight of this devastation—barns flattened, villages reduced to ash—reminded him that war's price was paid in more than just soldiers' lives. There were always innocent casualties who paid the price for living in the wrong place at the wrong time.

Reaching the base, they flew over the control tower and fired their red flares, announcing the presence of wounded aboard. After they landed, Caruso watched as medics tended to Walsh and laid him carefully on a stretcher then whisked him away. Just a few months ago, Caruso had been the one on the stretcher. Walsh would have a long road ahead, if he made it. Caruso remembered hearing him talk about his daughter back home, how she loved to bake cookies for him before he shipped out. The thought of her waiting for a father who might never walk again tightened his chest.

⁂

The group tramped to the debrief in silence, with only a few scattered comments speculating on Walsh's chances of survival.

"Do you think he'll make it?"

"If anyone will, he will. He's a tough soldier."

Caruso stayed quiet during the discussion, his mind consumed with grim thoughts about Walsh's fate. These men couldn't possibly grasp the enormity of what was in store for the injured airman. Explaining it to them would only deepen their already heavy burden of worry. He briefly wondered if Helen would care for him at Stoneleigh, then forcefully pushed the thought aside.

Sergeant Devaney from Intelligence met them as they neared the debriefing room, puffing on their cigarettes. They robotically relayed their mission details, their eyes glassy with emotion.

Afterward, they were each offered a shot of whiskey. Caruso downed his in one gulp and noticed that the top turret gunner pushed his away. "Hey, buddy, can I have yours?" Caruso asked.

"Sure." The airman slid it over in front of Caruso. "I've flown with Walsh for months. I can't think of drinking at a time like this. Help yourself."

"Thanks." Caruso quickly took the glass and tilted back his head, hiding the tremor in his fingers. The brown liquid burned as it went down, a fleeting warmth that blurred the edges of his swirling mind.

His thoughts spun like a carousel. Only whiskey could slow them down—at least for tonight. He lit another cigarette, welcoming the dulling of his senses as he processed the day's events. He knew it wasn't a solution, but it was the only one he had right now. A nagging voice in the back of his mind wondered how much longer he could rely on borrowed peace.

CHAPTER TWENTY

A few days later

CARUSO'S NAME RIPPED through the darkness, yanking him from another half-formed nightmare. His body jolted upright before his mind could catch up, a film of sweat clinging to his back. Another mission. Again. Always.

It never stopped.

He exhaled hard, rubbing his eyes. The night had been like all the others—fragments of sleep stitched together between haunting visions of getting trapped in the turret. He was so damn tired. Of the missions. Of the war. Of himself.

When the morning call came, he dragged himself from his cot, heading to the latrine before the others, who were still sluggish in their beds. Thoughts filtered in as he showered. He could feel his comrades' frustration like a heavy fog. He didn't need to hear them to know they were tired of him. Hell, he was tired of himself. He toweled off and dressed, then made his way to the mess hall.

ග

"Anyone else gonna address this?" Perch's voice sliced through the barracks, his frustration clear as he glanced around at his crewmates. "Because I swear, if Caruso wakes me up one more time screaming, I'm going to start yelling back. Maybe then he'll get a taste of what it's like." Another night disrupted by shrieks and screams—a daily occurrence linked to Caruso, though Perch had yet to confront him directly.

"Caruso's sleep always seems erratic," Max said. "I can barely rest myself without an extra pillow over my head. His tossing and turning—and shouting—it's like he's fighting a battle in his dreams. Surprised he hasn't fallen out of the sack."

"I don't think he even knows he's doing it," Perch said, commenting on Caruso's dark circles and the persistent tension in his face.

"And those eyes," Frankie said, shuddering. "They seem almost haunted."

As they walked to the latrine, their conversation turned to finding a solution.

"It's becoming unbearable!" Frankie said. "Just as I drift off, he starts again. The strain of being over here is bad enough, but I need to get some sack time!"

"Well, *I* can't be the one to confront him," Ray said flatly. "Max, maybe you should."

Perch nodded his head. "Yeah, I think Max should do it. He's the most mild-mannered of all of us. He can always find a way to deliver news that's hard to swallow. How 'bout it, Max?"

Max frowned, rubbing the back of his neck. "Look, we could talk to him…" He hesitated, eyes flicking to Caruso's empty cot. "But what if it makes things worse? What if he just shuts down completely?"

He exhaled through his nose, weighing his words. "It already seems like he's a loner. If we gang up on him, it'll just push him further away." A beat passed before he added, "I'm thinking about talking to Chaplain Richards. He's experienced in this kind of thing. Clearly, Caruso's going through something. Maybe he can help him."

"Well, we've got to do something. It can't go on like this," Frankie said under his breath.

"You're right. But it's not just about us; it's about helping Caruso, too. I'll speak to the chaplain and see what he suggests," Max said.

The chaplain would help. Max believed that. But as he glanced at Caruso's empty cot, a gnawing thought lingered.

What if it wasn't enough?

After the mission and debrief, Max drifted from the group of battle-scarred fliers recounting their narrow escapes. Fueled by urgency, he sought out the chaplain's office. Rows of bombers rested heavily on the hardstand, their battle scars glistening under the sun. Max quickened his pace.

He reached the chaplain's door and hesitated. Would Caruso even listen? Would he see this as help—or betrayal? He took a slow breath, squared his shoulders, and knocked. The door opened almost instantly, as if Richards had been expecting him.

"Max, come in, please." The chaplain's warm, understanding smile set Max slightly at ease as he motioned to the seat across his desk.

Max sat, his hands clasped tightly together. "Sir, I… we're worried about Caruso. He's been drinking and smoking a lot, and having nightmares, shouting and tossing in his dreams.

It's affecting everyone, but more than that, we're concerned about him."

Richards nodded, his expression serious yet filled with empathy. "I appreciate you coming to me, Max. It's not easy to see someone struggle and not know how to help."

"It's just…" Max paused, searching for the right words. "He seems to be in trouble. Caruso looks like he's carrying the weight of the world on his shoulders, and it's more than the usual worries we're all dealing with. And his eyes… they don't seem to find rest, even in daylight."

The chaplain leaned back, intertwining his fingers. "War doesn't just wound bodies, Max. It leaves scars that aren't always visible."

Richards leaned forward, folding his hands. "Some men walk away with medals. Others walk away with ghosts. And Caruso? He's carrying more than his share of both. He's been through hell—not just once, but twice. First, his combat injury on his third mission, then in the months of rehabilitation. He just returned recently—coming back must feel like walking into the fire all over again. It's a lot for anyone to readjust to."

Max nodded, feeling a mixture of relief and concern. "Is there anything we can do? We feel so helpless."

"First, understand that your being here, showing concern, is already doing more than you know. But let me talk to Caruso. There are options, Max, resources that we can explore to help him. The Army has ways to help soldiers in this situation. It's important he knows that he's not facing this alone. And sometimes, the most powerful thing you can do for someone struggling is to remind them they're not a burden. A kind word, a shared laugh—it can mean the difference between despair and hope."

Max nodded and stood, feeling lighter, yet carrying a new weight of responsibility. Acknowledging his concern for Caruso had been the first step, a step he'd avoided before. Now, he felt compelled to act, to support his comrade in any way he could. "Thank you. It means a lot, not just to me and the other fellas, but I know it will to Caruso, too."

Caruso was out when Max returned to the barracks later in the day. Snafu trotted in beside him as if he owned the place, as if he hadn't spent most of his waking moments mooching scraps from every barracks on base. Still, he always seemed to find his way back to theirs.

"What did the chaplain say?" Perch asked eagerly, reaching down to scratch Snafu behind the ears.

"He thanked me and said that Caruso's injury on his third mission was severe—he's only just come back to battle now, and might be struggling to adjust."

Perch exhaled sharply, dragging a hand down his face. "Hell. We've been looking at this like he was just being difficult, but..." He trailed off, shaking his head. "Thanks for talking to him, Max."

"My mother always said it's easy to misjudge people based on first impressions," Max said. "Over here, I've found most of the fellows are good people just trying to cope with doing their job. Caruso's probably no different.

"Maybe the tense look on his face was never meant for us—maybe it's just fear. Fear of being back. The injury sounded serious; he's lucky to be alive."

Frankie let out a low whistle. "Man... and here I was just thinking he was being a jerk. Didn't even consider..."

Max nodded. "None of us did. But maybe now, we can help instead of just complaining."

"You've got a good heart, Max," Perch said. "Always looking for the best in people, even when it's hard. The chaplain will know how to help him."

For the first time in weeks, the tension in the barracks eased, just a little, like a sigh of relief.

CHAPTER TWENTY-ONE

TODAY MARKED CARUSO'S seventeenth mission, and the debrief still echoed in his ears. Each mission stretched out in a slow crawl, the monotony only occasionally shattered by the planning of the Christmas party. Anticipation of the joy they'd be bringing was a ray of sunlight through the relentless slog of battle.

But he was still only less than halfway done, and his original crew had gone home three months ago. At the beginning of the war, twenty-five missions were required for a tour of duty; then the Army, in all its wisdom, had increased it to thirty, then thirty-five. Since he'd been back, he'd never had the same assigned crew; every single time there was at least one airman he hadn't worked with before. In today's mission, there was a new radio operator on his very first raid in England. The fellow had done okay, but Caruso didn't like the thought that his life was in the hands of someone who'd never even flown a mission before.

It seemed like every time he stepped into that turret, he panicked, with each experience worse than the last. His heart pounded so hard it reverberated through his whole body, and he was lightheaded and dripping with sweat by the time he extricated himself from his bubble. His only respite came when he was safely on the ground. But even that relief was short-lived: his thoughts would quickly shift to the next mission and the gnawing uncertainty of whether he could perform. He wasn't sure how he was going to make it through.

Flicking the remnants of his cigarette into the ashtray, Caruso's hand trembled as he reached for another. He patted his pockets. Nothing left. His fingers tightened into a fist before he let them relax, exhaling sharply. When had he smoked the last one? He could have sworn he still had some left.

The bourbon felt cool in his shaky grip, its warmth a temporary solace as he downed another that sat abandoned on the counter. It was then that he noticed the five empty shot glasses in front of him. How had he gotten to this point, telling himself it was just to steady his nerves? His hands trembled as he took it in.

The realization sat heavy in his gut, a quiet unease creeping over him. His thoughts reeled, dark and dizzying, like a plane spinning out of control.

He felt like he was on the verge of falling into a black abyss. He looked around at the other men, laughing and talking over their smokes and drinks. The idle chatter in the room was something he just couldn't relate to. It was as if he were watching himself in a mirror.

"What troubles you, Caruso?" The voice, gentle yet commanding, belonged to Captain Tom Richards, the chaplain. Caruso lifted his hooded eyes and met the chaplain's gaze—a haven of empathy in a sea of turmoil.

The bottled-up feelings overflowed, and his eyes filled with tears as his emotions suddenly broke free. "I'm not sure I can make it, sir," he confessed, each word spoken aloud making the reality more overwhelming. "I just don't know how I'm going to get home. And… I need to get home. I can't go in that ball turret again. I'll never survive it."

The chaplain paused briefly, weighing his words. "Listen, you're a damn good soldier and you *will* make it home. But you need more time to recuperate."

Caruso's face was tight and his eyes wide with panic as he shook his head. "I can't, sir. I need to get back out there. It's the only way I'll make it home. I can't stay here a day longer than I have to."

"Sergeant, I'm ordering you to a flak house and then we'll figure things out. You'll get home, son. I'll see to it myself. But we need to do this right. I'm not going to send you back up in the air until you're ready. Your body has healed, but your mind needs recovery. I've spoken with Captain Gannon. It's all arranged. You leave tomorrow for Ebrington Manor. There, professionals will help you get back on track." He reached out and shook Caruso's hand. "This will turn around for you. You gave your all for the US Army Air Forces, and we'll do the same for you. Don't give up on yourself, son."

The elephant-like weight that had been hanging over him suddenly lifted. Maybe this was just what he needed.

Ebrington Manor was located about two hours from Polebrook, close to Chipping Campden in Gloucestershire. Prior to the war, it had operated as a country house. As the jeep rolled through the quiet countryside, Caruso couldn't stop the gnawing thought that he was abandoning the men who still had to fly. He could picture them, tightening their gear, stepping into the planes, their faces hardened by the same fear he carried.

What kind of man left them behind? And yet, another part of him—a smaller, quieter part—whispered that maybe he wasn't abandoning them. Maybe he was just surviving.

They passed a stately stone church, standing like a sentinel guarding its sacred grounds. The manor emerged like a grand dame, its majestic presence stark against the lush background of the countryside. Caruso's awe was tangible as they swept through the gates, the elegance of another era standing in defiance of the specter of the conflict. It was hard to believe there was a war on. The gloriousness of the place showed no evidence of it.

At Caruso's knock, a torrent of barking heralded his arrival before the door swung open, revealing a striking blonde juggling an enthusiastic dachshund. "Good afternoon, and welcome!" Her voice was warm and melodic. "I'm Evie Sanders, and alongside my husband, we manage this estate. We're honored to have you with us. And this," she said, looking down at the dog in her arms, "is Schleppy. We so appreciate you making the long journey from the United States to support the war effort. Come in, come in!" She stepped aside to let him pass. Her simple gesture, making space for him as if he already belonged, felt unexpectedly profound, chipping away at the barriers he'd erected around himself.

"Consider this threshold a step away from your past battles to a moment of peace, Sergeant," Evie said, her voice soothing, the scent of fresh baking wafting through the doorway. "You've entered a sanctuary away from the front lines. Ebrington Manor, with its centuries-old walls, now serves a new purpose: to offer soldiers like you a place to rest and recover. Here, we hope you'll find some relaxation and comfort." Her words painted a compelling picture of the manor's mission, intertwining the past's elegance with the urgency of the present.

"To further distance you from thoughts of war, you'll be provided with civilian clothes. You'll wear uniforms only for dinner. We have a large staff here to attend to your every need. Should you find that you have any health or stress-related concerns, a medical officer is available to provide any necessary emergency care or professional advice.

"The American Red Cross ladies will serve as your hostesses and will assist you with recreation and dining. The Red Cross also manages the civilian staff that runs the house and maintains the grounds. If you have any needs that aren't being addressed, please don't hesitate to come to me directly. It's our goal to provide you with a home away from home, where you can enjoy some much-needed relaxing and luxurious pampering.

"My husband, Arthur, will be here shortly, and he's looking forward to meeting you. He was in the jewelry business before the war, and since we had to close the store, he's been at a loose end. He can be shy, but he loves people. Your arrival is actually helping *us*!" Evie said, smiling. "He'll be thrilled to have another airman in the house! But you better watch out: he can hook you into talking about yourself, and before you know it, you've missed whatever it was that you had planned to do!

"Let me show you to your room and give you a chance to unwind and clean up a bit from your travels. You must be tired!"

Caruso looked around, incredulous. It was like entering Wonderland. He was certain he could get used to life in this place. He followed Evie up the stairs to his room, the opulence of the manor a sharp contrast to the war-torn environments he'd grown accustomed to.

ꟹ

Refreshed after a hot bath, Caruso descended the stairs to the sitting room, his steps slow as he absorbed the warmth of his temporary retreat. A lush boxwood garland adorned the mantle, with white candlesticks interspersed that cast a gentle, welcoming light. In the corner, a majestic Christmas tree commanded the room, its branches laden with twinkling lights that danced across shiny ornaments in a kaleidoscope of colors. The tree reached ambitiously to the ceiling, a symbol of hope and celebration, quieting the strain of war. Evie, her movements gentle and deliberate, was setting a tray on the coffee table, its cozy offerings of steaming tea and cookies promising a refuge from the world outside.

"I love to prepare food, so I hope you love to eat!" She beamed, placing the tray down. "I'm happiest when we have guests I can cook for, and even with the rationing, I've found ways to make food that everyone seems to enjoy." She nodded to the baked goods on the tray. "These are speculoos biscuits, and once you've had them, you will dream of them for the rest of your life! They're my grandmother's recipe. At Christmastime, we imprint impressions on them like these have, but in other seasons, I just make them plain. The sugar rationing put me in a bit of a pickle, so I started growing sugar beets and managed to eke out some sugar from the crop, even if it was a bit makeshift at first. I got better at it as time went on. And I form the biscuits smaller now, to make them stretch."

She smiled, her eyes gleaming. "I'll bet someday bakeries everywhere will be selling them, but for now they are my special secret and gift to you. I hope you enjoy them."

Caruso reached hungrily for the pale yellowish cookies and took a bite. His eyes met Evie's. "This is the best cookie

I've ever had," he said. "Don't tell my mother, though. I've always told her that she makes the best cookies—but she never made anything quite like this!"

Evie's engaging smile put him at ease, and Caruso was taken in by her charm. Schleppy stationed himself close by, ready to retrieve any dropped crumbs. When none were forthcoming, he ran to get a tennis ball, bringing it to Caruso's feet and dropping it, looking up expectantly.

"Schleppy, are you trying to tell me something?" Caruso asked, his eyes twinkling.

"Oh, don't let him bother you. He would play catch all day if he could. He can be a bit tiresome after a while. It's our own fault. When we were cooped up here in the house before we opened it to the military, playing catch with him was something to entertain ourselves. And now, it's become his favorite pastime."

"Where did the name Schleppy come from?" Caruso asked between bites.

Evie's musical laughter tinkled like wind chimes. "Well, the word '*schlep*' is Yiddish, meaning to lug or drag something. When Schleppy was a puppy, he just would *not* walk; he wanted to be carried everywhere." She smiled at the memory. "So, we had to schlep him around the house, or he'd make such a fuss.

"And that," she said, laughing, "is how Schleppy got his name! Actually, Schleppy is just a nickname. His full name is Baron von Schleppenheimer. Don't you think that makes him sound sophisticated?"

"Oh indeed," Caruso said. "And if you don't mind me saying, that's an awfully big name for an awfully little dog!"

Being in someone's home again was almost surreal after all this time. The warmth, camaraderie, homey smells… the whole gleaming house, so different from all the weathered buildings in London and the cities surrounding them. It reminded him of home, which had often been filled with friends. And always a dog. Although Evie didn't look much older than Caruso, he felt a sense of mothering from her, making him feel safe and comforted. It was a refreshing feeling.

Their banter was interrupted by the sound of a door opening, and a short, stout man with a full head of salt-and-pepper hair and a bushy mustache walked in, his eyes on Evie. "My darling! I see you've found yourself another soldier to feed!" He looked at Caruso with a conspiratory wink. "I've got to keep my eye on her, or one of these days I fear she'll run off with one of you!"

Evie walked over to the man, linking her arm in his. "Not a chance, Arthur. But let me introduce you: this is Sergeant Caruso, from an air base in Polebrook. This is my husband, Arthur."

"I hear you were in the jewelry business, sir," Caruso said, shaking Arthur's hand.

"Yes, yes. I bought, sold, and repaired jewelry for many years. A very interesting career." Arthur paused as he peered deeply into Caruso's face, seeming to search for the right words, finally settling on a story about a watch he once repaired. "Each piece has its role, no matter how small," he said in conclusion, locking eyes with Caruso in a moment of silent understanding. He was really talking about people, about Caruso himself. In Arthur, Caruso sensed a kindred spirit, someone who understood the importance of each individual's contribution to a larger cause.

"We had a young sergeant here last month," he said, his voice tinged with pride. "He came in like a tightly wound spring, hardly said a word. But by the time he left, he'd found his laugh again. Not sure where he is now, but I like to think this place gave him back something he'd thought was lost."

Caruso was just beginning to recognize that the war hadn't totally stripped away everything. As he continued to talk and exchange stories with Evie and Arthur, he felt a subtle softening inside, an unraveling of the tension in his body that he'd grown so accustomed to. Here, in this unexpected refuge, their kindness stitched back pieces of himself he hadn't fully realized were threadbare. It sparked a flicker of curiosity about what the rest of his stay might reveal, making him wonder which forgotten parts of himself might reemerge in this sanctuary.

"When we closed the shop, I thought I'd lost myself," Arthur said, his voice low. "What's a jeweler without his tools, without the customers who come in smiling and leave with something precious? But Evie… well, she reminded me that people aren't defined by what they do. They're defined by how they live, how they carry on. I think you'll find that here, Sergeant."

The warmth of Arthur's words merged with the glow from the Christmas tree, its light reflecting off the decorations and filling the room with a comforting radiance. Settling into this newfound companionship, Caruso felt a gentle hint of hope that healing might be possible. But he couldn't help but wonder: could a place so removed from the front lines truly mend what had been broken, or would the darkness of war find him even here?

CHAPTER TWENTY-TWO

AFTER DINNER, THE men and their hosts settled into the sitting room. A Victrola spun jazz classics, filling the air with the vibrant sounds of the Dorsey Brothers and Glenn Miller. Caruso sat in a quiet corner, his gaze fixed on the flames, their hypnotic motion lulling him into thought. His solitude, however, was short-lived.

Charlotte, one of the Red Cross volunteers, interrupted his reverie, holding out a hand with a sly grin. "Come on, Sandy!" Her voice was teasing and warm. "Your tapping feet are betraying you. Let's dance."

"I don't know…" Caruso began, shaking his head. But the good-natured insistence in her eyes left him little choice.

He stood reluctantly, feeling the eyes of the room on him as he let himself follow her lead. As the rhythm seeped into his muscles, he gradually relaxed, to his own surprise. When the song ended, the other men clapped enthusiastically. "Wow, Caruso, you have hidden talents," one said. "You're better than any of us! Where'd you learn to dance like that?"

Caruso, his face reddening, rubbed the back of his neck. "Well, believe it or not, my mom taught me. She said it brings joy into a home."

As the night wore on, the dancing gave way to games and quieter conversations. Eventually, Caruso excused himself and made his way to his room. It had been a long day, and he wasn't sure what to make of it all—Charlotte's easy laugh, the warmth of the room, the surprising pleasure of a dance. For the first time in months, he wasn't dreading what sleep might bring.

✤

The rich aroma of cinnamon toast and coffee greeted Caruso as he descended the stairs the next morning. He lingered at the doorway of the dining room for a moment, letting the scene wash over him. The clatter of silverware, the hum of voices, the smells of breakfast—it was all so achingly normal, so far removed from the chaos of war. He allowed himself a rare smile as he took a seat.

"Looks like you're settling in," Charlotte observed, setting a place in front of him.

"Yeah… I think I could definitely get accustomed to this life." The luxury of his surroundings wove its spell around him as he listened contentedly to the snippets of conversation of the men at the table.

The opulence of Ebrington Manor was still almost overwhelming—its thick carpets, ornate furnishings, and walls lined with paintings of stern-faced aristocrats. The grandeur of the place made him feel like an intruder at times, but the kindness of the hosts and volunteers chipped away at that discomfort.

The Red Cross women, Mary and Charlotte chief among them, were more than just attentive hosts. Their gentle banter and cheerful efficiency wove a sense of home into the manor, providing the men with a respite that felt genuine. Caruso hadn't realized how much he'd needed it until now.

ൻ

After breakfast, as the soldiers scattered to their activities, Caruso was called into the living room, where Dr. Sotelo awaited. The psychiatrist sat across from him in civilian clothing, his demeanor unexpectedly ordinary—almost disarmingly so.

"Good morning, Sandy," Sotelo began, his voice warm, encouraging trust. "Although we usually avoid war talk here, I understand you've been having a rough time. How are you feeling today?"

Caruso hesitated. "Fine, I guess," he said automatically, although the tension in his shoulders betrayed him.

Sotelo studied him for a moment before continuing. "Why don't we start at the beginning? Tell me what made you decide to enlist."

Caruso hesitated, then took a breath. "After Pop died, everything changed. My mom remarried, and then there was a baby, and…" He paused, staring at the floor. "I started to feel like I didn't belong anymore. Like I'd lost my place."

Sotelo nodded encouragingly. "That must have been hard for you."

Caruso nodded. "It was. I knew my mom still loved me, but now she had my new pop and the baby. I wasn't ready to move on. My first pop's death left a hole in my life that I didn't know how to fill." He looked up, his expression thoughtful. "I guess enlisting felt like something I could do to figure that out—to find where I fit."

"I see. How did your family react to your decision?"

"My mom was very upset. She said she had already lost one person and didn't want to lose her only son. But my stepdad said it was my decision to make. I think he saw how lost I was and thought maybe the Army would help me find myself again."

Caruso smiled faintly. "And it did, for a while. I liked my crew; we worked well together. We were like a family, in a way. We all trusted each other. That's something I hadn't felt since Pop died."

Sotelo's words were tinged with kindness. "And then you were injured."

Caruso nodded, a slow and heavy motion. Then, carefully, he began to unpack the war—his injury, the months of rehab, his crew going back to the States, Helen's betrayal, and the overwhelming fear he felt every time he climbed into the ball turret.

The mere mention of Helen tore open the scar of a wound that had never properly healed. The pain of her deception felt like a shard of glass lodged deep within his palm, a persistent reminder of faith forsaken and shattered beyond repair.

Sotelo listened intently, his questions gentle but probing. "It sounds like your injury and all that followed shook more than just your body. It's shaken your sense of self, your place in the world."

Caruso nodded, the words resonating in a way he couldn't quite articulate. "Yeah," he said finally. "Everything changed after I got hurt. It's like I'm standing on the outside, looking in."

Sotelo nodded, his expression understanding. "It's in these times of vulnerability that we find our strength, Sandy. Rebuilding trust isn't just about others. It's about trusting yourself again, your ability to overcome not just the battles in the air, but the ones within. Is there anyone you feel close to on base?"

Caruso looked up. "I did make a friend when I first returned to base. His name is Calvert. He's been a good buddy to me. But I don't see him very often, since we're in different lines of work."

"What drew you to a friendship with Calvert?"

"I met him after I was discharged from rehab and assigned to ground duty for a while. He's easy to talk to, a real good fella. He supported me when my relationship with Helen fell apart. And even though he's not aircrew, he's helped me to keep trying with my missions."

"And what do you offer in that friendship?"

Caruso thought for a minute. "I think he likes that he's made friends with an airman. It was something he always wanted to do, but a physical limitation interfered."

"But wartime's difficult for everyone. How have you supported him as a friend?"

"His mom just passed away, and Calvert thought it was because she was worried sick. But I helped him see it wasn't his fault. I told him about losing Pop, and I think it helped, having me to talk to about everything."

"What about the fellows in your barracks, or on the crews you've flown with? Do you feel close to any of them?"

"Not really. The crew I fly with is always changing. I pretty much keep to myself."

"Do any of them know about your struggles on missions?"

Caruso shook his head. He'd never risk telling any of them. It would only make things worse, he was sure of it. He thought of Bob Smith, who usually suffered in silence. Caruso assumed he should do the same.

The two continued to talk. "Sandy, I want to assure you of something," the physician said, placing his hand on Caruso's arm. "Everything you've experienced since your injury is perfectly normal. The fact that you lost one support when your pop passed away when you were a child, and then another major support when your crew finished up their missions while you were in rehab, has added to your natural inclination to pull away from others and protect yourself when you feel hurt. The difficulty you had with the woman you were seeing was probably linked to all of that as well.

"It's a journey, Sandy. Finding your way back doesn't always mean returning to who you were before. Recovery isn't a straight path. It'll feel like one step forward, two steps back at times. But even those steps back are part of the process—they show you what you still need to heal. It's all about finding a way forward and discovering who you are now, after what you've been through.

"Tell me, what's your first thought when you open your eyes in the morning?" the physician asked, leaning in.

Caruso's answer was immediate. "That I've got to get through these missions, or I'll never get home."

"Sandy, your purpose in life can't just be how to get through the day and get back to what you consider your real life at home. There's more to this life than marking time to get to the other side. You were put on this earth to learn how to live fully—to find meaning, and to influence others in ways that matter. Like throwing a pebble into the water, the impact of your actions will ripple outward and touch others. That's how you continue—and how your story goes on and on." Sotelo smiled. "A person isn't always measured in days lived. It's an important thing to learn.

"During this week, I want you to make a point of talking and opening up with the other men." He paused. "I'm not asking you to tell them all your war stories; that's not what this is about. It's about building relationships with others.

"Trust is a two-way street, Sandy. Everyone wrestles with discouragement, no matter who they are. It takes courage to act in the face of difficulties. No one else can run the race for you, but they can support you, so you know you're not running alone. We're all in this together. Shutting others out only makes it worse. Do you understand what I'm saying?"

Caruso was silent for a few moments and then nodded. "It's like with Calvert. We trust each other. And that helps us both."

Sotelo smiled and nodded. "You're spot on. Try my suggestion, and I'm going to check in with you towards the end of the week to see how it's going. Is that a deal?" He held out his hand.

Caruso's grip on Sotelo's hand was firmer than he expected. "Deal," he said, more to himself than to Sotelo. It dawned on him that he had already started opening up in this gentle refuge. He was beginning to realize that facing the war within might be the only way he'd ever be strong enough to face the one outside.

Caruso took a deep breath as he left the session with Dr. Sotelo. The psychiatrist's words lingered, resonating with a truth he had never really thought about. For the first time, he allowed himself to consider that healing wasn't just about getting through his missions, but about discovering things within himself. It felt like a great pressure had been slightly eased, even though the path ahead was still cloaked in uncertainty.

Reflecting on the conversation, Caruso felt a combination of relief and apprehension. Opening up about his fears and past had been unexpectedly cathartic, but the vulnerability it left behind was unsettling. Outside, the well-kept gardens and chirping birds seemed almost mocking in their serenity—too calm, too whole, for someone still so fractured inside. Could he truly piece himself back together, or was this newfound hope just another fleeting illusion?

❧

Later that day, Caruso and Aaron, one of the other airmen, ventured toward the stables, eager to gallop through the open air of the countryside.

At least, Aaron was eager.

Caruso, on the other hand, wasn't so sure. He hadn't spent much time with the fella, and the idea of making small talk one on one, pretending to be at ease, felt exhausting. It was easier to keep his guard up, to avoid the expectation of camaraderie altogether.

Then again, wasn't that exactly what Sotelo had called him out on? *Maybe trust isn't something you just decide to have. Maybe it's something you practice, step by step, until one day, it's not so damn terrifying.*

Still, trusting people and trusting a half-ton animal were two different things.

Aaron didn't seem to sense his unease, chatting easily as they walked. "I used to be petrified of horses. My sister made me ride one when I was ten, and I fell off right into a patch of nettles. Took me years to get back on one," he admitted.

"And today's the day you decide to try again?"

Aaron shrugged. "Well, we're already risking our necks in the sky. Figured I might as well face something a little closer to ground."

At the stables, Briggs, a mahogany-coated horse, was saddled in the unfamiliar English style. Caruso's first attempt at mounting without a saddle horn was a comedic battle of wills. As they left the area, Aaron was unceremoniously thrown, but his laughter filled the air.

An open meadow beckoned, and Caruso eased his grip, letting his horse surge ahead while Aaron fell behind. But soon the saddle started slipping, rocking unsteadily beneath him. He gripped the reins tighter, knowing that fighting against it wouldn't help—but relaxing felt impossible. He wasn't used to letting go of control. That, more than the horse beneath him, was the real challenge.

He finally succeeded in coaxing the horse to stop before climbing down. Stranded, Caruso began leading Briggs back to the stables. He couldn't help but think how much this moment mirrored his life—trying to find balance and control in foreign territory.

Evie approached on her own horse, a vision of calm competence oblivious to Caruso's disarray. "Aaron saw what happened. Can I give you a hand?" Her kind smile vanquished his wounded ego. "He didn't throw you, did he?"

"No, but the saddle was slipping, and I was going with it."

Evie's laughter, genuine and understanding, filled the space between them. "I'm so sorry. That saddle was meant for repair. Here, let me," she said, dismounting. "You take M'Lady, and I'll ride Briggs bareback."

Caruso gingerly mounted Evie's mare, still shaking his head at his own misfortune. "Guess I'll be paying for this tomorrow."

Evie effortlessly removed the offending saddle and, after handing it to him, hopped up on his horse. "Okay, hand me the saddle and we'll take it back."

Aaron, catching up, smirked. "At least you lasted longer than I did."

Evie grinned as they rode back toward the stables. "Briggs has a knack for humbling cocky soldiers. Consider it a rite of passage."

Caruso exhaled a laugh, feeling the tension loosen in his chest. Maybe this day hadn't been a total loss after all.

As they recounted their misadventures to the other airmen over dinner, Caruso smirked. "Briggs and I have an understanding now. He keeps me humble, and I get to feed him all the carrots he wants."

Later in the evening, Caruso felt himself drawn to a group at a card table, their laughter punctuated by occasional barks from Schleppy, who roamed optimistically from group to group in search of dropped crumbs.

As the hands were dealt, Caruso found an opening to share an anecdote about his dog, Cracker Jack, who once played dead for so long that his mother nearly called the vet. "You should have seen the relief—and then the annoyance—on her face!"

Laughter erupted, the connection between the men growing stronger with each shared story. It was a simple moment, but it started to break down the wall Caruso had built around himself since his injury.

As the night wore on and stories gave way to silence, Caruso found himself no longer at the edge of the room, or the moment. Something had shifted—just a little, but enough. Enough to wonder what else might change, given time.

He wasn't sure what tomorrow would bring—he rarely was anymore. But as he watched Schleppy trot from one circle of men to another, tail wagging, Caruso realized he was no longer bracing for impact. For tonight, at least, he was willing to trust the ride.

CHAPTER TWENTY-THREE

THE RHYTHMIC PITTER-PATTER of drizzle against the train's windows offered Caruso a rare moment for reflection as he headed back to base. *Funny,* he mused, *how a place full of strangers can quickly feel like home.*

His ten days at the manor had been a pause in the relentless grind of war. It hadn't been a vacation; it had been something deeper, like nurturing a struggling plant with fertilizer.

He thought back to Father Mulcahy's words during a Sunday service on base, where he shared the pulpit with Rabbi Kappelman and Reverend Barber.

"We all want to feel a sense of control," Father Mulcahy had said, his Irish brogue wrapping around the words like a comforting blanket, his eyes twinkling with mischief. "Ah, that would be nice, wouldn't it now?" Despite his short stature, Mulcahy's words were the kind that took root in your bones. Caruso knew he'd carry them with him always, and they had a habit of surfacing just when he needed them most.

Caruso's lips twitched into a faint smile at the memory. Control—it was something he'd chased relentlessly, only to see it slip through his fingers again and again. Hearing it from the priest had been oddly comforting, as if the admission that control was an illusion made it easier to bear.

"The truth is," Rabbi Kappelman had added, "we have to trust in something greater, in the divine guidance that steers us through our trials."

Reverend Barber hadn't soft-pedaled their struggles. "There will be times in this war when moving forward seems impossible. Yet in those moments, we must find the strength to take just one step. That's all—just one step. And like a child clutching a parent's hand, we can take courage in holding tight to God."

Their words had found a quiet place in Caruso, as if waiting to bloom in their own time. It reminded him of who he was, who he'd been before the war began. Memories of evenings in the kitchen with Mom and Pop, his mother humming over a pot of sauce, his father's hearty laughter, the reassuring weight of his hand on his shoulder. Those moments had been his sanctuary.

Caruso gazed out the window, the English landscape unfolding before his eyes. All the color seemed drained from the sky, leaving it a silvery gray, like the rinse water from his paintbrushes back home. Typical of the English weather: damp and dreary.

Yet as his eyes glanced upward, he saw it: the rainbow. *Was it a sign?* Caruso wasn't sure, but something about the sight of it stirred a quiet hope in his chest. Perhaps, with faith and perseverance, he'd find his way through.

Polebrook Air Base

As Caruso approached the barracks, a wave of anxiety gripped him. Seeing the weathered building brought back the familiar tang of oil and damp fabric, the creak of cots and muffled snores that had been the soundtrack of his life here. Just a few months ago, this place had felt like a prison, each day dragging him further into despair. What if the changes he'd experienced at the manor didn't last? What if the peace he'd found there crumbled under the weight of war?

He hesitated at the threshold, gripping the rough strap of his duffel. Taking a deep breath, he squared his shoulders and stepped inside. The musty smell of the barracks—oil, sweat, damp blankets—enveloped him. It was a far cry from the scent of fresh-baked bread and polished wood at Ebrington Manor. But it was familiar, and for the first time, he didn't flinch from it.

A dozen faces turned toward him, uncertainty flickering in their eyes. Max paused for a moment, as if bracing for the snarling, defensive man who had left for the flak house ten days ago.

Instead, Caruso caught Max's eye and smiled.

"Welcome back, Caruso," Max said, stepping forward and holding out his hand. His voice was warm but carried a hint of surprise. "It's good to see you."

As their hands clasped, Caruso felt something settle within him. Once, he would have bristled at the attention; now, he found comfort in this display of brotherhood, a testament to his transformation. "Thanks, Max. It's good to be back."

Max tilted his head, studying him. "You look swell—well rested. How was the flak house?"

The other men were watching now, curiosity flickering in their eyes. None of them had ever been to a flak house.

"You wouldn't believe me if I told you!" Light danced in Caruso's eyes, a spark absent before, as he recounted his time at the luxurious estate. "That place—it was like stepping into a dream. They treat you like royalty. Civilian clothes, no talk of war, every comfort you can think of. And the food!"

"Sounds like paradise," Bob Smith said, leaning forward. "How do they keep you from thinking about the war?"

"I don't know, but I'll tell you… it works. You start to relax without even realizing it. The people there are incredible—so warm, so kind. It's like they made it their mission to remind us of what life feels like outside of all this."

He told them about Evie and Arthur, Mary and Charlotte, and the other Red Cross volunteers. "They don't treat you like soldiers," he said, his voice softening. "They treat you like you're part of something again. Like you're home." He chuckled, his eyes sparkling. "They even had a dog there, a dachshund named Schleppy!"

"Schleppy?" Max laughed. "*Schlep* is Yiddish. My mom used that word all the time—it means to carry something."

Caruso nodded. "Exactly. They said that as a puppy, he wouldn't walk—he wanted to be carried everywhere. So, they named him Schleppy."

The men laughed, and Caruso joined in, his face lighting up in a way they'd never seen. One of the newer fellows, Al Cantrelle from Louisiana, let out a slow drawl between laughs. "Reckon that pup's got it figured out better'n we do." For a few minutes, the barracks faded, and it felt like home again—just a bunch of fellas trading stories over laughs.

"There was only one drawback," Caruso said, tossing his duffel onto his bunk.

"What's that?" the men asked in unison.

He grinned. "After sleeping on those beds, this bunk will feel like I'm lying on rocks."

The men dissolved into laughter, and for the first time in what felt like forever, Caruso felt like he belonged.

He glanced at his watch. "Listen, fellas. I've got to go meet with the flight doc. He has to approve my return to battle. See you later."

Caruso walked out, leaving the others in a flurry of conversation about what they'd just witnessed.

"Wow," Max said. "Looks like that stay really did him some good. Did you see? His eyes were clear, his hands were steady, and his entire manner was different!"

"Yeah," Bob said, nodding. "He was so upbeat and calm! No more of those large bags drooping halfway down his face. He looked like a different person."

Perch laughed. "How could he not? That place sounds spectacular!"

"Yes, that, but I mean… he's like a different person. It's unbelievable," Max said. "I'm glad. I hope this turns things around for him. I was really worried about him. He didn't seem right."

"Yeah, I hope this change in him is lasting," Perch said, looking off in the distance. "He's really been through a lot."

Before meeting with the flight surgeon, Caruso stopped by Chaplain Richard's office to express his gratitude.

"Santo, welcome back. I've been thinking about you and praying for you. How are you, son?"

"Better, sir. That place… it was exactly what I needed. I didn't think I'd ever find peace again, but I found it there."

The chaplain nodded, his expression serene. "It's important to find moments of calm amidst the storm. They remind us of who we are, and who we're fighting to become."

"Thank you for everything, sir. I don't know how I'll repay you."

"Live well, Santo. That's all the repayment I need."

❧

Captain Gannon greeted Caruso with a firm handshake. "Welcome back, Sergeant. How are you feeling?"

"Good, sir. My stay at Ebrington Manor was the best thing I've ever done. I'm ready to get back to my missions."

The doctor leaned back in his chair, his expression thoughtful. "Last time, you told me the same thing. But it turned out you weren't ready. I don't want to make that mistake again."

Caruso's stomach dropped as dread filled his chest. "What do you mean, sir?"

"I mean you're being reassigned. No more ball turret. You're moving to the left waist gunner position."

Relief flooded Caruso's chest, and he broke into a grin. "Thank you, sir. I won't let you down."

"I'm confident you won't. Now, get some rest. You'll likely have a mission tomorrow."

"That's fine, sir. Thank you again." He saluted and walked out the door, scarcely able to believe what he'd just been told.

That night, as he lay on his cot, staring up at the barracks' ceiling, he let out a slow, steady breath. The cots hadn't changed; the springs still creaked, the mattress was still lumpy, but something inside him was different. For the first time in a long while, he felt steady. Strong. Ready. He was no longer the man who had left for Ebrington Manor, worn and frayed at the edges. He'd found a new resolve, a quiet fortitude that made him believe he might just make it out of this war after all. One mission, one day, one breath at a time.

CHAPTER TWENTY-FOUR

January 1, 1945

THE START OF a new year at Polebrook Air Base brought with it not just the promise of fresh beginnings but also the long-awaited Christmas party organized by Calvert and his friend Edwin Birtwell, who worked in the photo lab processing films from missions. Although air raids had delayed the holiday festivities, excitement now coursed through the base. Each airman carried gifts labeled with the names of the youngsters they were meant to delight, their spirits buoyed by the promise of spreading joy.

The main hangar, usually dominated by clanging tools and the metallic scent of fuel, had become a winter wonderland. A towering tree, adorned with handmade decorations and colorful paper chains, rose proudly at its center. For one day, the hangar was no longer a staging ground for war—it was a haven for celebration.

"You really pulled it off, Birt!" Calvert said, elbowing his friend in the ribs. "The kids will love it. And is that cologne I smell? Trying to impress someone?"

Birt flushed slightly. "What can I say? It's my favorite. My mom sent it from home; it used to drive the ladies wild."

Calvert rolled his eyes. "Well, don't distract them too much. We've got work to do!"

The low rumble of an approaching bus silenced their banter. As the vehicle pulled up, the men lined up outside to greet the guests. The doors swung open, and children spilled out, their laughter cutting through the crisp winter air. Calvert and Birt were the first to step forward, their roles as hosts lending them a sense of purpose beyond their usual duties.

Searching the mass of young people disembarking, Birt's grin widened when he spotted Valerie, the schoolteacher, descending the bus steps. He had met her at a Red Cross coffee social and had been all too happy to be the liaison with the school during the party planning process. She was tall and slender, dressed in red velvet, her blonde hair tied back with a matching bow. "Let me assist you, ma'am," Birt said, offering his hand with a flourish. Valerie's cheeks reddened as she took it, her eyes twinkling.

"Thank you, Edwin," she said softly. Together, they guided the young ones toward the hangar. Birt, camera in hand, snapped pictures of the children's beaming faces as they ran around, mesmerized, surveying all the decorations.

Stepping off next was Dorothy, a shorter woman with wavy shoulder-length brown hair and striking emerald eyes that seemed to shimmer with an almost ethereal light. Calvert couldn't help but be drawn in, his eyes lingering a moment longer than intended. Her gaze reminded him so much of his sister Evelyn's—steady and kind, with a quiet strength. *Lyn would love this,* he thought, feeling a pang of homesickness. *I wonder if she's celebrating somewhere, somehow, amidst all this madness.*

Clearing his throat, he found his voice. "Welcome, ma'am. I'm Corporal Calvert P'Pool, one of the organizers. We're honored to have you here." He gave a slight, respectful nod. "Despite the missions throwing us off schedule, seeing this come together has been worth every effort." He paused, looking around at the youth darting around gleefully. *How much we all need this*, he thought. *A moment of normalcy in a world turned upside down.*

Her warm, genuine smile eased the slight tension in his stance. "Pleased to make your acquaintance, Corporal. I'm Dorothy Beaumont. And this"—she gestured toward the bustling children—"is just smashing. The children are over the moon; they've been talking about it for weeks."

As they walked toward the hangar, Calvert's usual confidence wavered. He fiddled with the buttons on his jacket, a nervous habit he hadn't indulged in since his arrival at Polebrook. His mind raced for the right words, feeling an unfamiliar self-doubt. "You teach at the school, then?"

Dorothy shook her head, laughing lightly. "Oh, no, I'm just an office secretary. Valerie, bless her, twisted my arm into coming today. She thought it might do me some good."

The slight tremor in her voice didn't escape him, and Calvert hesitated. "I hope I'm not prying, but… has it been a difficult time?"

Her smile faltered, and her voice dropped to a near whisper. "My husband was killed in the war almost a year ago."

Calvert's chest tightened at the raw grief in her eyes. Without thinking, he stepped closer, gently placing a hand on her arm. "I'm so sorry, ma'am. Truly."

For a moment, she looked startled by the unexpected intimacy. Then, as tears began to well up, Calvert pulled her briefly to him.

When they parted, Dorothy wiped her eyes and gave a shaky laugh. "Forgive me, Corporal. I didn't mean to carry on so."

"Not at all," Calvert said earnestly. "You're not alone in this. My mother passed away just a short while ago. It was sudden, and I wasn't there. That's something I live with every day."

Dorothy's gaze softened, her tears abating. "I'm so sorry for your loss. The holidays… they have a way of making these absences feel even heavier, don't they?"

"They do," Calvert agreed. Then, offering her his arm, he added with a small smile, "But maybe today we can distract ourselves. Watching these little ones enjoy themselves might do us both some good."

Dorothy hesitated, then linked her arm with his. "I'd like that," she said softly. "And please, call me Dorothy."

He smiled. "And you can call me Calvert."

Inside the hangar, the children's eyes grew wide as they took in the festive decorations. Popcorn garlands glimmered gold, and twinkling lights cast a warm glow. At the room's heart, a large hand-printed sign proclaimed: "HAPPY CHRISTMAS FROM THE 351ST."

The children dashed between tables, exclaiming over every detail. One boy, his glasses slightly askew, clutched his toy plane tightly as he looked up at the soldiers with both admiration and curiosity. A girl with pigtails tugged at Valerie's dress, her voice a whisper. "Will there be pudding, Miss?"

Valerie laughed. "Patience, Annie. First, we eat supper."

Soldiers escorted the children to the mess hall, where tables were laden with turkey, stuffing, and potatoes. Red Cross women flitted between the rows, pouring drinks and ensuring the children had everything they needed.

A loud squeal pierced the cacophony of voices in the mess hall. Startled heads turned toward the sound. Peeking from behind the wall, a short, trim man in a red and green outfit and a red pointed hat greeted the merry crowd. "Hello there! I hope you liked your supper! But *I* think they forgot my favorite part: dessert! Now, where did that chef go?"

Calvert recognized Caruso's familiar Philadelphia accent, which added to his elf-like charm. The boys and girls, giggling gleefully, pointed and shouted, "He went out that door!"

The elf paused dramatically, peering around the room with exaggerated suspicion before creeping to the back door, playing to the children's delight. In less than a minute, he returned with the chef in tow, followed by the Red Cross ladies wheeling carts loaded with plates of mince and pumpkin pies. Tiny hands met in enthusiastic applause, their cheers of delight floating through the air, eyes aglow with the wonder of the unexpected banquet of treats.

Ice cream—made from powdered milk—appeared like a bit of magic. The children paused, puzzled by the cold white scoop set before them, a rarity in wartime England. One brave boy took a tentative bite and broke into a grin. The rest followed, giggles rising like birds startled into flight, wonder melting into joy.

"This is just lovely," Dorothy said, leaning toward Calvert. "Look at their faces. They haven't seen this much food in… well, probably since they can even remember."

"That's why we do it," Calvert replied, watching a boy clap his hands in delight. "These moments remind us why we're over here."

Meanwhile, Caruso the elf wove through the youngsters, laughter bubbling around him. Each joke and playful gesture felt like a tiny victory—proof of how far he'd come from the shadows he'd once lived in. A smile tugged at his lips as he caught Calvert's eye across the room. This silly costume, he realized, was more than just holiday fun. It was proof that even in the face of war, he could still choose a moment of gladness. They were all far from home, yet moments like these knitted them into a makeshift family bound by their shared experiences—good and bad.

After the children finished their dessert, their laughter and chatter filled the air as they made their way back from the mess hall. The transition to the hangar was seamless, their excitement undimmed by the brief walk. Their anticipation was tangible, each wondering what surprise awaited them next.

"Ho ho ho!" Father Christmas boomed as he pulled up in a sputtering jeep. Dressed in the traditional red suit, he sported a belly that looked suspiciously like a balled-up pillow. "Happy Christmas to y'all!" he bellowed in a thick southern drawl. The voice was unmistakably that of Al Cantrelle, from Caruso's barracks. His thick Louisiana accent peppered his every word. The kids swarmed around him, laughter and delight filling the hangar as he made his way to the chair by the tree. It was impossible to tell who was having more fun.

One by one, names were called, and each child received a carefully wrapped gift—candy, gum, or small trinkets the soldiers had gathered from home. The children's shrieks of glee rang out, filling the hangar with a joy that seemed to erase, if only for a moment, the oppression of war. As Calvert surveyed the scene, warmth bubbled up within him. *This is what it's all about*, he mused. *Amid all this darkness, we've managed to bring a bit of light.*

"Ho ho ho, y'all, I seem to have two more gifts here!" Father Christmas extended his arm, then stroked his beard theatrically. "Let's see who they can be for…" He made a show of adjusting his glasses as if to improve his eyesight. "Hmmm…" He looked out at the young faces. "Can you help me? Is there a Miss Valerie here? And… a Miss… Dorothy?"

Giggling, the children pointed in unison at the two ladies as if on cue. "Over there!"

Valerie and Dorothy raised their eyebrows in surprise as Father Christmas approached first one, and then the other. "It seems that you both have been very good this year! Father Christmas has brought you a gift."

"Let us see! Let us see!" The clamoring young voices were a small chorus. Valerie opened hers first, gasping in delight at the Shalimar perfume nestled inside the box. "My favorite! Thank you, Father Christmas!" Her eyes twinkled as they rested on Birt.

Birt smiled as he saw her face light up. He'd noticed an empty bottle of the perfume at Valerie's flat and had asked his parents to send him some. The package arrived just the week before. There'd been more than a little ribbing when his buddies saw that he had received some ladies' perfume.

"Your turn, Miss Dorothy!" The children clapped with radiant cheer. Dorothy opened her package and lifted out an elegant hand-knitted beige scarf. She held it up, admiring the intricate stitches, running her fingers thoughtfully over the soft wool.

"Oh, my goodness! Thank you, Father Christmas!" she said. "It's just beautiful!"

She looked over at Calvert, who was beaming. "I'd asked my mother to knit something as a Christmas gift. When I got it, I was so surprised at the detail she put into it. I didn't know who would be getting it, but now that we've met, I think it was meant for you. It looks like that was what my mother was hoping, also," he said, conspiratorially. "It's quite the work of art, isn't it? She loved to knit and was very good at it. She even held knitting classes."

Dorothy's smile wavered, her gaze dropping to her lap as a shadow crossed her face. "How can you part with this?"

Calvert reached out and gently touched Dorothy's hand. "Dorothy, my mother has knitted me many a scarf. She would have wanted you to have it. I think she considered it a way to support the military effort. I'd be so happy knowing that her beautiful work is being worn and treasured, and she'd be over the moon, too. There was nothing she loved more than to see her knitted garments being used. Just think of her when you wear it, that's all I ask."

Dorothy looked up, her eyes brimming. "This was such a thoughtful gesture, especially when you didn't even know who the recipient would be. All this effort into helping complete strangers have a lovely holiday." She looked into his eyes. "You're a very good and kind man. Your mother sounds like she was a proper gem, knitting away for the likes of us. I'll cherish it, I will. And I'll think of her every time I wear it. That's a promise."

As the youngsters' laughter continued, the elf, with a mischievous glint in his eyes, waltzed back into the room. "Father Christmas must be on his way. Say goodbye and thank you!"

The boys and girls complied with shouted goodbyes and thanks as Father Christmas touched his hand to his hat in farewell. After a few false starts, his jeep roared to life. "Remember to be good in the coming year, and kind to your parents! I'll see y'all next year! Ho ho ho!"

The children went back to their gifts, until the elf began hopping around the room, a twinkle in his eye as he seated himself at the piano. "Come gather round, everyone! Let's sing some carols! Do you know 'Jingle Bells'?"

"Yes! Yes!" Squealing and huddling together, their eyes gleamed with excitement.

Caruso struck the first chord, his voice rising in a warm baritone. The youngsters joined in, and the room erupted in jubilant harmony as the men and women lent their voices to the chorus. For a brief moment, the world outside faded, leaving only warm companionship and the power of music.

As the party wound down, Valerie and Birt approached Dorothy and Calvert, who were looking on while sipping some tea. "What a lovely gathering you two have put on," Valerie said with a contented sigh.

"It's been a real pleasure. I sincerely mean that," Calvert said. "You don't realize until you're away how much the holidays mean to you. Back home, Christmas was a time of gathering, of family. Here, with all the reminders of war, these moments become all the more precious. There isn't a lot to look forward to from day to day, but it's times like these that make it worthwhile."

At that moment, the bus driver entered the hangar and approached the group. Calvert and Dorothy got up to get everyone ready to go, leaving Valerie and Birt at the table. Valerie turned to Birt. "Thank you so much."

Birt gently took her hand, pressing a tender kiss into it. "Allow us the honor of escorting the children to the bus," he said, his words still carrying a lingering hint of the day's magic. He looked into her eyes and said softly, "I hope to see you again soon."

Valerie smiled warmly at Birt. "I would like that, very much."

Calvert and Dorothy shepherded their charges toward the bus, where Valerie and Birt assisted them up the stairs. As the last child climbed aboard, Dorothy turned to Calvert with a smile. "This has been just splendid."

Calvert nodded, his voice soft but earnest. "Meeting you has been an unexpected treat. Sometimes, you never know what's around the corner, and in wartime, it's rarely something good. Today was an exception. I'm glad you decided to come."

"Me too," Dorothy said, her voice tinged with sincerity.

"Would it be too forward to ask if I might see you again?" Calvert asked, hope flickering in his eyes.

"Most definitely, Calvert… I'd like that very much."

As the bus pulled away, Calvert stood with Birt and Caruso, watching the taillights disappear. "For a few hours," Caruso said, breaking the silence, "we weren't soldiers—we were just people."

Calvert nodded. His voice was quiet as he said, "Yeah, a little bit of hope in these hard times. That's what it's all about."

The three stood in quiet understanding before turning back to the hangar, the echoes of the children's laughter lingering like the last notes of a cherished song.

CHAPTER TWENTY-FIVE

Week of January 28, 1945

CARUSO HAD BEEN back for a few weeks, and the change in him was unmistakable. He woke each morning without the weight of nightmares, his demeanor softened, and he greeted his comrades with a smile that was becoming less forced.

Max had been quietly supportive since Caruso's return from the flak house, creating space for trust to take root. One afternoon, while the two were alone in the barracks, Max finally broached what had lingered unspoken for weeks.

"Caruso," he said, tentative, "I noticed something. Your nightmares—they've stopped, haven't they?"

Caruso nodded, his gaze dropping. "Yeah. Getting out of the ball turret helped. So did the time away. I didn't think it would, honestly."

Max hesitated. "The chaplain mentioned something happened… but he didn't say what."

Caruso gave a dry huff. "That's probably for the best." He leaned back, arms folded. "Let's just say it messed me up more than I let on. Physically, yeah… but mostly here." He tapped his temple. "And here." A light touch to his chest.

Max nodded, his expression unreadable. "I understand. Maybe not the same way… but I do."

Caruso glanced over, surprised.

Max shrugged. "You ever wonder if we'll know who we are after this? When we're not crew, or gunner, or just trying to survive?"

"All the time."

A silence settled between them, not tense this time, but shared.

"There was someone at the rehab place," Caruso said. "A nurse. Helen."

Max raised a brow.

"She helped. A lot. Got me through the worst of it. I thought maybe… I don't know. But it wasn't meant to be."

"Still," Max said, "sounds like she left her mark."

"Yeah." Caruso's voice was barely a whisper. "She did."

Max leaned back on his bunk, staring up at the ribbed ceiling. "Well, for what it's worth, I'm glad you're back. Not just here. But *back*."

Caruso didn't speak right away, but nodded. "Thanks, Max." He cleared his throat. "Anyway, seeing others far worse off at Stoneleigh made me rethink my own self-pity. There was this one fella, Walter. Just stared. Never spoke. The nurses wheeled him outside every day, hoping for something."

"Did they get it?"

"One day, he turned his head and said he was thirsty. Just two words. You'd think it was a miracle."

"But?"

Caruso shook his head. "Nahh. He was still… gone. Dependent for everything. I couldn't stop thinking about what kind of life he had ahead. And what his family would get back after all this." He rubbed his temples. "It was like staring into a mirror of what I could've become. Maybe that fear is what pushed me to fight back."

Max nodded, his voice low. "This damn war… it takes everything. Not just lives. People come back forever changed."

"Yeah," Caruso said. "Getting back in the plane, facing it again… it's still hard. But I had to."

"Did the rest home offer counseling?"

"They tried. But it was mostly physical recovery. The meds for nightmares just made me feel worse. In the end, I had to find my own way. Chaplain Richards helped. More than anyone."

Max leaned forward. "What about your crew?"

Caruso's eyes misted. "Good men. They visited before shipping out. I was proud of them. But damn, it was hard to watch them go. I hope I run into them again someday."

Max placed a hand on his shoulder. "You've been through hell, Caruso. And you came out the other side. I admire that. This life—it's not like the ads say. Everyone wanted to be a pilot, right? I went to flight school. Washed out. But I like being a radio operator. Still doing my part."

Caruso nodded. "All this… it changed the way I see things." A shadow passed over his face. Yet in talking to Max, he sensed the first threads of a brotherhood forming, faint but real. He remembered what Dr. Sotelo said about trust. Maybe that's what this was.

After Max left, Caruso sat alone, their conversation settling like embers cooling from a long-burning fire. Outside, the low murmur of the base went on, steady and indifferent. He stood, the memory of their talk still warm in his chest, and stepped outside.

Every day, he thought, *brings me closer to who I was… or maybe to who I'm becoming. Maybe that's what this war does—reshapes us in ways we never expect.*

ক

A few days later, with missions scrubbed due to weather, the men gathered in the Red Cross Club, waiting for the guest of honor. Paul Lucyk, one of the base's gunners, had just married Betty, an English woman he'd met at a coffee social, and his friends had organized a small celebration in their honor. The room was warm and lively, with bunting strung overhead and a makeshift cake the chef had cobbled together with whatever rations they could spare.

Laughter and music filled the air as Paul entered, his grin stretching from ear to ear, Betty's hand clasped tightly in his. Caruso watched the couple for a long moment, struck by how Paul's eyes never left Betty's face, how she seemed to glow in the light of their happiness.

Paul was one of three men to survive a crash in the Channel. He still walked with a slight limp, but the light in his eyes signaled that all was right in his world. He looked like a man who had already faced death once, and had found some peace in spite of it.

Caruso wondered if he'd ever find himself in that place—surrounded by friends, with someone to call his own, a future that felt more certain than fleeting. For now, though, he let himself be swept up in the celebration, tucking the moment away like a small flicker of hope for the road ahead.

ক

Later, Caruso was playing cards with Rapoport when Max walked in, a smile on his face as he ripped open an envelope and became engrossed in a letter. A photo dropped out from the folds, and Al Cantrelle picked it up with a whistle. "Mmm, mmm! What have we here? You've been holding out on us, Max! Who's this beauty? My, my!"

Max's face reddened as he snatched the photo back. "Just a girl I know. Sister of a buddy from home. Nothing to get all worked up about."

"Um hmm…" Al winked. "I know how that goes, my friend. And you can tell that hogwash to somebody else. I can tell by that look: you're sweet on her. Nothin' wrong with that. Ya know what, Max? Take whatever good feelin's you can find. From what I've seen in my short time here, they are few and far between. We could be a puff of smoke tomorrow. Enjoy what you can. Did she just write you outta the blue?"

"No. I ran into her brother when I was on pass in London. He and I used to play basketball at home. His sister Margaret had a crush on me back then, but she was too young to even think about. He said she's a nurse now and gave me her address. I wrote her to let her know her brother was doing okay."

"Well now, you must be the most thoughtful fella I know, takin' time outta the war to check in on a girl. How selfless of ya!" Al said, teasing.

"Alright, alright," Max chuckled. "He did show me her picture and… well, I gotta admit, she grew up real pretty."

"I'll agree with ya there, my friend, that I will. No harm in rekindling old feelin's, no harm at all. Life's too short. I'm jealous!" Al slapped him on the back and handed over some tape. "Put that photo up where you can see it. Let it keep you goin'. Lord knows we can use whatever inspiration we can find over here!"

Caruso stood back, a silent observer. The lightheartedness felt distant, a contrast to his own unsettled thoughts about Helen. "Hey, fellas, I'm going to get some air. See you all later."

The door slammed behind him, the warmth of the room fading into the cold night. Engines hummed in the distance, and laughter spilled faintly through the walls. The weight of his thoughts settled around him like snowflakes finding a place to rest.

Inside, the others exchanged glances. "I think he's still smarting from a romance that didn't work out," Max said. "Probably too soon for him to think about falling in love again."

"He's different, though," Perch said, "since he came back from that flak house. Remember how he was when we first arrived?"

Max nodded, his eyes far away. "Makes you realize how easy it is to judge a fella without knowin' what he's been through. I used to think Caruso had it easy, flying over with his crew instead of being crammed onto a troopship like the rest of us. But after hearing what he's been through—the injury, losing his crew, flying again—I see now he's been carrying more than I ever realized."

He paused. "You know, most of the time, when a fella snaps, it's not about you. It's about whatever's goin' on inside him. That's what my mom used to say: *Only the soup knows what's in the pot.* And she's the smartest woman I know."

CHAPTER TWENTY-SIX

February, 1945

THE FEBRUARY CHILL of England permeated their bones, an unwelcome yet familiar presence. Near the control tower, the ground crew huddled together, their breath visible in the cold air. The distant roar of aircraft engines announced the bombers' return, cutting through the pewter skies over Polebrook.

Caruso, his cheeks reddened from the cold, paused and squinted into the haze. Beside him, the ground crew shifted expectantly, their eyes scanning the sky as the bombers emerged from the fog, shadows against the clouds.

The planes prepared to break from the group one by one, a routine they'd performed countless times. Yet today, as the men on the ground watched, the synchronized ballet faltered. Two planes peeled off simultaneously, their paths intersecting with a horrifying inevitability. A collective gasp erupted but was lost in the screech of colliding metal. The sky exploded in a blinding burst of red fury, debris cascading down.

John Leasure's wrench hit the ground, unnoticed. His trembling hands rose to his mouth in a feeble attempt to hold back his horror. One of his buddies, Robert Sollers, a fella who could find laughter in even the darkest of times, had been up there. Leasure's words, choked by sobs, cut through the air. "Just this morning, we…" His voice trailed off, the reality too stark, too immediate. Only the day before, Sollers had swelled with pride that his brother Buck was in aviation school in Alabama. "Damn this war!"

Leasure remained dazed and immobile, his eyes fixed on the trails of smoke tracing where his friends had flown moments before.

"How?" John Montgomery's voice broke in anger and despair. "To survive the enemy and then…"

The air was thick with the acrid smell of burning fuel as emergency crews swarmed the wreckage. Pieces of fuselage jutted out of the scorched earth like broken bones. A helmet lay half-buried in the snow, charred and unrecognizable. Somewhere in the distance, a soldier retched violently, unable to bear the sight. Caruso didn't go to the crash site—he couldn't—but from where he stood, he saw enough: twisted metal, shattered remains of what had been two planes, two crews, just moments before.

As the afternoon wore on, the men gathered in small groups in an attempt to calm their emotions. Whiskey did little to dull the sharpness of their grief. One of the downed planes carried Al Cantrelle and his crew, who had been in Caruso's barracks for barely over a month. A familiar emptiness opened inside Caruso, but this loss cut deeper than any before.

He stood frozen in the cold, unable to tear his eyes from the burning horizon. The wind carried the scent of charred metal and something else: something final. Around him, voices rose and fell, a chorus of shock and grief. And in that stunned silence, Caruso's mind drifted to Al.

He had been so full of life, so vivid in personality, that the void left behind felt unbearable. His jolly portrayal of Father Christmas. The playful ribbing—seasoned with that distinctive Louisiana twang—about Max's blossoming pen-pal romance with Margaret, always bringing roars of laughter to the barracks, lightening even the grimmest moments. His pride in his siblings all serving their country. His wit, once a guiding light, now extinguished. Caruso hoped Al's family knew how deeply he had touched everyone on base—how his humor always lifted the spirits of even the most down-and-out soldier.

When posing for photos, he always tilted his head a little to the right, claiming with a wink that he was showing off his better side, which he believed to be his left. Everyone in the barracks argued that both sides looked the same, but he'd just say, "Gotta put my best side forward; you never know who might be looking!" What a card he was. He left an empty hole in Caruso's life that no one else would ever quite fill.

Caruso's conversation with Dr. Sotelo back at Ebrington Manor sprang to mind, when he said there's more to this life than marking time to get to the other side, and that life isn't always measured in days. He still remembered his words: *Your purpose on this earth is to learn how to live a full life that has meaning and influences others in a positive way. Like throwing a pebble into the water, your life's impact will reverberate through the lives of others. And that way, your life goes on and on.*

Al had one of those lives he was talking about, Caruso realized. *His life rippled outward, touching everyone around him. In the short time he was with us, he really left an impression, and we were better men for having known him. Will I ever leave a mark like that? In the end, will I be remembered not just as another name, but as someone who mattered?*

In the days that followed, the base mourned, their sadness enveloping them like a dense fog. The arrival of the film *Combat America*, featuring their own 351st Bomb Group, had offered a welcome break from their melancholy. Clark Gable's time among them, once a novelty, now underscored the depth of their shared experiences.

As the film had rolled on, Caruso found himself wondering what Al would've said about it. Probably something cheeky about Clark Gable's mustache, or how Hollywood didn't quite capture the smell of sweat and fear inside a bomber. But beneath the jokes, Al would've been proud. This was their story, after all—the story of all the men who fought, lived, and died to see it told. The screening sparked conversations and memories, but for Caruso, the film was a tribute—to their lasting bond, their sacrifices, and the stories that would outlast them.

Alone on the edge of the airfield, Caruso gazed up at the vast expanse of stars. The cold didn't seem as biting, nor the darkness as oppressive. *Combat America* had reignited something in him and the others. It personified the spirit that tied them all together, and a belief that their sacrifices were part of a larger story.

Memories of Al, and all the others who were gone, filled him with a profound sense of loss and resolve. As he stood there, he thought about those mornings when he'd first awoken, momentarily expecting to hear Al's southern drawl booming through the darkness like it always had, before the harsh reality settled in anew. The anguish that followed those moments made him yearn for the safety and comfort of home.

But there was strength to be found even in these memories. Friendships formed in the Army, intense and quick, borne out of necessity, offered a unique bond. They garnered support from one another and shared a connection no outsider could truly understand.

Eventually, the deepening chill reminded Caruso it was time to head back. He shoved his hands into his pockets, and his breath fogged in the night air. As he reached the barracks, he thought of Al tilting his head for the camera, winking. *Gotta put my best side forward.* A faint smile formed on his lips. Around him, the base would keep moving, keep fighting, and in that movement, Caruso found a small measure of peace. The ache in his chest reminded him: some people stay with you, no matter what.

CHAPTER TWENTY-SEVEN

March, 1945

WHEN THEY WERE standing down from missions, weekends offered a rare chance to blow off steam. For those who stayed on base, if the weather was poor, Saturdays meant writing home, playing cards, or watching a movie. But on sunny days, the men opted for baseball, biking to town, or just soaking in the rare warmth.

Max, with his tall and gangly stature, was great at shooting hoops, though one of his favorite on-base physical activities was a spirited game of baseball. During Army training, it had always been fun to get the fellas together for a game. Tournaments were well attended, with some men placing bets on various parameters. Max gazed at the field on base, and for a moment, it became his hometown's dusty diamond, with laughter ringing out as his younger self swung at pitches from his older brother Harry. He shook the memory away, the bittersweetness of it fueling his desire to win, not just for the game but for the piece of home it brought, even here in England.

Today was one of those uncharacteristically warm and sunny days, and a few of the men gathered outside on their makeshift baseball field. Ken Craumer, the gunnery instructor, was already out with a few others, trying to drum up enough players for a game—not a difficult task on this fine day. He loved to play the odds and was always looking for some angle to get a bet going. When he won, which was often, his grin would light up the sky, no matter how much or little he won. For him, it was the thrill of the win. He was even known for betting on himself.

"Hi there, Max. You in?" Kenny's eyes twinkled with mischief. Although he feigned modesty, Kenny was probably one of the best athletes on base, having played many sports back in Pennsylvania, and played them well. Max had once told Caruso that he'd always imagined that he, too, could have been on a college team, had he had the opportunity.

Max glanced at Caruso, who nodded in silent agreement to play.

Caruso tried to hide his smirk as he began to relish the win before the game even started. Raising his eyebrows, his eyes moved over Max and his crew, trying to give a somewhat ambivalent look intended to relay his hesitancy. "Well, why not, Ken? We've got nothing else to do. I see you need more people, so maybe we'll all take you on."

As the game progressed, the crowd swelled, each play drawing cheers and gasps. By the ninth inning, with the score tied, the air was charged with tension. Each pitch, hit, and catch was no longer about the game; it was a tribute to their resilience, their teamwork, and the rare joy of playing beneath a clear English sky.

Frankie led off for Max's team but quickly fell, sending a fly ball straight to right field for the first out. The sharp crack of the bat shattered the air. For Caruso, it echoed like a distant gunshot, a sound that sent an involuntary jolt through his chest. For a second, his mind faltered, an image of flak tearing through the sky flashing before his eyes. He instinctively pulled the brim of his cap down, as if the brim could shield him from the memory. Under its shadow, his face was a mask of composed neutrality, but his eyes darted briefly, a vestige of past reflexes not so easily brushed away. Then, with a steadying breath, he forced himself to clap, his hands stinging against the cold as he willed the moment to pass.

Kenny flipped his cap backward, a signal to everyone that he meant business. "Alright, fellas, let's see if you've got what it takes to take me down," he said, his grin as cocky as ever. Even losing a month's pay in a bet wouldn't dent his confidence—he'd just chalk it up as a "lesson learned" and double down next time.

He wound up, and Caruso stood ready at the plate, eyeing the pitcher's grip and stance, trying to size up the pitch before it rocketed toward him. Then, showing patience, he earned a walk, eyeing the bases with the zeal of an opportunist.

Perch was next, smashing a triple deep into the gap and sending Caruso sprinting home. The crowd roared as they edged ahead, 3–2. Jimmy Brady kept the fire alive with his own triple, bringing Perch in and padding the margin. Max grounded one to second, enough to bring Jimmy across. 5–2.

An infield error put Ray Youngberg on base, and a single sent Max charging across the plate.

A grounder to the shortstop led to an easy toss to second, bringing the inning to a close.

Watching their team tussle in celebration, Caruso felt a sting of nostalgia mixed with relief. "You know, Max," he said, half to himself, "a few months ago, I couldn't have enjoyed this. It's strange how some days still feel like borrowed time, as if these shared moments might slip away at any second." Max clapped him on the back with a nod, his understanding evident. They sauntered over to collect their winnings from Lester Rhein, serving as the bookie, their spirits high among the backslaps of victory.

After the game, Kenny's group made their way over. "I sure underestimated you fellas," he said, a note of genuine respect in his voice. "I'm not used to losing. Next time I'll remember to check who I'm betting against."

Caruso laughed, the sound easy and light. "Kenny, you had no way of knowing. A lot of us played ball under the fierce sun back home. Took a bit to shake off the rust, but we've still got it," he said, offering a handshake that bridged the gap of competition. "Great game. And this break from the routine? Couldn't have asked for better."

His gaze momentarily lifted to the clear skies, marveling at the day's gift. *What a change I've felt over these past few months*, he thought. *I remember feeling alone around all these faces that I didn't know very well. And now, here I am, a part of their group.* He turned to his friends. "How about celebrating at the Red Cross Club with some refreshments?"

Ken's response came with a playful smirk. "Appreciate the offer, but I've got plans to shine tonight. And I've got to get some sack time before then. I plan to win a different kind of game with my lady!" He strolled away with a wink and a confident stride.

Caruso's smile faltered, his gaze turning distant as thoughts of Helen surfaced.

Max, catching the subtle shift in Caruso's expression, was quick to respond. "Hey, Caruso, the Red Cross Club sounds great to me. Celebrate our win?" His voice carried a tone of solidarity that cut through the awkward silence.

The gratitude spreading across Caruso's face was apparent, a quiet recognition of shared understanding among friends. Nodding, they all agreed to Max's proposal, the decision wrapping them in a sense of unity as their steps lightened, leaving the field with its memories of sunlight and victory behind. As they walked toward the Red Cross Club, Caruso stole one last glance at the field, quiet now in the fading sunlight. These moments—shared laughter, competition, and brotherhood—reminded them of life beyond the war. They didn't know what tomorrow would bring. But for now, they had this, and it was enough.

CHAPTER TWENTY-EIGHT

IT WAS MID-MARCH, and Ray Youngberg, the left waist gunner on Max's crew, secured a three-day pass. Max seized the opportunity and approached Caruso about the next day's mission. "Hey, Caruso, why don't you join us on tomorrow's sortie? You'll get home quicker with every extra mission under your belt," he said, hopeful that the weather would hold.

The following day, the serene morning weather gave way to a stormy afternoon, diverting the returning aircraft from Polebrook. Most of the planes went to Colerne, near Bath, but with their fuel depleting, Max's crew made an unexpected landing at a base in Bassingbourn, near Cambridge. They took advantage of the base's liberty bus to transport them into the city.

"This isn't just a detour," Max said, his eyes lighting up. "It's a chance to step through history."

Cambridge, shrouded in persistent drizzle, granted them an unanticipated holiday. Venturing into the heart of the city, Max, Perch, and Caruso took in the grandeur of the university, as imposing in reality as in reputation.

"Wow, I can't believe we're here in Cambridge! My brother Harry told me all about this place. The thought of who may have walked these paths before us is overwhelming," Max said, his voice tinged with reverence.

Perch shrugged. "Well, I'm not much for history, but maybe they have a decent pub around, at least."

Their journey through the city's storied streets led them to the Eagle, a place as rich in history as the university. The pub was warm, dimly lit, and crowded with airmen. The walls groaned under the weight of history. Caps, photographs, and squadron insignias cluttered every available space, like echoes of the men who had come before them. The scent of ale and pipe smoke hung thick in the air.

As they stepped inside, Perch let out a low whistle. "Now this is a proper pub."

"Better than anything in Polebrook," Max agreed, shaking the fine raindrops from his jacket.

They found an open space near the bar, the wooden ceiling above them darkened with age and something else: names. Scorched, scratched, and inked into the surface, messages stretched overhead like a chaotic, sprawling roster of the men who had passed through.

"Fellas, look up there," Caruso murmured, tilting his head. He traced a few of the letters with his gaze, trying to picture the hands that had made them.

Perch squinted. "Think we could add ours?"

"Damn right, we could," Max said. "We should."

They were still studying the ceiling when Perch nudged them. "Hey, there's an interesting one." He pointed to an inscription, neater than the rest: *Rules are for the obedience of fools and the guidance of wise men. – D. Bader*

Caruso stared at it, then glanced at Max. "Douglas Bader?"

Max nodded. "The man himself."

Perch frowned. "That the guy who—"

"Flew with no legs?" Max finished. "Yeah. Got grounded, refused to stay down."

Perch shook his head slowly, incredulous. "And here I thought we were stubborn."

Caruso's fingers brushed over the sleeve of his jacket. "Imagine that. Being told you're finished, that you'll never fight again, and then climbing back into a cockpit anyway." His voice was quiet, laden with something unspoken.

Max studied him for a beat before clapping a hand on his shoulder. "Yeah. That's guts. He kept flying combat missions until they finally shot him down—and threw him in Colditz, the prison for Allied officers who wouldn't stop trying to escape."

A voice interrupted them. "If you're thinking of leaving your mark, I'd hurry."

They turned to see a waitress balancing a tray of pints. She nodded toward a nearby table. "Those fellas over there sent you these." She set the beers down. "Initiation, of sorts. Next time you see a new airman writing his name up there, you buy him one."

Caruso picked up his pint and turned toward the group who had sent the drinks. They raised their glasses in silent acknowledgment.

"Well," Perch said, setting down his beer, "guess we'd better make it official."

A few minutes later, with the encouragement of onlookers, each man took his turn. The smell of scorched wood filled the air as Caruso etched his name into history. *A tribute to the man who taught me how to stand up and keep going, no matter what*, he thought as he wrote his inscription: For Pop by Caruso—351st BG 3/12/45.

It was just a mark in the wood. Just a name among hundreds. But somehow, it felt like more. He thought of Al, and all the others. Names lost to the sky. Maybe this was their way of holding on, of saying "We were here."

Max lifted his glass. "To the men who came before us."

Caruso raised his. "To the ones who never quit."

Perch smirked, lifting his pint last. "And to the poor bastards flying tomorrow morning."

Their glasses met with a quiet clink, the warmth of the toast settling into their bones.

Outside, the cobblestone streets shimmered under the drizzle, the spires of Cambridge cutting sharp against the gray sky. For a moment, Caruso let himself believe that, even in war, some things—*some places*—were meant to last.

CHAPTER TWENTY-NINE

End of March, 1945

CARUSO'S NAME SLICED through the darkness, yanking him from a rare, comforting dream. He blinked into the cold barracks and then checked the time: three a.m. *Here we go again*, he thought.

Today he was flying with Perch. Caruso liked him—he always seemed to have the knack for cracking a joke at just the right time to ease the tension. Max always said Perch was a fantastic gunner: very focused and driven. He was glad to have him on his crew that day. Max had a three-day pass and had gone to London with a few of the other fellas to celebrate Passover.

They made their way to the briefing room, where the colonel made a speech about what great crews were sitting there in the room. Caruso cringed, thinking that the colonel was buttering them up for bad news. When the curtain finally opened, the room erupted with a litany of cursing. The knot tightened in his stomach, the word "Berlin" on the briefing map looming like an ominous apparition. A cold sweep of fear crept up his spine, and the room seemed to spin.

He touched his chest pocket for his crucifix. Suppressing a wave of panic, he immediately started patting all his pockets, searching. Nothing. Running his fingers through his hair, he anxiously awaited the end of the briefing, his heart pounding.

"Hey, buddy…" Caruso nudged Perch with a tense shoulder, urgency written in his eyes. "I need to go back to the barracks. Forgot something critical."

"There's no time. You know you'll catch hell if you're not on the plane with the rest of us. What did you forget?"

"My crucifix. I never fly without it." Caruso looked him in the eye. "I can't fly without it."

"Damn it, we're on a tight schedule!" Perch shook his head vigorously. "You can't. Listen, I've got one. I'll give you mine." He reached into his pocket and pulled out a rosary. "Just don't lose it. It's my nonna's and she'd kill me."

Caruso was momentarily speechless. All the men had their lucky charms, their special routines or keepsakes that they hoped would protect them. It was unimaginable that Perch would loan him his; he didn't think he'd have been able to do the same.

"No, no… I can't." Caruso stumbled over his words, flustered by the utter stupidity at leaving his crucifix in the barracks.

"Caruso. Take it." Perch's tone was firm as he stuffed the rosary into Caruso's chest pocket and began walking away.

Caruso's hands trembled as he fingered it in his pocket, struggling to swallow past a suddenly tight throat. "Thanks, Perch. You're a lifesaver."

"Here's hoping!" Perch looked back over his shoulder with a wink and a grin.

The takeoff and formation were flawless, all good signs. Making their turn onto the initial point for Berlin, they were six minutes from the target—it seemed the longest six minutes of his life. Tension creased his forehead. In an instant, a barrage of flak filled the sky, and suddenly a flame appeared near the bomb bay of an adjacent B-17, igniting the fuzes of the five-hundred-pound bombs it carried. A massive explosion obliterated the plane and everyone in it, leaving an empty sky where the plane had once been.

Before he had the chance to fully absorb what he had just seen, their aircraft jolted. Like watching a motion picture, the plane began to vibrate and slide, moving perilously close to a neighboring bomber. In what seemed like just a moment, they were losing altitude and falling below the formation.

The aircraft shuddered violently, plummeting faster, a swift, cold foreboding—they were easy prey now. The intercom buzzed, snapping Caruso back to the grim present. "Pilot to crew. Two engines are failing, one leaking oil and the other smoking badly."

A second report from George, the radio operator, soon followed. "Radioman to pilot. There's a tear in the left wing. Our oxygen system's been hit and we're losing oxygen."

The pilot's response was swift. "I'm going to drop us down below ten thousand feet so we can breathe without the masks."

Caruso's heartbeat raced. As they continued to lose altitude, the intercom squealed and the pilot's voice came on again, the tension cutting like a knife: "Jettison what you can!" They began throwing out non-essential equipment including guns and ammunition, to lighten the aircraft and stay airborne as long as possible.

As they continued, their fuel dwindled to fumes, their predicament dire. The pilot's voice crackled once again through the intercom. "Crew, it's decision time. Bail out, or push to the Channel? I don't see any way we can make it back to base."

George's reply was immediate, the strain in his voice evident through the static. "Radioman to all. Let's push these engines as far as they'll go. I don't want to end up being the guest of the Germans today if I can help it." Agreement was immediate, the crew's resolve united in the face of uncertainty.

"Alerting the base and Air Sea Rescue now," George said, setting to work with focused determination.

Reciting the rosary, Caruso finally saw the blue-gray coast come into view. They were at seven hundred feet, the fuel level almost imperceptible. George's assured voice sounded the mayday call, notifying Air Sea Rescue of the aircraft's position and updating the pilot that their rescuers had a fix on their location. "Radioman to pilot. Radio key tied down."

"Brace for impact." The pilot's voice was a blend of command and reassurance. George, Perch, and Caruso, along with Smithers, the nose gunner, closed all the windows and braced against the walls in the radio room, heads down for protection. In those last seconds, he didn't pray. He just thought of home.

The aircraft's tail grazed the water with a shudder that coursed through the fuselage, sending a reverberating tremor under Caruso's feet. Then, with a violent lurch, the nose plunged, unleashing a rush of water that slammed against the windows, momentarily engulfing their world in a frothy white blur.

The frigid bite of the water seeped through their clothing as they clambered out over each wing, their movements hurried and desperate, their breath visible in the frosty air. Quickly inflating their Mae West life vests, they scrambled to release and inflate the life rafts located on either side of the plane. Perch and Smithers quickly got in one raft, along with the pilot, navigator, and ball turret gunner. George and

Caruso got in the other with the right waist gunner, copilot, and bombardier. Caruso watched, heart tight, as the waves swallowed the plane in large gulps, adrenaline quickly overshadowing his emotions.

The raft rocked violently, swells of four to five feet challenging their fragile nest. The copilot's voice pierced the roaring of the waves. "Bail the water!" As he lunged for the pail, Caruso's fingers wrapped tightly around its slippery handle, scooping and hurling seawater overboard. Desperation lent strength to his efforts, but the sea was relentless, and water continued to seep into their life raft through some flak holes in the corner.

"Do we have the repair kit?" Caruso asked.

The copilot's response was grim. "Negative. Unless the other raft has theirs."

Craning his neck for the other dinghy, Caruso's breath caught in his throat—it was nowhere in sight.

"We're going under!" Caruso's voice cracked with tension and despair.

"Stick with the boat as long as you can. Rescue's already on their way," the bombardier instructed, his tone remaining steady amid the chaos.

Clinging to their sinking dinghy, Caruso had lost all feeling in his fingers, the pervasive chill weaving its way into his bones, his mind rapidly becoming sluggish in the frigid water around him. Abruptly, a sharp, wet slap across his cheek jolted him back to the moment. As his eyes slowly refocused, he saw the lifeline from the Air Sea Rescue boat. Relief washed over him as he grabbed the line with both hands and was pulled aboard.

The boat's cabin was a haven of warmth for Caruso and seven others from his crew. Caruso blinked rapidly as his eyes swept over each man in turn, embracing them fiercely, his eyes questioning the fate of Perch and Smithers as the workers continued their search. The three rescued men from Perch's dinghy had fallen into the water and lost sight of their two comrades in the chaos.

The rescue team's hunt for the two missing aircrew was to no avail. The waves were now about six feet. Caruso clutched the rosary that Perch had given him just a few hours before, a lifeline of a different sort. The weight of Perch's absence squeezed his heart as tears ran silently down his cheeks.

Caruso was released after a few nights' stay at the base hospital. When he entered the barracks, the sight of Perch's empty bunk was a sucker punch to the stomach. Seeing his stripped cot underscored the void where laughter, camaraderie, and the very essence of Perch used to fill the air. Caruso could hardly breathe. How could he face Max?

He couldn't.

As he turned to walk back outdoors, Max stopped him, his brows knitted with worry that made him appear older than his twenty-six years. "How are you holding up, Caruso?" The weight of unspoken fears hung between them.

"They didn't find Perch?"

Max's gaze drifted away for a moment, seeming to compose himself before meeting Caruso's eyes with firm determination. "No word yet, but Perch is the cat with nine lives. I'm not giving up on him."

Caruso's face paled, the concern lining his forehead. "He didn't have his rosary. He gave it to me because I forgot my crucifix."

"It's not your fault, Caruso," Max said gently, touching his arm. "Look, we got into this war knowing what we were in for.

There aren't any guarantees. Perch knew that… he knows that. I met with the chaplain. We've been praying for his safe return. You take Perch's rosary and do the same. Don't you give up on him; I'm not. If anyone can survive out there, it's Perch. And the captain told me they're still out there looking."

Snafu looked up at Caruso, whimpering, and Caruso picked him up, snuggling him to his chest absently. His voice wavered, a whisper lost in the wind. "I need… some air." He couldn't meet Max's eyes, overwhelmed not just by his own grief but by the steadiness of the hand that briefly squeezed his shoulder—a quiet message of solidarity. Clutching Snafu tighter, he stepped out into the waning light of dusk, the oranges and pinks of the horizon bleeding into the sky's deepening canvas. The little dog, a small warm weight in his arms, trembled slightly, mirroring the torrent of feelings bubbling within him. The barracks behind him cast long shadows across the ground, the events of the past few days clutching deep within Caruso's soul.

The base was quiet, its usual hum of activity missing, mirroring the emptiness that now filled Caruso. Only the distant sound of a jeep engine and the occasional muffled voices carried by the wind broke the silence. The world felt suspended, caught between the chaos of the day and uncertain promises of tomorrow.

Caruso's eyes were drawn to the sky, where the first stars were twinkling in the darkening night. *Is Perch looking at the same sky, wherever he is?* A pang of longing struck for his missing comrade. His chest constricted tighter, as much by the loss of Perch as by Max's unwavering and unexpected support. The thought circled back like an unending loop: *How does he hold on to hope like a lighthouse beacon in the dark? When all the odds are against his friend—my friend—being alive?*

Standing alone, Caruso felt the storm of emotion building inside him. Snafu, pressed against his chest, provided some consolation, a symbol of the ties that bound him not just to Perch, but to all the men he flew with. The cold bit at his cheeks. Inhaling deeply, he tried to settle the turbulence of his emotions.

As night fell, Caruso thought about Max's steadfast loyalty. In that moment of solitude, he realized brotherhood wasn't just about shared laughter or battle cries; it lived in quiet understanding, shared grief, and the unspoken promises to keep moving forward as one, no matter what. He'd always associated brotherhood with the men physically by his side in the aircraft. But Max's optimism and refusal to give in to despair showed him that their connection stretched far beyond those moments in the air. It was about finding hope in the bleakest times through each other's strength. Individually they would crumble, but together they were a formidable force.

Max's faith in Perch's return and his support of Caruso had shown him the depth of his character. Caruso hadn't realized this until now, seeing Max rise above his own grief to offer solace. The selflessness was unspoken but present in every gesture and silent companionship.

Caruso turned toward the barracks as his eyes misted, Snafu nestled in his arms. Frost was beginning to form on the grass, tiny crystals glinting in the last light, reminding him of life's fragility. The dog nuzzled into his chest, his warm beating heart a reprieve from the cold.

The sound of his boots crunching on the hardened earth filled the evening silence. He passed under a bare tree, its branches stripped yet reaching, a monument to the cycle of life.

Caruso walked back with determined steps, buoyed by the understanding of their unshakable bond in this experience. It was a realization that would change how he faced the days ahead, hopeful for Perch's return and strengthened by the solidarity he felt with Max and his comrades.

CHAPTER THIRTY

THE BARRACKS WERE hushed, dawn's light faintly filtering through the grimy windows as whispered prayers rose to meet it. Max lay awake, each breath a fog of worry. Another day with no word from Perch.

The memories of their training, when Perch's quick wit had carried him through moments of doubt, felt painfully fresh. Max could still picture them standing together at the New York gangway, freshly minted airmen brimming with anticipation for the adventure ahead. Perch had filled their arduous sea journey to Great Britain with tales of his mother's authentic Italian cooking and promises of sharing it once they were home. They'd talked endlessly about futures made possible by the GI bill, their dreams taking shape with each passing mile. Now, those dreams hung heavily in Max's heart, a reminder of all that had been lost.

Max forced a smile as Frankie's voice broke through the stillness. "How's the world treating you today, Max?"

"I feel as empty as a tin can." Max's voice was heavy with worry. "I'm doing my level best for Caruso's sake, but it's eating at me, thinking Perch is out there somewhere, needing our help."

Jimmy Brady, their top turret gunner, chimed in with a hint of optimism. "Perch always talked about his guardian angel. Maybe she's watching over him now."

Max nodded, methodically straightening his bunk, clinging to any sliver of hope. "Last night, I dreamed I was searching for Perch in the sea. I saw him in the distance but couldn't reach him…" His voice trailed off as he folded a blanket with mechanical precision. "Perch is the kind of person everyone's drawn to. Remember how he lifted our spirits on that awful troop ship? And when we were stuck in Cambridge, he was laughing about living forever and burning our names in the ceiling of the Eagle.

"We were best friends from the start. We've always been twin souls, despite our different faiths—his Catholic, mine Jewish. We were surprised to find how similar our religious upbringings and rites were. I'm praying with all my might that his provides him the stamina to get through."

He sighed, glancing skyward, his words a whisper. "Just hold on, Perch. We're trying to find you."

Frustration spilled over as he slammed his trunk shut, startling Snafu. Max paced with restless energy. "Why did he volunteer for an extra mission when we're almost done?" The captain's assurances replayed in his mind: they were doing all they could.

Frankie placed a calming hand on Max's shoulder. "I heard the Spitfires and P-47s went out again today, sweeping over the Channel. They'll find him."

By early afternoon, with no updates forthcoming, the tension thickened like fog. Desperate, Caruso sought out Calvert in the cluttered Intelligence office, surrounded by maps and dispatches. The hum of radio chatter filled the dim space.

Taking in Caruso's strained appearance, Calvert got up and guided him to the door. "Let's get some air, talk outside."

Once secluded, Caruso's words tumbled out. "Everything's unraveling. Perch and I… we were supposed to finish this trip together."

Calvert listened intently as Caruso recounted the harrowing mission over Berlin—their forced ditching in the Channel, their life rafts struggling against the choppy waters. "He lent me his rosary because I'd forgotten my crucifix. Now I can't stop thinking it brought him bad luck."

Caruso's eyes were glassy with unshed tears as he pleaded with Calvert. "Please, talk to your captain. We need more eyes out there. We can't just sit here."

Calvert nodded solemnly. "I'll talk with Captain Flemming now. We'll do everything possible, you have my word."

"Thank you, truly," Caruso said, his whispered gratitude mingling with his anguish. "I'll never forget this."

❧

As the day wore on, each tap of Caruso's pacing echoed through the nearly empty barracks, accentuating the dragging seconds. He glanced at his watch. Time crawled. Each tick of the second hand thudded like a drumbeat in his chest.

Max approached, his voice soft but firm. "Caruso, they're doing everything they can. I checked with the CO just yesterday, and he promised updates would come as soon as there's any word."

"That's not enough!" Caruso's voice shook, desperate. "He needs us! He could be freezing out there! We need to do more, now!"

Seized by a sudden resolve, Caruso grabbed his jacket and stormed into the biting cold. The frost stung his cheeks, but he barely felt it as he made his way along the path. He needed answers, guidance—anything to shake this suffocating helplessness.

The small chapel was dimly lit, its silence stretching heavy and wide like the sky above. Caruso hesitated at the threshold before stepping inside, the familiar scent of candle wax and wood polish calming him ever so slightly.

Captain Richards, seated in a back pew, looked up and gestured for Caruso to join him. "Something's on your mind," he said, his voice warm but perceptive.

Caruso sat beside him, clutching the rosary in his hand. "It's Perch. He's out there—maybe hurt—and we're just sitting here. I-I can't shake this feeling that I should've done something differently. That I failed him somehow."

The chaplain listened intently, giving Caruso the space to let his thoughts pour out. When he finally spoke, his words were steady and deliberate. "We don't always have control, Caruso, even though it's human nature to feel like we should. What you can control is how you carry your faith—for yourself and for Perch. Believe that he's fighting to come back to you, just as you're waiting to welcome him home."

Caruso swallowed hard, the words settling into his chest like a fragile weight. "But what if he doesn't?" His voice cracked as he stared down at Perch's rosary.

Richards placed a reassuring hand on his shoulder. "Then you carry him in your heart, as you already do. But until you know, don't give up hope. That hope matters—for you and for him."

Their conversation left Caruso with no concrete answers, but it did bring a flicker of solace. As he left the chapel and made his way back to the barracks, the rosary in his hand felt like a tether—to Perch, to faith, and to the small sliver of control he could hold on to.

⁂

Later that evening

Caruso entered The Rose & Crown, the door slamming shut behind him. Calvert, nursing a pint, looked up at Caruso's worried silhouette framed in the doorway.

"Any word?" Caruso's voice was tight, his eyes intently searching Calvert's face for any hint of news.

Calvert's response was measured yet hopeful. "We've dispatched more planes. They're combing the last known coordinates and the surrounding areas, based on the weather and water currents." He glanced at Caruso's leg, bouncing with nervous energy. "They're doing everything they can. We have to trust them to do their job!"

Caruso's grip on the rosary tightened. "The weather's turning worse tonight." Concern creased his forehead. "I haven't stopped praying."

"Keep at it," Calvert said, standing to place his hand on his comrade's arm. "Look, these men are the best we have. Flemming will move heaven and earth to find him. You know we always look out for our own. I'll let you know the moment there's any news."

Caruso smiled weakly and thanked his friend, then returned to the barracks, each step sluggish with the burden of waiting.

⁂

The next afternoon, Caruso was a bundle of pent-up energy by the control tower, pacing back and forth, his footsteps quick and erratic. The faint hum of arriving aircraft drew his eyes upward, as he briskly rubbed his hands together in anticipation. Transfixed, he counted each plane as it landed, ensuring all had returned, each maneuver executed with precision. Every moment stretched, loaded with the tension of waiting—for news, for Max, for a chance to finally exhale.

As the debrief room began to empty, Caruso spotted Max and couldn't contain himself any longer. His previously charged pacing erupted into a burst of exhilaration as he crossed the room in long, eager strides. "Max! You'll never guess—" His words tumbled out, breaking under the emotion, as he quickly closed the distance, the reason for his anticipation written clear across his beaming face. He flung his arms around Max, hugging him and jumping up and down simultaneously. "They found him! They found him! He's alive!"

"Really? He's alive?"

"Yes! Yes!" Caruso laughed, tears mingling with joy. "He survived! Can you believe it? Our prayers were answered!" Reaching into his pocket, Caruso pulled out the rosary and waved it aloft, grinning. "I've had this thing with me since we lost him. I slept with it. It's a miracle!"

A brief stunned silence was quickly shattered by cheers and clapping that swept through the crew. Caruso, overcome with relief, looked at Devaney, the intelligence officer, who nodded with a smile, acknowledging the good news. He had taken the debrief report on the day that Perch was lost. Caruso caught Max's eye, a broad grin breaking across his friend's face. In that moment, Caruso saw the same flood of relief and gratitude that he felt himself.

Max and the crew were abuzz with questions. "Is he okay? Where's he been? Where is he now? Is he coming back?"

"He's in the Army convalescent hospital, the same one I was at, and he's going to be okay. After they capsized, he and Smithers somehow managed to get the dingy turned over and get themselves back in. Unfortunately, Smithers died of exposure out at sea. Perch got picked up by a fishing boat and they took him to Hythe. He was in rough shape, but after they got him stabilized, they sent word, and we went to pick him up."

Caruso's words stumbled out, tripping over his emotions, as he barely managed to string together a coherent sentence. His laughter, blended with his tears, wasn't just a release; it was a victory cry over the tumultuous sea of uncertainty they'd all been navigating. Around him, the room erupted in celebration, a shared catharsis. But even as relief washed over him, a part of him remained anchored in what had transpired: a man lost, the war's ever-present shadow. Smithers' death was no less tragic, even if they'd barely known him. War didn't discriminate when it came to those it claimed.

Yet now, all that mattered was the gratification he felt—as tangible as the rosary he still clutched in his hand. Amid the lingering darkness of the world conflict, this was a rare burst of sunlight, a moment to cherish.

Caruso paused, fixing his eyes on the string of beads in his fingers. Each one seemed to represent the trials they'd endured and the prayers they'd whispered into the void of the unknown. Gently, he lifted it to his lips and kissed it, a silent thanks to the heavens.

He had his friend back.

CHAPTER THIRTY-ONE

Early April, 1945
Stoneleigh Rehabilitation Center

"GOOD MORNING, SERGEANT," Helen said as she stepped into the room, her voice a calm contrast to the sterile hum of the ward. "I'm Helen. I've reviewed your records, and it seems you've had a rough go of it. How are you feeling today?"

The airman managed a faint smile. "Well, considering everything, I'm just glad to be here. And you can call me Perch; everyone else does."

Helen chuckled softly. "Perch. That's an unusual nickname. How did that come about?"

He shrugged. "My last name's Del Percio, but it's a bit of a tongue twister for most, so Perch stuck. Makes life easier."

Helen glanced down at the chart before meeting his gaze. "I see you're from the 351st in Polebrook. I… I had another patient from there a while ago." She hesitated, as if searching her memory. "Santo Caruso. Do you know him?"

Perch's brows lifted, eyes widening. "Caruso? Oh, my goodness—you're Helen!"

Helen's cheeks flushed as she straightened. "Yes." She was silent for a moment, her face unreadable as she met his eyes. "How is he doing?"

Perch sat up slightly, his voice taking on a sharper edge. "Better than he was, but it hasn't been easy for him. I'll tell you this—he really fell hard for you. You broke his heart."

The words landed with force, and Helen's hands tightened on the chart. "That was never my intention," she said quietly, glancing away as emotion flickered behind her eyes. "I wanted to explain myself, but I don't think he wanted to hear it."

Perch's tone was insistent, his New York straightforwardness cutting through. "He deserved the truth from the start, Helen. Not half-truths."

"It was more complicated than that." Her voice trembled slightly, a mix of defensiveness and regret. "I wasn't trying to hurt him, Perch."

"Well, you did," he shot back. "And I'm not sure why you're here telling me all this. You're married. The person you should be talking to is your husband."

Helen's gaze dropped to the floor. "That's not possible."

Perch frowned. "Why not?"

A long pause. "He came back," she said slowly, "but not for a reunion. He wanted a divorce. He found someone else."

Perch let out a low whistle. "So what are you hoping for?"

"I just want him to know the truth," she said, her voice firm. "I should've told him sooner—I know that. But I was still sorting through the mess. I didn't want to reach out to him until I could be sure of what I had to say. What he chooses to do with it… that's up to him."

Perch studied her for a long moment. "That's fair," he said at last. "But don't underestimate how deep that wound went. He was really torn up."

Helen looked down, then back at Perch. Her voice quiet, she said, "I know I hurt him. But if I can talk to him, maybe he'll understand."

Perch sighed. "Well," he said, his voice losing some of its edge, "that's for Caruso to decide, not me. But he doesn't need his heart broken. Again."

"Hearts are indeed fragile," Helen conceded, her eyes dropping to her hands. "But we can't let the fear of getting hurt again keep us from falling in love. All we can do is trust ourselves to make the right choices." She met Perch's gaze once more before adding, "But you're right, that's something that only Sandy can decide."

Perch nodded, a trace of a smile on his lips. "At least we agree on that one thing." He watched as Helen's eyes flickered with a mix of defiance and vulnerability. He knew all too well how war could entangle not just the body but also the soul in battles far from the front lines.

When Helen left, the last look she gave Perch wasn't one of regret, but of uncertainty. As the curtain swayed behind her, Perch sank back on the pillow. The war had twisted so many lives—his own included—but Helen's love for Caruso wasn't something he could untangle. Maybe that was the point. Some things, like war itself, didn't have easy answers.

The sun was sinking lower in the sky when Max and Caruso's familiar voices broke the silence like a warm gust of wind.

"What some people won't do to snag a room with clean sheets and a comfortable mattress!" Max clapped Perch on the back, grinning.

Caruso's smile was radiant, lighting up the room like a sunrise. "You have no idea how happy I am to see you, Perch!"

Perch chuckled. "It's good to see you both."

"We were all worried sick. Especially Caruso," Max said, his tone light, his eyes speaking volumes. "He felt terrible about taking your rosary—he was convinced it was his fault you went missing."

Caruso reached into his pocket and handed the beads to his friend. "I've never been so happy to give something back that I borrowed."

Perch smiled absently, turning the rosary over in his hands. "It was touch and go for a long time. After Smithers died from exposure, I wasn't sure I was going to make it back. They told me when the fisherman found me, I was unconscious."

Caruso nodded. "Yeah, I heard that when they brought you in, they weren't sure who you were. I guess you lost your dog tags in all the chaos."

"The whole ordeal really makes you appreciate life and all it has to offer," Perch said. "Speaking of which…" Disbelief and concern pulled at his features. "Guess who I ran into here?" His voice lowered. "Helen."

An awkward silence followed as Max and Caruso exchanged glances. "Did you speak to her?" Max asked.

"Yes, we talked." He looked at Caruso. "She's got something she wants to say to you. I'm sure you'll be hearing from her soon." He hesitated. "She really cares about you." He closed his eyes and shook his head slightly, as if trying to shake loose the weight of her words.

Caruso's posture didn't change, but his gaze dropped, fixed on a spot on the floor. When he finally spoke, his voice was quiet. "That was a long time ago."

Perch studied him. "Doesn't mean it didn't matter."

Caruso gave a noncommittal nod, his jaw working as if there was more he wanted to say but couldn't find the words.

A muscle twitched in his jaw, and his expression closed like a door.

Max caught the shift and stepped in gently. "You need your rest, Perch. We just wanted to stop in and say hello."

"Thanks for dropping by, fellas. I appreciate it."

Caruso patted him on the shoulder. "Anytime, Perch. You just focus on getting better. We all want you back, fit and fighting." With a final nod, they left, and Perch was left alone with his thoughts.

The room grew quieter in their absence, broken only by soft voices, nurses' footsteps, and the occasional rattle of a passing cart. Turning the rosary beads over in his hands, Perch thought of the day he'd given it to Caruso—how he'd joked that it would bring him luck. Now, it felt like a thread connecting them all, something fragile yet unbroken in a world full of chaos.

He stared at the space where his friends had stood, his thoughts drifting to everything they'd all endured. He remembered the cold bite of the Channel wind, Smithers' pale face, the silence of the waves. He blinked it away, focusing on the sunbeam now warming his wrist. Outside, the clouds were breaking—just enough for light to find its way back in.

CHAPTER THIRTY-TWO

End of April–beginning of May, 1945

ALL SQUADRONS HAD been called together for a big announcement. Rumors were swirling that their tour of duty in England was ending, and the men were hopeful that they'd finally be able to go home. The customary clamor of the large group gathering was replaced with hushed conversation.

"Ten-hut!" The men stood at attention as Colonel Carter approached the front of the room. The room immediately quieted as the men took their seats to hear the news.

"I'm happy to inform you that missions are hereby discontinued. The European war is ending!" The room erupted with clapping, hooting, and loud cheers.

The colonel raised his hand, gesturing for the men to quiet down. "This doesn't mean your Army obligation is over. I want to remind you of the Adjusted Service Rating Score. This is a point system to determine the next assignment for each of you. Under this policy, each of you will receive one point for every month of military service, and if that service was overseas, another point for each of those months as well.

Decorations are valuable—each battle star or other decoration adds five points to your total. For those of you with children, twelve points will be awarded for each dependent child, though we cap this at three children. Initially, you'll need a total of eighty-five points to be eligible for demobilization. Those who meet the threshold will be prioritized for return as transport becomes available, unless you have special skills that are still needed. If that's the case, six extra months is the intended maximum time required.

"This will all be reviewed with you in more detail by your CO, at which time it will be determined, based on your status, when or if you'll be discharged or reassigned.

"We'll also be requesting volunteers to participate in some extra flights. We're planning some food drops to Holland. Their people have been suffering from starvation for a long time. More details to follow on that. Also, we anticipate a need for some revival flights to pick up POWs and return them to their homelands."

Caruso let out a slow breath.

At last.

The media's reports intensified daily. No more missions! All the men on base huddled around radios, waiting for the next update on the official end of the war.

"Hey, fellas," Frankie said, looking up from the *Stars and Stripes* newspaper he held in his hand. "Here's a little more information about the food drops the colonel spoke about. Apparently, the Germans have agreed to designated corridors to allow bombers to fly at low altitude to drop food to the people in Holland without being fired upon. The Dutch have been on strict rations for four years."

"Can the Germans be trusted not to fire?" Caruso asked, his tone skeptical. "We'd be sitting ducks if they decided to attack. After surviving the war, I'm not sure I'd risk getting shot by the Germans while dropping food rations."

"It says here that these Mercy Missions will be carried out by several air forces including those from Britain, Australia, Canada, New Zealand, Poland, and the United States. Ours are going to be called Operation Chowhound."

"Well, Frankie, with a name like that, it seems like just the mission for you!" Max laughed. They'd all called Frankie a chowhound at one time or another, due to his appetite that seemed like a bottomless pit.

"I thought so, too. I'm going to sign up."

Several days later, Frankie stumbled back, weary yet elated from his Chowhound experience. As he approached his comrades, his eyes glistened with excitement and humility, and his voice cracked slightly with emotion. "Fellas, you won't believe what it was like. Imagine, after all this time, to be able to bring these people something good." He paused, collecting his thoughts. "As we flew low, Holland looked like a patchwork quilt. The Dutch had spelled out 'Many Thanks' in tulips!"

Frankie blinked his eyes rapidly as he relived the experience. He described how the crowds had gathered, their faces upturned not in fear but in gratitude, waving as the planes passed overhead. "There was this moment when I realized that what we were doing was more than a mission. For once, we weren't bringing destruction. We were bringing relief—and hope. You could feel it, the connection between us and the people down there." His usual bravado seemed softened by the memory.

His friends listened, rapt, as Frankie recounted every detail. He spoke of the nervous tension that had gripped them as they flew, vulnerable, half expecting enemy fire that never came. "The risks faded into the background. Those faces… all those arms waving… it was something else.

"And you know, for that little while, the war seemed miles away, with just us and the Dutch. It was like a thank you for all the times they risked everything to help smuggle our men back to England from enemy territory.

"After we got back, they told us that with everyone's combined effort, over five and a half thousand planes delivered over eleven thousand tons of food. There was another ground-relief operation, too, that brought food in by trucks to about four million people in the western Netherlands. It was heartwarming."

Something profound stirred in Caruso upon hearing about the message in tulips and the crowds waving their thanks. Throughout the war, their missions had been about destruction from a distance, the results measured in objectives destroyed, not lives saved. Listening now, he realized they had also been unwitting messengers of hope: their bombs had paved the way for this very moment of peace and relief. It was quite a revelation. They'd endured the horrors of conflict for the chance to see humanity restored, offering salvation even as they inflicted destruction.

As Frankie finished, his comrades sat in respectful silence, moved by the vivid picture he'd painted. A newfound sense of optimism lingered—a brief interlude that seemed to bridge directly into Caruso's own contemplations. The day's triumphs and Frankie's story about the faces of the grateful

Dutch stirred something in him. He wasn't just reckoning with war and survival anymore—but with the possibility of what came after. It was a quiet reminder that even amid devastation, there could still be restoration. That thought sparked another: maybe what Helen wanted to say could help restore what they'd lost.

⁂

A few days later, Jimmy Brady was hunched over the desk, pencil in hand and deep in thought. "Hey, fellas… we need eighty-five points in the Service Rating Score to get home," he said, looking down at the paper on his desk. "So let me get this straight. Every month we've been in service gets us a point, and another if it was overseas, right?"

"Exactly," Caruso said. "And those medals we earned? Each one's worth five points. Plus, fellas with kids get twelve points per kid. Three kids max, though."

"Looks like being a father finally pays off, huh? Just need to hit that magic number, eighty-five, then it's home sweet home," Frankie said.

"I just tallied mine up," Jimmy said. "I only have eighty-three. Anybody have two they want to sell?"

"Fat chance of that, Jimmy. But if you've fathered any babies out there, just one will put you over!" Caruso said.

Jimmy tilted his head, placing his finger on his cheek theatrically as he chuckled. "Hmmm. Maybe I'll find someone who will let me borrow one of theirs, just for a while."

"Or maybe we can find some London lassie with a child who will attest to your contribution!" All the others joined Caruso in the laughter, their mood light and jovial.

❧

Later in the day, Caruso sat down to write a letter home.

Dearest Mom & Pop,

Have received your most welcome letter.

From the time I wrote you last, I told you that I had finished my missions and was coming home. Now I have some bad news to tell you. With the war over, the Army has a point system to decide who gets to return to the States first. I'm not sure when I'll be home.

Don't worry about me, I'm not flying anymore, so everything is fine.

I don't have much more to say. All is well here, but I miss you all. I have received the picture, and I think you all look swell. Caroline has grown so much I hardly recognize her!

This is all for now. I will write you soon.

Love, Sandy

He folded the letter, but his thoughts didn't settle. His gaze drifted to the dim outline of the barracks outside, the quiet a poor match for the restlessness knotting in his chest. Finally, he opened the drawer and pulled out the letter from Helen. It had arrived the week before. He'd read it. Reread it. Ignored it. Tried to forget it. And yet, here it was… still waiting. He unfolded it again and read slowly, the paper soft from handling.

Dear Sandy,

Perch told me that you had stopped by for a visit. I was so sorry to have missed you. I have so much I want to say.

I know my actions over the past few months have likely put you off, and I want and need to explain myself.

But this is something that deserves to be said in person.

You may not want to see me, and I wouldn't blame you. But I would very much like to see you. I know I've made a dog's dinner out of everything, but I owe you the truth.

If you know when you'll have free time on base, I can arrange to travel to you. Otherwise, I would look forward to your visit to Stoneleigh when it's convenient, and I will make the time for us to talk.

I don't blame you if you're cheesed off, but I implore you to hear what I have to say. It might seem like flogging a dead horse, but it will help you understand my behaviour, if you're at all interested.

I know I've really botched things up. Nonetheless, I would like to apologise in person, if you'll give me the chance.

Yours,

Helen

"'Yours,' she says." Caruso crumpled the letter slightly in his hands. The words struck him as disingenuous—or maybe wishful. Either way, they stirred something he wasn't ready to name.

Still, the fact that she'd sent him a letter surprised him. Despite what Perch had said, he'd never expected to hear from her again. Why was she even bothering? Folding the letter and placing it back in the envelope, he laid it on his desk. Even with his eyes buried in a magazine, they kept drifting to the envelope on the desk.

Rising again, he picked up the envelope, fingers tracing its edges as he turned it over in his hands. Helen had been the one bright light during his time overseas. Had it only been because of his vulnerability after his injury and his crew going home? He didn't think so, although certainly that could have been part of it. Her support through his recovery, urging him on when he was ready to give up, had been a lifeline. But the look in her eyes, and the electricity between them… that had been unmistakable. Yet despite the obvious attraction, her indecision at every turn had been puzzling and frustrating. She'd already torn him in two; did he want to risk more heartbreak?

He shook his head, tossing the letter back onto his desk. What was the point? She'd made her choice, and it wasn't him. Maybe she just wanted to ease her conscience, to smooth over the mess she'd made of things. Perhaps she simply wanted to be friends. *Friends? After everything? I'm going home soon. Why reopen old wounds?*

He pulled his magazine toward him again, flipping a few pages without seeing the words. But the envelope stayed in his periphery, tugging at him, despite every reason he had to let it go.

But war had a way of putting everything into stark perspective. He'd seen men lose their lives in an instant, plans interrupted and futures stolen. It made the pull toward Helen feel both urgent and terrifying—a chance to reclaim something real in a world that had taken so much from so many.

He sat for a long while, ignoring the banter of the men in the background, as the light filtering into the barracks grew dim and the afternoon waned. He wasn't the same man as the one he'd been at Stoneleigh, or even afterward at the dance. So much had happened since then.

When he'd first come to England, he saw himself only as a part of the trusted crew he'd trained with, rather than an individual gunner in his own right. When he was forced to return to base alone after his rehabilitation, with the help of Dr. Sotelo, he slowly learned that he had strengths he hadn't even been aware of. He also learned that this brotherhood of comrades extended far beyond just the small circle of his crew. He'd found that their strength lay in their mutual support and trust for each other; they each contributed to each other's lives in ways they didn't fully realize.

Caruso wasn't sure if reconnecting with Helen would be positive for either of them, after all this time. Nor was he even sure, at this point, what he was hoping for. But the fact remained, despite it all, he was in love with her. He replayed Calvert's advice from so long ago in his mind, back when Caruso was so distraught in the pub after realizing she was married. *War makes a mess of things—it's not always about loyalty or disloyalty. Sometimes it's just survival,* he'd said. He shivered, the persistent chill of England creeping into the walls of the barracks.

Then he grabbed his jacket and walked out the door.

Caruso arrived at Supply and found Zeus just leaving. With a bribe of a carton of cigarettes and a promise of more the next week, the soldier agreed to take him back to Stoneleigh.

"I really appreciate your driving me, Zeus."

"Is fine." He smiled. "I believe in love."

Caruso shrugged. "Love is a complicated matter," he said.

"Not complicated if following heart." Zeus's broken English pierced Caruso's trepidation.

"Ah, well, perhaps, but it takes two people, and not everyone follows where the heart leads."

"Trust the heart," Zeus said, persistent. "Best compass."

They rode the rest of the way in silence, the truck bouncing roughly over the dilapidated roadway. Caruso was surprised to feel his heart racing and hands trembling. As he reread the letter from Helen, it dropped to the floorboard. Retrieving it, he licked his dry lips. What did he have to be nervous about? He looked out the window, taking in the changing landscape as they neared Stoneleigh. Finally, the facility slipped into view, and they entered the driveway.

"I won't be long," Caruso said, rushing out of the vehicle before it had fully stopped.

Approaching the building, he pulled open one of the double doors easily, remembering how he used to struggle with the weight when he was a patient. He smiled at the memory. He had come a long way.

And now, home was within reach.

He walked down the long hallway until he finally came to the nursing lounge directly adjacent to his old room, which now sat empty. Helen was just emerging from the medication room when she saw him. Her eyes danced, her face aglow.

"Sandy!"

Caruso couldn't help himself. He felt drawn to her but was compelled to hold back, leaving him momentarily frozen. His crooked grin belied the tension etched across his forehead, while his eyes spoke silently of uncertainty.

Helen walked briskly toward him. She started to reach out to embrace him, then stopped herself and held her hands tightly in front of her. "It's good to see you. I wasn't sure if you would come."

Caruso nodded as he raked his hand through his hair. "Well, I wasn't sure if I would, either. But I decided to hear you out."

"Thank you, Sandy. That means a lot to me. Come." Caruso flinched slightly as she reached out and touched his arm, guiding him to his old room.

Was he imagining the spark?

The familiar scent of her perfume hit him like a wave, stirring memories of their times together. The fragrance had always been her signature, lingering long after she left the room. Back then, it had comforted him. Now, it felt like a weapon, prying open feelings he wasn't ready to face. He shook his head, fighting to keep the perfume from overwhelming him, grounding himself in the present. "I guess we've come full circle," he said, avoiding her eyes and taking in his surroundings. "We're back to where we started."

"No, we're not, Sandy," she said, her eyes shining with emotion. "You've come such a long way. You've regained your strength, and you're almost home. I'm so proud of you."

Caruso's hands clenched and unclenched at his sides. "It's a strange choice of words—that you would say you're proud of me. Wasn't I just another patient?"

"That's where you're wrong. You're far from just another patient. But there are some things I need to tell you. Come and sit down."

Caruso remained standing, the knot in his stomach tightening. "I already know. You're married."

"Let me tell you." Her tone was pleading. Seeing him nod, she took a deep breath as she struggled to meet his eyes. "My husband was in the RAF when we married. I knew it would be difficult for him to be away so often, and then, when the war started, it was much worse."

Caruso's voice was low, edged with a hint of accusation. "You made vows to him."

"Yes, I did. But please, let me tell you. When he went off to war, there was already some distance between us, but there was so much danger involved, I was dreadfully frightened for him. We'd known each other for years. Even if we weren't exactly in love anymore, I still cared for him."

Caruso was silent.

"Then I got a cable that he'd gone missing. They didn't know if he was dead or alive. It was seven months of not knowing. During that time, I found myself drawn to you in a way I hadn't expected."

"You were still married."

"Yes. And this is no excuse, but he'd been away for over two years. I'd poured myself into my work to avoid thinking about things. And when I met you, our connection was undeniable. Perhaps some of it was loneliness, but that wasn't the whole of it, by any means. I wrestled with it, Sandy, and that's why I acted the way I did. When I was with you, I couldn't help being drawn to you. But every time I pulled away, it was due to guilt—because I knew I was falling in love with you.

"I had no idea he was even alive that day he came to Stoneleigh. I was gobsmacked. He looked well, but a bit knackered after his travels. He showed up out of nowhere, said we needed to talk, and asked me to skive off work. Everyone knew he'd been missing, so they didn't mind when I asked for a few days off."

Caruso clenched his jaw, unsure whether to feel sorry for the man—or jealous.

Helen looked away. "My colleague told me someone popped in to see me. From her description, I knew it was you."

Her voice faltered. "I'm sorry that's how you learned that I was married."

Caruso's gaze flitted across the faded wallpaper, lingering on a crack in the windowpane, anywhere but on Helen, as her words filled the room.

"So, what did he have to tell you?"

"I thought maybe he wanted to rebuild things between us. Instead, he told me he'd fallen in love with someone else and that she was pregnant. He wanted a divorce immediately so he could marry her and raise the baby." Her voice faltered, a mix of resignation and sorrow shadowing her features.

"I agreed. Everything was completed within a few months. I waited to write to you until it was all done."

"What a gentleman," Caruso said wryly, his arms crossed tightly across his chest. "How thoughtful that he wants to give the baby his name. So, is that what you wanted to tell me?"

"There's actually so much more. I wanted to tell you I'm sorry. It was wrong to allow myself to become smitten with you. Lonesomeness played a part, and you were such a wonderful listener, but that's no excuse. Being married meant upholding my vows, and I should have been honest from the start. But I was pulled to you, Sandy. I didn't want to lose what we had—even though I knew it was wrong."

As she spoke, Caruso felt a pang of recognition. He thought back to the flight doc—how he'd lied about his health, too stubborn to admit he wasn't ready, too afraid of losing the one thing that gave him purpose. Maybe Helen's choices weren't so different from his own.

Helen went on. "I was determined not to lose the bond I had with you. It felt like I'd been in a dark, stuffy room when suddenly, someone opened the window to let in light and fresh air."

He'd felt the same, once. In her presence, the war had seemed a little less dark, his burdens a little lighter.

"Not telling you straight away was a mistake, and for that, I'm truly sorry. It was wrong to come close to you and then keep backing away. I just didn't know what to do with what my heart was feeling."

Caruso gave a half smile. "Zeus was just telling me that the heart is the best compass." He wiped a hand slowly down his face. "I didn't come to talk everything through today," he said, glancing toward the door. "Just to see you. To see if this was even something I wanted to walk back into." He checked his watch. "But I did tell Zeus I wouldn't be long—he's waiting out front."

"Will I see you again before you go home?" Helen's voice wavered, a hopeful note threading through her tentative words.

Caruso's gaze drifted away, and for a moment, he seemed to lose focus, as if he were searching the corners of the room for an answer. His jawline tensed, a hard swallow visible before he managed a slow nod. His eyes darted toward Helen, skipping away before returning again. The silence stretched between them, his hesitation underscoring the gravity of his decision.

"With the war over, there aren't any more missions, so I'll be on base. Come by next Saturday and maybe we can spend the day together."

"That would be lovely." Helen smiled, her eyes glistening. "And thank you, Sandy, for listening. Again, I'm deeply sorry."

Caruso took her hands in his. "Until Saturday, then." As he kissed her lightly on the cheek and walked out the door, he felt the pull of conflicting emotions—bitterness and hope wrestling for footing. Yet, somehow, he felt a little lighter. As he stepped into the cool spring air, he felt something unfamiliar: not certainty, but the possibility of it.

CHAPTER THIRTY-THREE

May, 1945

THEY'D AGREED TO meet in Peterborough. It seemed right to step away from the base, away from the war, even if just for a day. Caruso climbed onto the bus that would take him into town, and, although it wasn't far away, the ride felt endless. Every minute dragged as Caruso checked the time repeatedly, his heart pounding in his chest. What would this meeting bring? Despite his reservations, the pull toward her proved irresistible. He'd decided to meet her, see where things could go, preparing himself for any outcome.

Earlier in the week, London had provided a welcome distraction with the post-war festivities. The streets had been filled with laughter and joy, but all the celebrating felt strange, with so much uncertainty dominating his future. Caruso hadn't been able to get his mind off Helen. He wasn't happy that she'd misled him, though he understood the intensity of what she'd been feeling, the mixed emotions. How could he not? He felt the same.

As the bus rolled to a stop, Caruso stepped down and scanned the small crowd, his eyes searching for one face. The town was bustling, but when he finally saw her, his breath caught.

Helen's smile broke through his uncertainty like a ray of light piercing the clouds. As she approached with a shy gait, he hesitated briefly before enveloping her in a tight embrace. The soft trace of Chantilly wrapped around him, stilling the whirl of thoughts in his mind.

They wandered hand in hand through the winding streets, losing themselves in conversation, each word a stitch mending the fabric of their connection. The town was alive with the sounds of chatter and the distant clanging of the bells of Peterborough Cathedral. Almost without intending, they found themselves at the entrance to Central Park, its familiar expanse welcoming them like an old friend. After sitting under the bandstand for a while to talk, they walked over to The Hand & Heart, the same pub that Helen had stumbled upon on the night of the dance.

Inside, the wood-paneled pub wrapped them in a cozy calm.

"I can't believe we're here," Caruso said, settling across from her. "Had anyone asked me if we'd ever be together again, I'd have said no."

Helen giggled. "Me, too. I guess it just proves that you never know what tomorrow may bring. Just when you're certain that something's impossible, suddenly… it's possible."

His smile faded slightly as he traced a finger along the rim of his glass. "For so long, I thought I'd been a fool. That you didn't care."

Helen's hands tightened in her lap. "Sandy, I did care—"

He shook his head. "I know that now. But back then, it felt like the end of the world. I tried to let you go, but I couldn't."

Helen's eyes softened. "Neither could I," she admitted quietly. "Every time I tried to write to you, I worried it was too late. But I had to try. Because the truth is, you were never just a passing moment for me, Sandy. You were… and still are… the only thing that's ever made sense."

Caruso stared at her, the walls around his heart beginning to crack. The tension between them settled into something softer. Fragile, but real.

He reached across the table, taking her hands in his. "I lost you once, Helen. I don't want to lose you again. But I need to know we're in this together."

Helen swallowed hard, her fingers tightening around his. "We are."

Caruso took a deep breath. "Then let's not waste any more time."

Helen's brows knitted slightly in confusion. "What do you mean?"

"Come home with me," Caruso said, his voice trembling with both hope and vulnerability. "Marry me." He held her gaze, waiting, bracing.

She blinked, her lips parting in surprise.

Seeing her hesitation, Caruso softened his tone. "It's sudden, I know. But I've carried this with me for months—this feeling that if I had the chance, I'd never let you go again."

Caruso's voice was barely more than a whisper, laden with emotion. "I love you. I've loved you through every moment we've been apart."

Her eyes welled up, but no words came. His eyes locked on hers, willing her to answer.

Finally, her voice broke through the silence, soft and trembling. "Oh Sandy… yes. I love you, truly I do. But this is all happening so fast. What if I don't fit in? What if your family thinks I'm too… British?" She smiled weakly, her voice trailing off as though she didn't dare speak her fears aloud.

Caruso laughed. "Of course they'll like you! You practically saved my life! They will love you no matter what. And I'll make sure you always feel at home."

Helen hesitated, then nodded, her fingers wrapped around his. "My heart says yes before my mind can even begin to catch up."

Caruso exhaled as relief coursed through him, but so did something deeper—a fierce determination to make this work.

Slowly, he reached into his pocket and pulled out a small box and opened it gently before her, revealing a gleaming silver locket nestled inside. It was intricately designed with delicate engraving and held a tiny photograph of Caruso in uniform.

"I won't know for a little while if I'm getting out for good or just being reassigned to a stateside base," he said gently, "but once I do, we'll make arrangements. I want us together. Really together.

"I got this to remind you of how much you mean to me, no matter how far apart we are," he said, his voice steady despite the storm of emotions within him.

Helen gasped, letting him fasten it around her neck, her hand lingering on the locket as if imprinting the moment into memory.

"Sandy, you are the treasure of my heart."

He leaned across the table, his voice thick. "And you're mine."

They'd found their way back to each other.

And this time, neither of them was letting go.

CHAPTER THIRTY-FOUR

The End of the War

CALVERT BURST INTO The Rose & Crown, face aglow. "Guess what? I finally got to ride in a B-17!"

"You did? How'd that come about?" Caruso leaned in, eager.

Calvert's grin was infectious as he brought his unexpected B-17 journey to life—a moment he'd long dreamed of. "I couldn't believe it, Caruso," he said, pride coating his voice. "Me, getting invited on an 'Observation Tour.' A chance to see the fruits of our labor."

Eyes sparkling, he described the sensation of boarding the iconic bomber, feeling its power and witnessing its capabilities firsthand. "It was like nothing I've ever known. Being inside, feeling the engines rumble—I felt part of something much bigger than myself."

He described the flight—soaring over the battered countryside, the weight of the war seen from the air. "It's a perspective you can't understand from the ground. It made me proud of our efforts, knowing we contributed to something so significant. It was over too soon, but it's a memory I'll carry with me forever."

He carefully retrieved a well-worn letter from the pocket of his bomber jacket. "I wrote to my brother about it," he said with a hint of reservation. "Never was good at putting feelings on paper, though."

Caruso clapped him on the shoulder. "But you told it here," he said, gesturing between them. "And that's what matters."

The moment held a bittersweet edge, underlined by the unspoken realities of war. Some stories might never be told beyond the confines of their duties, and some promises might remain unfulfilled. Yet, in the telling, the stories forged a bond that transcended the written word, capturing the essence of human connection amid the chaos of war, thousands of miles from home.

Caruso gave a faraway smile. "It's hard to believe the war's really over and we'll be back in the States soon." Lifting his glass to Calvert's with a wink, he began an age-old military toast. "To the land we love—"

"—and the love we land!" Calvert finished with a grin. The clink of their glasses rang out, a celebration of survival and brotherhood, echoing the promise of new beginnings.

As the men returned to the barracks, the pub's laughter faded behind them, and their thoughts drifted back to the war that had defined them for so long.

It was May 11, 1945, just three days after VE Day, the end of nearly six years of war in Europe. The day before, the Eighth Air Force had issued orders to the 351st Bomb Group in

Polebrook, directing them to fly thirty-eight bombers to Linz, Austria.

"They needed volunteers," Max said quietly to his comrades, the weight of his words settling over the room. "After all we've been through, I felt like I had to go. We were bringing home French officers, prisoners of war since 1940, from a camp adjacent to the Linz Luftwaffe Air Base in Austria, back to France. They called it a 'Revival Mission.' We were just a small crew of five, not sure what we'd find when we got there."

Frankie leaned in. "How was it?"

"Beautiful flight. Clear skies… and when we arrived, the officers were overwhelmed with relief and joy. They looked well, all things considered."

His expression darkened as he continued. "But nothing prepared us for the Mauthausen concentration camp, on the other side of the Luftwaffe Air Base. The smell of ash, the prisoners in striped uniforms, skin and bones. Their eyes followed us, as though they couldn't quite grasp that freedom had come at last. I wanted to say something to them, offer comfort, but what could I possibly say that wouldn't feel empty in the face of all they'd endured? We did what little we could, offering our food and water. They accepted it with such grace, it broke my heart."

Max paused, collecting his thoughts. "And then, later… to see the relief on the officers' faces when we crossed the border into France… that's something I'll carry forever."

Silence followed, each man tangled in his own thoughts. The war was over, but its grip lingered. Its memories would take a lifetime to unravel.

Max stood up, breaking the quiet. "I wonder when they'll send us home. I'm ready."

Caruso nodded as he thought of Al Cantrelle's family, and how fragile it all was. Losing Al, and almost losing Perch, had changed his life. Maybe that's why he'd said yes to seeing Helen again. If the war had taught him anything, it was this: holding back out of fear wasn't living—it was just surviving.

"Feels like forever since I've been home," Caruso said, the word "home" tasting almost foreign.

Max nodded, a tired smile on his lips. "Yeah, it's time."

As they drifted off to sleep, Caruso lay staring at the ceiling, his mind filled with images of home—how it looked, how it felt, how far away it still seemed. Whatever came next, it had to be better than what they'd survived. It had to be.

CHAPTER THIRTY-FIVE

June 8, 1945

THE MEN SAT in the briefing room in preparation for the day's flight, something Caruso had done countless times. But today was different. Mechanics, clerks, ground crew, and airmen alike sat together, all wearing their No. 1 uniforms, united in one thought: they were going home!

Caruso looked around at the faces of these men who, in many ways, had become like a second family to him. They looked years younger, their faces bright with relief and hope. In contrast to the customary groans when mission destinations were disclosed, all the men whooped and cheered when the map of their flight course was revealed. The intelligence officer, usually so stern, let the men have their moment of joyful anticipation before explaining the flight plan home. Caruso thought he might have even cracked a smile.

Lieutenant Higley, the weatherman, advised that some bad weather would be expected in the early afternoon, stressing the importance of departing before it rolled in, since it could scrub the takeoff. The plan was for the B-17s to be grouped into threes, departing in staggered groups.

When the debrief was over, they rode on the truck to the hardstand. They could've run there if necessary. It was hard to believe they were actually going home.

As they approached the aircraft, the sun glinted off its wings, creating shadows that danced jubilantly on the ground. Twenty men would be on Caruso's bird. Caruso glanced at Calvert, a smile beaming across his face.

"I got up early today, too excited to sleep," Calvert confided. "I can't wait to get back to the States. My family's been through so much since losing Mother." He removed his cap and took out the family photo he'd tucked inside, rubbing his thumb softly over the image—a ritual he'd repeated so many times it was starting to wear away the picture.

Unlike the bombers they were used to, the plane had been stripped of all the battle equipment, allowing more space for ten crew and ten passengers along with their duffel bags.

"Would you look at this!" Captain Joe Glover, the navigator, exclaimed as he boarded, his customary serious demeanor replaced with a wide grin. "If I didn't know better, I'd hardly recognize it as a B-17!" He glanced at John Montgomery with mock suspicion. "Gummy, did you stay up all night to make these changes?"

Gummy shook his head with a laugh. "Nope, but I made sure the men did everything right early this morning. No radar, but she's ready to go. Let's beat that weather." He couldn't suppress the big grin that kept sneaking onto his face. He was on their plane, too. Caruso knew that everyone felt close to Gummy. His attention to detail was meticulous when clearing the B-17s for flights every day.

Boyd Dobbs, one of the aircraft mechanics, climbed aboard, greeting Gummy with a handshake. There was an atmosphere of levity in the group that Caruso had never seen before. It seemed like the ranks had been stripped away, and they were all just men eager to get back.

Although the briefing had outlined which groups of three would leave when, their plane was delayed by a minor issue identified on the pre-flight check. Despite the lighter mood, Caruso sensed some anxiety among the crew about not taking off at the designated time. The pilot and copilot kept looking up at the sky and checking the clouds.

Zeus, always the gentle giant, climbed aboard with a broad smile. He'd confided to Caruso that he was most looking forward to being able to get some education paid in full by the Army. He was also hoping to be expedited for citizenship once he got back to the States. After greeting Calvert, he made his way over to Caruso, asking, "Everything work out?"

Caruso hugged him long and hard. "Yes, yes, thank you. And she's agreed to be my wife!"

"Just like our mamas said—things fall into place!"

John Leasure, another plane mechanic, scrutinized everything and gave the all-clear before pulling himself into the bomber.

Next came Edwin Birtwell, Calvert's co-planner for the Christmas party, camera in hand. He and Valerie had decided to tie the knot as soon as he could get leave to come back.

Caruso noticed Max boarding and ventured over, crouching down beside his friend. "So, today's the day!" he said with a wink. "Are you sure you're ready?"

Max laughed. "Oh yes. I can't wait to see the family again."

"Bet you're looking forward to seeing that pen pal of yours." Caruso chuckled.

Max nodded. "Yes. Margaret, my buddy's sister. Isn't it funny how life twists things around? I doubt we'd have reconnected if I hadn't gone to war. We've gotten so close through our letters. I guess time'll tell if that connection holds when we meet again, but I can't wait to see her.

"And I'm sure glad I don't have to take that dreaded troopship back home, like most of the other fellas. My only regret is not going home with my crew, but we'll meet again in the States. The hardest part is leaving Perch behind."

Caruso nodded. "I'm glad he's doing so well. But you're right. Saying goodbye wasn't easy. It was nice of you to give him your St. Christopher medal before you left." Caruso looked at him thoughtfully, one eyebrow raised. "Though I thought it was just us Catholics who carried those, not Jews."

Max laughed. "My brother Harry used to have a St. Christopher medal and I'd asked him about it. He said even though it was mostly Catholics who believed in him, he thought it best to cover all his bases. I figured it couldn't hurt. I made it out of here, so…"

He paused. "By the way, Snafu is being looked after by one of the fellas on base until Perch gets released, and I asked Tom at The Rose & Crown to take him after the base cleared out. Tom's happy for the company and said he could be the pub mascot."

"That's swell. Tom has a good heart."

Caruso nodded. "He's also keeping Calvert's trunk for him at the pub until Calvert can come back to get Dorothy."

They looked over at Calvert, snuggled into a corner, contentment shining across his face.

"Calvert and his lady make a good couple," Max remarked, his voice soft with tenderness and a touch of envy and admiration.

Sheldon Coons, all energy and New York charm, greeted Caruso and then turned to clap Max on the back. "Us New York boys stick together, huh?" He winked. Originally an armorer, he'd later become an instructor with the Link trainer, a type of simulation tool. Shel and Max first got to know each other at the Jewish services during the holy days, sharing a realization over the parallel battles of faith and war and how surreal it was that, even in the midst of chaos, they'd found echoes of their old lives.

Caruso next spotted Camille Devaney and Teed Smith, the intelligence officers from their debriefings. Devaney, a quiet Iowan who sometimes joked about his pre-war days in his father's funeral home, and Smith, eagerly awaiting a reunion with his wife, shared a look of mutual anticipation.

Lieutenant Higley climbed on, adjusting his cap as he scanned the faces. "Supposed to be on an earlier flight, but someone else needed it more," he said with a nod, relief softening his expression. Always one of the first near the control tower on mission days, he never rested until the last of the planes had returned.

Max leaned into Caruso and nodded at Rapoport, nestled in a corner, hands clasped beside his head as if he'd just won the grand prize. "He and I used to talk about missing some of the holiday rituals from home. Still, we kept our own traditions faithfully, hoping they'd keep us safe when we were flying." He winked. "They seemed to work!"

Kenny Craumer, their baseball nemesis, climbed aboard next, ready to trade his gunner's gear for a coach's whistle. His dreams of a peaceful life coaching sports back home were a stark contrast to the harsh realities of war. Caruso realized in that moment that they all carried hopes of simple joys and new beginnings.

Lester Rhein, from their barracks, pulled himself onto the bomber. Typically serious, today there was a noticeable lift in his posture, as if he were finally releasing some of the burdens he'd carried. Though they'd never flown a mission together, their paths often crossed in the barracks and over cups of coffee at the Red Cross Club.

A Pennsylvanian with seven siblings waiting back home, he ambled over to Caruso and Max, holding up a jagged piece of flak. "I never told you this, but this could've been the end of me," he said, "if not for my mother's prayer book in my chest pocket." He retrieved the book, its pages pierced nearly through by the shrapnel. "Imagine me telling my mom her prayers shielded me all the way over here." Awe filled his voice, tying faith, family, and fate into a single, powerful thread.

Next came Paul Lucyk, climbing aboard with his signature grin. "Lucky rabbit's foot still working its magic, huh?" someone teased.

"Survived December of '43, didn't I?" Paul chuckled, patting his pocket. Caruso flashed back to the party they'd thrown him when he married his sweetheart, Betty, an English woman. "The baby's due, any day now!" His announcement added to the glow on his face. "Figured the sooner I get out of here, the sooner I can get back and be with my family!" He said "my family" with a deep pride in his voice, eyes shining with the anticipation of fatherhood.

Bob Smith, the biggest prankster on base, almost glowed as he came aboard. Even with his fear of flying, he always kept things light, but it turned out he'd been doing some real heavy thinking about the future. He'd confided to Caruso that he was contemplating the seminary—a surprising path for the barracks' clown who'd once pulled the water-bucket trick.

Lieutenant Howie Hibbard gave a thumbs-up as he boarded and moved toward the pilot seat amid cheers. "We made it, fellas!" he crowed. "And soon I'll be seeing my wife, Mary! It's been a long year and a half over here!" Caruso had heard the English ladies were disappointed when they learned that this handsome young pilot with his wavy hair and all-American looks was already taken, but there were plenty of other soldiers ready and willing to take his place on the eligible list.

He'd also heard a story about Hibbard's narrow escape when his plane suffered severe damage after being shot full of holes during a raid over Germany, prompting him to sound the bail-out alarm. It was miraculous that he'd made it back alive. Those experiences contributed to the relief emanating from his body as he passed by Caruso.

Joe Robinson, with his bushy eyebrows and small, pointed nose, was right behind him; he was their copilot today. "Fellas, it's my honor to assist in getting us back to the good old US of A! And I don't know about the rest of you, but I can't wait to get home and see my family, especially my wife!" Joe had flown as many or more missions as Howie. Like Max, he'd participated in a revival mission at the end of the war, flying some POWs back to France. He'd been just as affected by the experience as Max had.

Caruso felt a strong tie to each of the men on board, regardless of how little or well he knew them. As he looked at them, he realized that each of their stories reminded him of the connection that tied them all together—forged in the fire of war and emerging strong as tempered steel.

He got up from his position next to Max and crossed over to Calvert. "How do you feel, my friend?"

Calvert's face was serene, with a look of wistfulness. "I looked for Captain Flemming this morning to say goodbye. He'd been so good to me. But I couldn't find him, so I left him a note. I hope he'll visit if he ever finds himself in Kentucky."

Caruso nodded.

"You know," Calvert continued, his voice softening, "as I scribbled my farewell, I couldn't help but recall one late evening in the operations room, when Captain Flemming was hunched over his maps. He looked up and gave me a nod of trust. That one gesture, to me, cemented my place among those shaping the course of the war—a responsibility I've carried ever since."

"It's true, Calvert," Caruso said. "Everyone's role—whether in the ground or the air—was equally important in the success of this war." He smiled. "I learned that when I worked with you."

As the engines came to life, they both situated themselves for takeoff.

Calvert fingered the bomber jacket Caruso had given him before tucking it into his duffel. "You know, Caruso, this jacket feels like an extension of me—kind of an emblem of honor and a reminder of my evolution during my time here in England."

Caruso nodded. "We're all changed men."

When the green flare was fired, the aircraft echoed with more whoops and hollers, and the plane started to taxi forward. The ground crew gave a final salute as they rolled by, the unspoken goodbye heavy in the air.

The men settled into soft chatter, weaving memories with future dreams. Calvert looked out the window as they slowly gathered up speed, the tall grasses by the runway bending as if to wave goodbye. A tightness built in Caruso's throat as Calvert blinked rapidly, as if caught off guard by the sting of unexpected tears. As the plane lifted off, Caruso took in the green expanse of England below them, a patchwork quilt of memories and battles fought. He was so proud of what they'd accomplished here. A surge of emotion welled up inside him: elation and nostalgia, and an overwhelming yearning for home that he felt in every fiber of his being.

Calvert interrupted his thoughts. "It's like my chest aches at the thought of leaving Dorothy behind. You must feel the same about Helen. Dorothy and I vowed this separation would be nothing more than a small dot in the trajectory of the long life we'd build together."

"Yes," Caruso admitted. "It'll be hard to be apart. But knowing we have a future makes it all bearable."

"I wonder if Dorothy heard our engines as we took off, or saw our plane…" Calvert's voice trailed off, a pensive smile tugging at his lips.

Their daydreams dissolved when cheers erupted from the men, who were laughing and joking about all their plans for when they got home, each forecasting a bigger and better idea than the one before:

"When I get home, I'm eating a whole plate of blueberry pie—and then seconds!"

"Always the chowhound!" someone teased, laughter bubbling around them.

"Here's to never having tea again!"

"Don't rub it in. I'm leavin' my wife over here. And when I see her again, I'll have a new baby!"

"Hey, Glover's baby is nine months, and he hasn't even met her yet! That pile of gifts over there in the corner is for her. I'll bet she's going to be a daddy's girl!"

The banter continued, light and jubilant, as they flew over the fields of England, so picturesque, it could have been dropped from a painting. Caruso looked out, wanting to memorize every feature so he could relay it to his family back home. He knew he'd remember this moment always.

❧

Soon, they all settled in for the first leg of their flight. Their route was from Polebrook to Anglesey, Wales, where the aircraft would refuel. From there, they would cross over to Iceland, then Goose Bay, Labrador, and finally head to Bradley Field in Connecticut.

"It's almost unimaginable to think of being back in the US once again, safe and sound. Sitting here, feeling relaxed and at peace, I think about what you airmen must feel, having danced with death every day you flew," Calvert remarked.

Their conversation dissipated when John Leasure picked up the guitar he'd managed to bring on board, strumming the opening chords of Billie Holiday's "I'll Be Seeing You." To Caruso, it felt as though the cabin itself stilled, the song's soft melody weaving through the air.

Suddenly, he wasn't on that B-17 anymore. He was back in that dimly lit dance hall, Helen's hand resting in his, her eyes shining with a love that seemed to hold the whole world together. The memory was so vivid he could almost smell her perfume and feel the softness of her hair as he pulled her closer.

John's singing filled the cabin, and it felt like the first green shoot pushing through the frozen ground of winter, a quiet promise of healing, of life waiting on the other side. Caruso watched Calvert's eyes droop, lulled by the warmth of the melody and the hum of the engines. His friend fought to stay awake, determined to memorize every detail, but in the end, sleep claimed him, carrying him closer to home.

CHAPTER THIRTY-SIX

June 8, 1945
North Wales

THEIR AIRCRAFT APPROACHED the air base in Anglesey, Wales, enveloped in a dense veil of fog and low visibility. Even the seasoned crew couldn't escape the nerves that came with flying blind. Seeking guidance from Valley Air Force Base, they flew inland toward Barmouth, misled by the deceptive glow of city lights and the faint line of the railway below. Sky and earth dissolved into each other, the world outside a disorienting wash of gray.

"Pilot to navigator. Turning back to get on course. See anything?"

"Navigator to pilot. Visibility's zero. Rechecking our heading now."

"Pilot to navigator. I think I see something ahead, but it's pea soup out there. I can't be certain if it's…"

The pilot's words were sharply cut off by the copilot's urgent voice. "MOUNTAIN! Pull up! Pull up!"

The engines strained, a desperate plea for altitude. The pilot gritted his teeth, yanking the controls with everything he had, sweat blurring his vision. The lumbering bird began to ascend but then jolted violently. The screech of metal against rock filled Caruso's ears, followed by an ear-splintering *whoosh* and a searing heat surrounding him. Then, everything plunged into blackness and silence, as if an invisible hand had lifted the needle off a record, mid-song.

CHAPTER THIRTY-SEVEN

PERCH AND HELEN stood together in the quiet hush of Cambridge Cemetery, the wind weaving through the trees like a soft lament. Perch's face was pale but resolute, his fingers curled tightly around the rosary beads that Caruso had once carried so close.

"He saved my life," Perch whispered, his voice rough with memory. "I want to make sure this goes with him, so he's never alone. They were my nonna's, but I know she'd approve."

Helen's eyes shone with understanding. She reached out, her fingers brushing Perch's arm, a gentle comfort. "I'm sure he'd appreciate that," she said, her tears falling freely.

Perch nodded, his gaze steady on the casket. He spoke with the undertaker, his voice low and urgent, asking that the rosary be placed inside before the burial. The man nodded solemnly, and Perch closed his eyes, feeling the finality of it all.

He fingered the St. Christopher medal around his neck, a parting gift from Max. Max had gotten it from his brother Harry and had promised Perch he could return it when they met again. Of course, neither of them had imagined that Max would never come home.

He thought about all these lives lost—men who had survived the damn war, only to be lost on the way home. The cruelty of it cut deep. The sight of the twenty caskets was almost too much to bear. He knew every one of those men.

As the prayers were said and the earth was gently returned to its place, Perch squeezed Helen's hand, and she squeezed back. It was a silent promise that they would carry this memory forward, to honor the lives that had been lost and to hold on to the fragile threads of connection that still bound them all together.

CHAPTER THIRTY-EIGHT

HELEN SAT AT her desk, dread settling over her like a shadow. She picked up her pen, her hands trembling as she wiped away teardrops that fell across the page of her diary.

Tonight, the silence is almost too much. I've just returned from Cambridge, and my heart is so heavy it feels like it might sink right through me. There were no long speeches, no stirring words… just the murmur of prayers and the wind sighing through the trees. It felt almost like the world itself had paused.

Perch placed his rosary in Sandy's casket. I told myself that gesture was enough—a final kindness, a last act of brotherhood. But watching the earth fall back on him felt like a door closing on everything we'd shared.

I know that in many ways, Perch has it so much harder than I do. He knew every one of those men: some were in his barracks. Max was his best friend from training, and Perch feels like he's only alive because of Sandy. It only adds to my overwhelming sadness.

The war may be over, but today felt like the worst part was just beginning.

I keep telling myself that love is stronger than grief. That in time, memories will comfort me instead of bringing me pain. For now, I can only hold on to the echo of Sandy's laughter, his steadiness, and the way his hand felt in mine… even as the world feels cold and hollow.

CHAPTER THIRTY-NINE

December, 1945
Oundle, England

DOROTHY SAT BY the fire, her hands curled around the diary she'd kept since Calvert had first come into her life. The pages felt heavier now, as if sorrow kept weight.

> *I had so many hopes and dreams. Falling in love with a Yank seemed like the most beautiful twist of fate. We planned a life together in the States, a life that will now never come to pass. My Calvert isn't coming back for me. He's gone.*
>
> *On the morning he left, I heard the departing planes overhead. I tried so hard not to cry because I'd promised him I wouldn't. Instead, I pictured the reunion with his dear family. His father, still grieving the loss of his wife, would have been overjoyed to hold his son tightly again. Evelyn and Harold would have been so proud as their brother shared stories of his time overseas. But that, too, will never be.*
>
> *I wasn't able to pay my last respects at the cemetery in*

Cambridge, where he was laid to rest. I'd used up my petrol ration during our final days together, driving around the countryside—a cherished pastime I'll never regret. Perhaps it's for the best. I could never have said goodbye.

My life feels like a vacuum, as if the past several months were a beautiful dream with a cruel ending. How can something so miraculous as finding each other amid this terrible war turn so quickly into heartbreak? When a rainbow fades, you start to wonder if it was ever really there at all. That's how I feel about my brief time with Calvert. And now my future is as grey as the skies above. I don't know how I'll go on without him, but I must. For his sake, I must. He would want that.

It feels like the whole town shares my sorrow. Where once there was excited anticipation, now there's only stillness. The children who used to beam at earning chocolate or gum for mastering American slang now wander listlessly. Everything is so… quiet.

I remember when the Americans first arrived, we detested what we thought to be their churlish ways. Most of them, except Calvert, seemed loud and boorish. Now, after getting to know them, <u>and love them</u>, we understand them, and we appreciate their mannerisms.

The citizens of Great Britain have stumbled upon the realisation that they've been forever changed by the Americans, and things will never be the same. Those men we once barely tolerated are now mourned as if they had passed on, which I guess, in a way, they have.

In the pubs, there's talk about whether those Yanks think of us with the same wistful fondness we feel for them. They brought a playfulness to our lives, a brightness that cut through our reserve. It was refreshing to not always be so… proper. It's true that we Brits find comfort in the familiarity of our formalities. Yet, the mingling of our lives somehow seemed to have brought out the best in both of us. The boys across the pond wove themselves into our lives, bringing out something we hadn't known we were missing. Now that they're gone, the silence is deafening.

EPILOGUE

May, 2023
Dolgellau, Wales
PAT

Our car is one of the few navigating the quiet roads on the outskirts of Dolgellau, Wales, on this chilly morning. My husband, Stan, has reacclimated to driving on the left side of the road as we make our way into the tiny town center. He assures me he remembers the route from our last visit and doesn't need the GPS, but I connect it anyway so I can relax and let my mind wander about the day ahead.

As we drive, the dreamlike nature of this moment envelops me. Years of research, piecing together the fragments of these soldiers' lives, have led to this day. Meeting their families, after connecting through stories and letters, feels like we're bridging decades of history. I smile to myself, anticipating how the words and faces will come together, each a link to their departed loved ones.

Stan interrupts my thoughts. "I know you told me before, but remind me who's coming today."

I chuckle. It's true: I've already told him at least three times, but then, I know all these people, at least online, much better than he does.

"Matt Reeves will be there, of course."

"Of course." Stan nods. "If it weren't for him, we probably wouldn't even be here. Tracking down the family members would have been impossible."

"Absolutely. If our fallen relatives are a wheel, Matt is the hub that connects all the spokes," I say, smiling. "Without him, none of us would even know of each other. He's done so much research and even arranged for the memorial plaque—and he started this journey as a young boy. It's incredible."

My eyes crinkle as a smile crosses my face. "And Lisa is coming from New Orleans. She's the niece of Santo Caruso, the ball turret gunner. You remember her—we've been corresponding for over five years. And Anne, the niece of Calvert P'Pool, will be here from Kentucky. She's in her eighties now, can you believe it? She's been a wonderful resource with all the information she's saved, and has become a dear friend. Calvert was a corporal and part of the ground echelon."

"Right, and she's a historian," Stan said, recalling the many stories I've told him about my email friends over the years.

"Exactly. And then there's Bonnie, coming from New Zealand. She was just a nine-month-old baby when her dad, Captain Joe Glover, died in the crash. She never even got to meet him.

"Also, the relatives of Edwin Birtwell and John Leasure, who worked on the ground, and Bob Smith, an aircrew member."

Our conversation gets interrupted when we arrive at the florist in Dolgellau to pick up the flowers we ordered. I also brought a painted rock from home to leave at the site, my own tribute for the boys. As we leave the florist, a slightly built man with a shaved head, likely in his thirties or forties, approaches me, his eyebrows raised inquisitively. "Are you by any chance Pat?"

"Matt?" I ask, reaching out to shake his hand as he nods. Meeting such a dear, dear friend for the first time fills me with an overwhelming sense of excitement and gratitude. Without the internet, this would never have happened. I instantly feel comfortable with him. "I'm so happy to meet you, finally! Why don't you ride with us to the site? Our car's in the public parking lot around the corner. We planned to meet all the others there."

"That'll be fine," Matt said. "The fewer cars, the better; the roads around the site have really deteriorated."

As we walk the short distance to the parking lot, we notice several people gathered near the pay parking machine, their faces reflecting a mix of anticipation and solemnity. I approach them with a shy smile. "Hello, are any of you here to go to the 351st crash site?"

A slight woman with shoulder-length brown hair steps forward. "Pat, is that you?" she asks, with a trace of a New Orleans accent.

"Lisa!" I run to her, my arms outstretched. We embrace vigorously, tears instantly pricking my eyes.

My gaze then turns to an older woman in the group who is hesitantly stepping forward. "You must be Anne!" I say as she approaches me quietly. She reaches out her hand, and I pull her into an embrace, which she at first accepts tentatively and then draws me in tightly. This is probably the first hug she's had since Covid began, I realize. As we detach ourselves, we muse over the irony of our meeting. "Isn't it amazing that

I could have easily traveled to meet you in Kentucky, but our paths cross over here?"

"It's wonderful to finally meet you in person, Pat," she says, her voice carrying a lilting Kentucky accent as she smiles warmly. "And I'm so glad to be back here." We've only corresponded by email and never even talked on the phone, so her accent somehow surprises me.

Anne and her daughter Margaret visited this site years ago and met Matt. Her words about that first visit—"surreal and life-altering"—still resonate with me.

"Hi, Pat, I'm Bonnie," says another woman as she steps forward. She looks younger than her seventy-odd years, her face lighting up. "Joe Glover's daughter. I'm glad this trip finally came to pass."

"We tried to do this in 2020, to mark the seventy-fifth anniversary of the crash…" I say, turning to face the group. "But Covid got in the way." They all nod knowingly.

"Covid interrupted everyone's plans for a good long while," someone says.

The others take turns introducing themselves. "I'm sure I speak for all of us when I say I'm thrilled to be here," one of the family members says. "It's like finding a missing puzzle piece. Thank you for making this possible."

I search their faces, one by one. "It's really not me, it's Matt. He's been the catalyst for all this. Without him, I wouldn't have had anything to go on." I turn to Matt. "Thank you so much, Matt… for your interest, for your research, and for your dedication to honoring these men. If not for you and the plaque you had made, none of us would be here." Matt nods shyly.

"The only family member that I located that's not here with us is Joe Coons, the half-brother of Sheldon Coons, Jr.,"

I say to the group. "About a year into our email communications, Joe passed away unexpectedly. I'm thinking of him, and I know he's here in spirit. He was a nice, nice man."

As I look around at our group, I can't believe it. All these relatives and descendants from across the globe, gathered to pay tribute to "our boys." If they could see us now, they'd be amazed that relatives whom they've never met are here to honor them. And for those boys whose family members aren't here, I hope they know that it's only because I haven't found them yet. Every single person I was able to locate has arranged their schedule and made the long trek to be here.

Matt rides in our car, and the others follow closely behind as we make our way through the country roads into the farmland area that will lead us to the crash site. As Stan navigates the winding roads, my mind wanders—not just to the upcoming gathering, but to the deep sense of responsibility I feel. These men we honor today left an indelible mark not just in history, but on the hearts of those they left behind. Their stories, once at risk of being forgotten, are now kept alive in the voices of those who gather here. It's a poignant lesson of the enduring impact of memory and the power of collective remembrance.

I feel these reflections pressing on my heart as we prepare to step into a day of commemoration, bridging decades of history with our shared purpose in the present.

The rural road winds through serene countryside, interrupted now and then by the bleating of sheep. Every so often, Matt hops out to open gates between farmlands, allowing us to pass without disturbing the roaming livestock. We continue driving until we come upon a truck parked alongside a fence, where a man in a Kelly-green jacket stands talking to a young man. I suddenly remember, as if it were yesterday, when Stan and I first found the site on our own, six years ago, driving around and around until we serendipitously stopped in front of a fence that would turn out to be the gateway to our destination. The same young man I see now before me was the guardian angel who gave us meticulous directions on how to reach the site from this very place.

In this moment, I feel certain this is all destiny.

As the younger man departs, the other gentleman in the green jacket waves a greeting to Matt, and when we approach, they shake hands. "Let me introduce you all to John Lloyd," Matt says, turning to address the group. "It was John's father, Robert, who saw the plane go down and was one of the first on the scene to respond. Robert has since passed away, but John has continued to carry on the legacy from that day."

John himself has a quiet manner about him, but smiles broadly as he greets all the relatives that have come to visit. "John has been one of the unofficial protectors of this area," Matt says, "and prides himself on keeping the area in order and preventing looters from trying to rummage around illegally for crash-related memorabilia."

John joins us as we begin the walk to the memorial. The rocky path to the site is passable only on foot. John stops to speak, his soft Welsh accent carrying over the group. "This is an ancient road," he says. "It held up for a long time, but off-road vehicles and adventurers have worn it down. Now, to protect the area as much as we can, we only travel by foot."

We continue our leisurely walk. I reach out my hand to assist Anne periodically as we traverse the ruggedly uneven, pebble-filled footpath, dotted with small pieces of slate. The gravel crunches beneath our feet. We take care to avoid the potholes and sunken areas created by the outdoor enthusiasts who find racing along the rocky thoroughfare exciting.

The skies are the deepest blue, dotted with billowing clouds, and the mountain breezes are cool and refreshing. We're surrounded by spacious fields and rolling hills giving way to towering mountains. On either side of the trail are the dry stone walls so characteristic of these parts, first created in ancient times by piling rocks by hand, one above the other. Farm wire secured with wooden posts extends the wall height in some areas, to keep the herds in their assigned pastures. The sun is out, the air is crisp, and the sheep run up on the hills beside the path, pausing now and then to eye the strangers in their territory.

We look around in awe. The entire area captivates us with its breathtaking beauty. "I just love it here," I say to John. "The land really evokes a sense of tranquility."

John agrees. "Yes, I've always found it peaceful. When I become tense, my wife tells me, 'Go to the mountain; you'll feel better.' And I always do. There's something special about this place. My father always told me the same thing: *These men, and this place, are special. Preserve and honor the memories.*"

After about forty-five minutes of walking, the pathway inclines and curves slightly to the right, diverging from the stone wall. On our left, I'm drawn to a tiny babbling brook, a serene fragment of the mountain that claimed our boys.

As we gaze upward, Matt and John point out the scar on the mountain, where the impact from the crash is still visible, all these years later. "My father was outside and heard the plane circling low," John said, his gaze fixed on the scar. "He knew they weren't going to clear the mountain. He saw the accident and said he would remember the smell of the fiery crash for the rest of his life. He told me that after several hours, the Americans came to retrieve the fallen soldiers and that as they took them out of the plane, they laid their bodies on the crumpled aircraft. The sight of the long row of boots where the men were laid out on the wing stayed with him."

"I wonder how they got turned around and ended up over here," says John Leasure's nephew, his voice almost a whisper.

Matt has researched this accident for years. "A small compass error could have led them off course. Visibility was likely limited, so they were flying low to find a railway landmark—and then suddenly, the mountain was in front of them. The crash report shows that they were at high rpm, trying to gain altitude, but B-17s are too heavy to climb rapidly."

We're all quiet, picturing the pilot's panic in the final second. I wonder if the others on board even realized what was happening—or if it was all over in an instant.

We turn away from the mountain and face north, standing on the hillside overlooking farmlands further down and the estuary beyond. Barmouth Bridge is visible, with the town of Barmouth in the distance. We look out, spellbound, and then our eyes fall on the stainless-steel plaque that Matt had so kindly made so many years ago, hanging from the stone wall below us.

We descend the hill gingerly toward the memorial. The ground is green with growth but still uneven and downward-sloping, and there are large tufts of wheat-colored grass scattered around. Matt extends his hand to those who need some help with their footing. My husband gently places the wreath on the earth beneath the plaque. I insert the painted rock into one crevice of the stone wall.

A drawing of a B-17 is etched onto the gray metal and, below it, the words: "In memory of the twenty airmen of the 351st Bombardment Group USAAF killed in the crash of a B-17G Flying Fortress on this mountain 8th June 1945." Beneath it are the names of the twenty men. Each of us looks through the names, our eyes stopping when we come to that of our relative. The mood, though somber, is filled with peace and benevolence.

"It seems like such a heavenly place, with the sea in the distance, and the sheep grazing nearby," Lisa says as she takes in the vista, the breeze gently blowing her hair across her face as she speaks.

Unbidden, we gather in a semi-circle in front of the plaque, taking turns to share stories about our family members.

"Joe Glover was my dad," Bonnie says, touching his name on the memorial and passing around a picture of a lanky airman with dark wavy hair. "He was twenty-two when he navigated thirty-two bombing missions over Germany and a revival mission to pick up POWs. I never met him; I was just nine months old when he died. When I see Orion, the Hunter in the Sky, I think of him. I'd like to share a poem recited on Anzac Day in New Zealand to honor the fallen. At the end, please join me in saying 'We will remember them.'

"They shall grow not old, as we that are left grow old:
Age shall not weary them, nor the years condemn.
At the going down of the sun and in the morning
We will remember them.

They mingle not with their laughing comrades again;
They sit no more at familiar tables of home;
They have no lot in our labour of the day-time;
They sleep beyond England's foam.

But where our desires are and our hopes profound,
Felt as a well-spring that is hidden from sight,

To the innermost heart of their own land they are known
As the stars are known to the Night;

As the stars that shall be bright when we are dust,
Moving in marches upon the heavenly plain;
As the stars that are starry in the time of our darkness,
To the end, to the end, they remain."[1]

Bonnie looks up, cueing the group in their response. "We will remember them," we all say in unison. She inserts a single red rose into the wire running along the top of the stone wall.

I put my hand on Bonnie's shoulder. "That was lovely," I say, my voice a murmur. Looking around, I don't see a dry eye in the group.

"Max Marksheid is our family member," I begin, my voice faltering as tears spill down my cheeks. "We called him Mendy. He was a radio operator who flew over forty missions, plus a revival mission to pick up POWs after the war ended."

I take out a letter from my backpack. "Before I left for this trip, I contacted the 351st Bomb Group Association to let them know we were coming to the crash site. Soon after, I received a letter from a man who was Max's best friend."

My fingers tremble as I unfold the letter, pulling out a St. Christopher's medal on a silver chain and looping it over one of the fence posts. I read slowly, my voice wavering:

---

1 Binyon, L. (1917) *For the Fallen, and Other Poems*. London: Hodder & Stoughton. [Pdf] Retrieved from the Library of Congress, https://www.loc.gov/item/2021666957/.

"My name is Anthony Del Percio, but to everyone in the 351st, I was just 'Perch.' It was easier than trying to pronounce my last name. I saw in the Polebrook Post newsletter that you were coming to visit the memorial where some of my friends lost their lives just after the war.

"I was your Uncle Max's best friend. We met in training and were inseparable ever since. Max was a wonderful man, someone I always looked up to, though I never would have told him that. He was steady as a rock, and kind to everyone. He always looked for the good in people.

"Max and I went through a lot together—some terrifying moments, but plenty of good ones, too. He was Jewish, I was Catholic, but we often talked about how similar our faiths were. Family was important to both of us, and he cherished his family more than anything. I was thrilled to find a way to contact you, to let you know what a wonderful example he always was to everyone on base. He even adopted a little puppy we had as our mascot. His name was Snafu. When the last of us went home, a man from the local pub adopted him.

"I was in the rehab hospital when they left for home—otherwise, I might have been on that plane. I was deeply, deeply saddened to hear they never made it home. I knew all the men on board to some extent, and besides Max, there was one other man I was especially close to that I'd like to mention, Santo Caruso. When I was lost at sea, Caruso badgered all the brass to keep looking for me. I owe him my life, so please let his family know that he will always be remembered with great gratitude.

"Enclosed is a St. Christopher medal that Max gave me right before he left to go home. He said it was for protection and that I could return it when we met again in the States. I've kept it with me all these years and thought it would be fitting to send to you, to place at the memorial. I'd like to think that wherever they are now, this medal's blessings will finally reach them. Thank you, and thanks to all the families who have come to pay tribute to these brave and honorable men that I worked with side by side in the 351st. They are all heroes, the best of the best. I'm too old to make the trip, but rest assured I'll be there in spirit."

I nod to Lisa to speak next.

"Santo Caruso was my uncle," Lisa Jackson says proudly. "His sister, Caroline, was my mother; she was only three when he left for war. We called him Sandy. He was just twenty, a ball turret gunner from Philadelphia. After being injured on his third mission, he spent four months recovering and missed the chance to go home with his original crew. He flew thirty-nine missions." She pulls out a heart-shaped plaque with Santo's picture on it and attaches it to the stone wall, then turns to address the group, eyes glistening.

"He fell in love with his nurse, a woman named Helen. They had plans to be married, and before he left, he gave her a necklace as a token of his love." She gently fingers the heart-shaped locket around her neck, her touch reverent. "When Helen passed away several years ago, she left instructions for this necklace to be sent to our family. She said she had worn it every day, close to her heart."

Lisa pauses, gathering her emotions before continuing. "Receiving this locket felt like holding a piece of the past. More than just metal, it's a statement of love's resilience, of promises kept beyond lifetimes. Wearing it, I feel connected to Uncle Sandy, Helen, and the strength of bonds that endure beyond lifetimes."

One of the men in our group steps forward next. "How true. I'm so grateful to be here. Bob Smith was my uncle. He was from New York and was also only twenty. He was a waist gunner. One man on his crew recalled that every mission was an emotional struggle for him. He always feared he'd crash and burn on takeoff. Once in the air, he was as focused and efficient as anyone could be. He was also described as having a delightfully dry sense of humor. He had nine siblings. Two are still alive, and I'm also here on their behalf." He holds up some pictures of Bob so that all can see.

Anne Crabb clears her throat as she begins. "Calvert P'Pool was my uncle. He was thirty-four when he died. His job title was a clerk, but it seemed he did some work in the Intelligence Division. He always had a smile on his face. He fell in love with a woman named Dorothy while he was in England and had planned to marry her. Here's a picture of him," she says, holding up a photo of him in a bomber jacket. "He loved this bomber jacket and wore it all the time. We have no idea how he got it, because typically only aircrew had them, but this is probably another reflection of his gregarious personality and how well-liked he was. Someone apparently found a way to get him one. He was very proud of it."

John Leasure's relative begins, his words overflowing with raw emotion. "John Leasure was my uncle. Despite being only twenty-two, he had a job as an airplane engineer. He also loved music and used to play musical instruments with his family. My father, who was one of his two brothers, named me after him. John's other brother Ralph was in the Navy, and his mom wrote to both of her sons every week." He holds up a picture of John in uniform, and another of him with three family members, all with instruments in hand.

One of the other women in our group shares her family story with tender respect. "My uncle, Edwin Birtwell, known to some as Birt, was a skilled photo lab technician. He made sure that the photos from bombing raids were developed quickly and clearly to aid in planning the next missions. His work not only supported the missions but also captured moments of humanity—joy, love, and the unshakable spirit of those who served with him."

She lifts a small worn box filled with black-and-white photographs. "Before leaving England, he gave Valerie, the English woman he loved, a set of rosary beads blessed by Cardinal Cushing, symbolizing their planned future together. Though that future wasn't meant to be, he captured life and love amid the chaos of war in these photographs. Each picture tells a story, underscoring the depth of the connections made in the hardest of times.

"I found Valerie before she passed away, and when we met, she returned these photographs to our family. Meeting her was an incredible link to our past."

Holding up a photograph of a smiling couple, unmistakably in love, she says, "Though we may never know all their names, these images speak of Birt's ability to see beyond the war to the personal stories of those who lived through it.

"These photographs aren't just a bridge to our past but a memorial to the lives they touched, the moments they cherished, and the love that remains timeless. Through Birt's lens, we get a glimpse of the enduring spirit of those who served and dreamed of a peaceful tomorrow."

I pull out the papers in which I have documented bits and pieces about the other men who don't have family representatives here with us today. I've researched them all, the best I've been able. For some, I have photographs that I show to the group.

"I met Sheldon Coons' half brother online a few years ago, and he sent me these pictures," I say, pointing to

Sheldon's name and passing the photos around. "He was twenty-three years old and was from New York. He was originally an armorer, but later became a Link Celestial Navigation Trainer Operator, which allowed the crew to train using simulation.

"Joe Robinson, twenty-six, was the plane's copilot and flew twenty-one missions before taking part in a revival mission to pick up POWs." My fingers rest on the cold metal inscription of his name on the plaque. "He left behind a wife.

"Ken Craumer, twenty-four, was a gunnery instructor from Pennsylvania and a talented athlete," I say, pointing to his name and showing his picture. "His class ring was found at the crash site and Matt was able to return it to his family—a reminder of the life he left behind."

I look down at my notes. "Lester Rhein, a top turret gunner from Pennsylvania, flew missions alongside Bob Smith, whose bravery we also honor today. After his death, his mom sent photos of him to the families of the other men, creating a tribute to their shared sacrifice.

"David Rapoport, twenty-three, was a ball turret gunner from Philadelphia," I say, my fingers resting on his name. "He flew thirteen missions plus a revival mission to pick up POWs. He's now buried in Beverley National Cemetery, and his grave isn't far from where our uncle, Mendy, is laid to rest. We visited the graves last year.

"John Montgomery was a crew chief from Oklahoma, and ensured the aircraft were airworthy for every mission.

"Paul Lucyk, twenty-six, was a waist gunner from Massachusetts. He married an English woman, Betty Harrison, while stationed overseas. Betty was pregnant when he left Polebrook, and their baby was born on the very day of the crash.

"There were three intelligence officers in the group. Dick Higley was twenty-nine, married, and from Berkeley, California." I hold up a picture of a handsome man in military attire. "He entered the military as an intelligence officer after three years of college. He worked as a meteorologist when he was in England and did all the weather forecasting for the missions. Matt learned in a letter from family that he'd given up his seat on an earlier flight to another airman who had a family emergency in the US.

"The next two intelligence officers were both from Iowa, so they may have known each other. Teed Smith was forty years old and married. He and Camille 'Jiggs' Devaney, thirty-seven, were likely involved in debriefs after the missions. Camille had a fiancée, Leona, who was waiting for him back in the States.

"Morris Lizewski was thirty-eight and from New York. His role was Duty Soldier II, so he likely did heavy manual labor, unloading trucks, maybe driving them as needed. He was from Poland and wasn't a citizen when he was drafted."

I place my fingers on another name on the plaque. "This is Howard Hibbard. They called him Howie, and he was from Indiana. He was twenty-six and married, and was the pilot on the plane. He flew thirty-eight missions. His last mission was in November of 1944; he may have been a trainer after that.

"And finally, here is Boyd Dobbs," I say, showing his picture to the group and pointing to his name on the plaque. "He was forty-seven and originally from Texas, but moved to Oakland, California. He was an airplane mechanic, working on all the planes with John Leasure to make sure they were safe to fly before they went back up in the air."

"They were all so brave," Lisa says. "And they did their jobs so well, and so proudly. They really were from the greatest generation. Hearing about them and seeing their pictures has been wonderful."

"Yes," Anne Crabb says. "To have made it through and then to die on the way home while their family was anxiously waiting for them is unimaginable. My family was never the same after this loss. I'm sure that's true of all the families."

Tears prick my eyes and threaten to overflow again as I gaze at the plaque that Matt created almost thirty years ago. It's astounding to think that "our boys," so young, gave their all for the war effort without hesitation. They, along with countless others in uniform, succeeded because they worked selflessly together. I reflect on our world now, with so many factions within our "United" States going their own way, with their own agendas… Have we learned nothing in these eighty years? The Greatest Generation knew that unity, compassion, and shared purpose were the keys to overcoming adversity. In our fractured world, their legacy reminds us of the power of coming together for a common cause—a lesson we must strive to remember and uphold.

Our boys live on, I realize. There's more to this life than the years we are given. Though their lives were cut short, their memories remain alive—in their families, their families' families, and now with us. These men lived with a conviction that transcended their time on earth—a belief in solidarity, sacrifice, and striving for something greater than themselves. They remind us that immortality isn't found in fame or fortune, but in the way we live, the impact we leave behind, and the lives we touch.

Max, Caruso, and Perch hoped to make their mark in the Eagle in Cambridge—but they achieved something far greater. Almost eighty years later, their lives are still etched into the hearts of those who remember and honor them. Their story, and the unity that brought them together, lives on as a monument to their courage, dedication, and enduring legacy.

As I play Anne's recording of "Hiraeth" on my phone, the haunting melody fills the crisp Welsh air, a tribute to their yearning and ours. In Welsh, *hiraeth* means "a longing, especially for one's country." It's the perfect word for today.

As the final notes fade into silence, I'm struck by the timelessness of the bond we share with these men and with each other. Their story isn't just a relic of the past, but a signpost for the future. In honoring them, we carry forward their spirit of harmony, compassion, and resilience, forging a path toward a future where such wars are no longer necessary.

"Let their memory be a blessing," my husband whispers.

As we join hands, it's as if I'm reaching out and touching the fingertips of the men themselves. I feel them here with us, and in this quiet moment, we are one.

REFLECTIONS

In England and Wales, more than half a century later, those who lived through the war years still gaze into the distance, smiles tugging at their lips as they recall the foreigners who captivated their hearts.

When American tourists visit, locals pause to step back in time, sharing recollections and heartfelt thanks to the boys from across the pond who changed their lives forever.

Polebrook Airfield is quiet now. Much of the land has been returned to its original owners, the Rothschilds, while a small portion has been lovingly preserved by grateful residents as a tribute to the men who helped secure peace in Europe. The thunder of B-17s is heard no more. Wildflowers grow in the cracks of the old runway, pushing through an area where the great planes once roared to life. The skies are clear (or as clear as skies can ever be in the UK), filled only with the sounds of birdsong.

But the memories endure—etched into the hearts of those who lived through those years and carried forward by every grateful soul who stops to remember.

AUTHOR'S NOTES

This story weaves truth and imagination—written to honor what was, and what might have been. These notes offer a deeper glimpse into the people, places, and memories that shaped this book—and the layered truths I uncovered along the way. Unless otherwise noted, the airmen's names have been left unchanged, though all conversations and character details are fictionalized. Any resemblance to actual persons, living or deceased, beyond those explicitly identified, is purely coincidental.

All of the men who perished in the crash on June 8, 1945, as they were returning to the States, existed in real life. This story is my attempt to honor their memory—to lift their names from the margins of history and bring them to life for the reader.

Santo "Sandy" Caruso truly was injured on his third mission in England, his very first week in the air. He was out of commission for almost four months, during which time the crew he trained with completed their tour and returned home. Helen, his love interest, is a fictional creation, meant to reflect the kind of bond that might have brought light during those dark months. I chose her name in honor of my mother, who passed away in 2024—just shy of her one hundred and second birthday. Although Caruso's mission records suggest he likely did spend time at a flak house during his tour, no official record was found. That portion of his story has been imagined.

The scenes involving the base hospital were imagined, as were the staff who worked there.

Stoneleigh Rehabilitation Center existed during the war and served members of the Eighth Air Force. Despite extensive research, I was unable to determine whether Santo Caruso was treated there. His time at Stoneleigh—and all the individuals at the facility—was fictionalized to reflect the very real trauma and recovery many men endured.

Max Marksheid was our family member, and the names of his relatives are accurate. Because little personal detail was passed down, most of his characteristics and personality were gently imagined to honor the life behind the uniform—a man we wish we'd had the chance to know.

Calvert P'Pool did, in fact, serve in the ground echelon at the 351st Bomb Group. Thanks to his niece, who graciously shared family stories, I was able to include several details from his real life. His mother did pass away while he was overseas. He proudly wore a bomber jacket similar to those worn by the flight crews—though how he acquired it remains unknown. What is known is that he wore it often, and fondly. He did fall in love overseas with a woman named Dorothy, and left a trunk with the owner of the pub he frequented, intending to retrieve it on a return trip. It is believed that the trunk was never reclaimed. Dorothy's diary entry is entirely imagined.

The character called "Perch" was inspired by the many airmen whose stories I could only glimpse in fragments.

Likewise, "Snafu" was imagined—drawn from the many dogs who padded faithfully through the lives of wartime crews—symbols of loyalty, comfort, and kinship.

Although flight surgeons served on base, Captain Gannon himself is an invented figure, representing the quiet guardianship of wartime medicine.

The Christmas party described in the story—held on January 1, 1945, for the children of Oundle—did indeed take place on that date. Research confirms that a holiday meal was served and that the men saved up treats to offer as gifts. Other details of the celebration have been imagined.

Edwin Birtwell's love interest, Valerie, was a real person. Years later, a family member was able to locate her, and she provided the box of his photographs, as described in the Epilogue.

The monthly dances with the local women from Peterborough and Oundle did occur when missions allowed. They were a cherished reprieve in the midst of the uncertainties of war.

The description of the Chowhound missions—in which American planes dropped food for the starving Dutch—is accurate, including the now-famous tulip fields where the Dutch spelled out "Many Thanks" in gratitude. So, too, are the revival missions, which rescued Allied POWs from prison camps as the war neared its end. Mission notes reflect that Max, along with many others, actually did participate in a revival mission.

The Eagle, the pub mentioned in the story, is real and remains a historic gathering place in Cambridge, England. During the war, it was a popular haunt for men in the air force, who often signed their names on the ceiling or left behind small mementos. Many of those marks remain today. It is unknown whether any of the men portrayed in this story ever visited the pub, but it felt true to include it.

There is reference to an airman named Albert who lost his life when his oxygen source became disconnected. My research confirmed that this tragedy did occur, though the airman's story remains largely lost to history.

The bomb explosion at Metfield Air Base, as described, was based on a true incident.

Though imagined, the scene involving the bomber's belly landing in the English Channel and Perch's rescue that followed echoes real emergency landings made by crews in distress.

The incident in February 1945 involving two planes colliding during landing at Polebrook Air Base did happen, though the conversations around it were fictionalized. One of the bombers carried a crew that included Al Cantrelle—a real radio operator who lost his life that day, though his personality and character traits in this story were imagined. All members aboard that aircraft were lost. The vast majority of them had only been flying missions in England for a month. The full crew included: 2nd Lt. Rheinhold Vergen, First Officer Robert Sollers, First Officer Stanley Dietal, Sgt. Francis Leonard, Sgt. Emerald Cutting, Sgt. Joseph Ventress, Sgt. Philip Singleton, and S/Sgt Robert Wheatley.

The second aircraft carried: 1st Lt. Edward R. Ashton, First Officer George Bowman, 2nd Lt. Donald Cornell, 2nd Lt. John F. McNeill, S/Sgt. John Folks, T/Sgt. James Allman, Sgt. John Nelson, S/Sgt. Bruce Cook, Sgt. Harold Wieland, and Sgt. John Connelly. All were lost.

During a visit to the Imperial War Museum in Duxford, England, I came across a metal-bound Bible inscribed with the words "May this keep you safe from harm." According to the placard, it had been found at the crash site in Polebrook where these two bombers collided in midair. The Bible was said to have been kept in an airman's chest pocket—close to the heart, where it might shield against bullets. The original owner is unknown.

The film *Combat America* really was shown on base shortly after that collision, although whether its timing was intentional remains unknown.

The crash that ultimately claimed the lives of the crew en route back to the States—the very event this book builds toward—also truly occurred. It has been recreated to the best of my ability, based on the limited records and witness accounts that remain. The airmen portrayed on that plane all perished in the crash. Each was real. Each had a family, a history, a story. The descriptions in this novel are drawn from every detail I was able to gather, however sparse.

I'm especially indebted to Matthew Reeves, whose work—begun years ago under the name Matthew Rimmer—was foundational. Long before I ever began writing this, he had already traced the outlines: identifying the men, locating the crash site, and reaching out to families through handwritten letters. It was because of his efforts that a plaque now hangs near the crash site, offering a place of remembrance for all twenty men. His dedication created the very framework on which this story could be built.

David Rapoport's first mission was in March of 1945, but for the purposes of the timeline, he appears a few months earlier than he likely arrived.

The religious staff portrayed in the story who served on base were fictionalized characters, although the chaplain, Tom Richards, was a real person who served in the 351st. His characterization and actions, however, are imagined.

Ebrington Manor also truly existed—a stately home converted to a flak house, offering rest and respite for airmen during the war. The individuals Caruso met there were entirely imagined. While no official records confirm that he stayed at Ebrington, the timing of his missions suggests he likely spent time at such a place. It is also noted in mission logs that his position changed from ball turret gunner to waist gunner following a period of leave, providing a clue that recovery was part of his journey. Of note, the names Evie, Arthur, and Schleppy were borrowed from a family who selflessly offered help many years ago in Dover, Delaware, when my husband's family needed it.

The memorial visit to the crash site did not occur as portrayed in the story. However, I have long imagined what such a gathering might feel like—standing in that quiet space with others sharing the same loss. Over the course of my research, I've come to know several family members through email. Their generosity in sharing memories, photographs, and story fragments helped shape the humanity behind the names. Their loved ones became more than casualties of war; they became sons and brothers.

This entire project, in fact, began as a desire to better understand the men and the crash that took their lives. What I first set out to write and what I ended up writing are two very different things. Over the course of many years of research, this story grew, and so did my love for the men I never met. I may not know every detail of their lives, but I know this: they mattered deeply. They still do. Any remaining errors or misunderstandings in this book are entirely my own.

My husband and I have visited the crash site several times—first on our own, and later with Matt Reeves and John Lloyd. Their graciousness in walking that sacred ground with us, and in opening their hearts to this work, will always be remembered.

ACKNOWLEDGMENTS

I owe a debt of gratitude to Lieutenant Charles (Norm) Stevens, whose firsthand accounts of his time in the 351st Bomb Group as a bombardier were invaluable in helping me understand the realities of life in WW2 England. Our correspondence was a privilege, and I remain grateful for the kindness and candor he shared.

To the families of the real airmen—especially those who entrusted me with photographs, fragments, and memories—thank you. Your memories allowed me to see your loved ones not only as airmen, but as sons, brothers, musicians, storytellers, and friends. This story is shaped by your generosity.

To Tawnya Caldwell, who provided invaluable help in the first stages of bringing this story to life. Thank you for showing me where—and how—to begin. Your guidance became a compass, helping the words find their way.

To my parents, who saw possibilities in me long before I could see them myself. Their faith in me still lights the path.

To my husband, Stan, who first told me the story of his Uncle Mendy, and who has walked every step of this journey beside me. Your confidence in my ability to undertake this project was the catalyst for everything that followed. Thank you for letting me chase every dream—including visiting the places our boys might have wandered. You trusted the story before I knew where it would lead—and you were the first to believe the gate would open, even when I stood before it unsure. Thank you for your love, your patience, and your steadfast support.

To Elizabeth Ward, Rachael Mortimer, and Jennifer Kay Davies—thank you for your editorial insight, precision, and care in shaping these pages.

And to those who helped me find our boys—

To Matt Reeves, who honored their memory before most had ever heard it. You held the first thread and carried it forward for so many years. Your research became the tapestry that helped this story take flight. I'll be forever indebted to you for the care, detail, and reverence you brought to this legacy, and for creating and placing the plaque that now quietly commemorates them all.

To Lisa Jackson, my first dear friend on this journey, who found Matt when I thought I never would. Your perseverance shone a light on all that would come after. I will always be grateful that Lt. Stevens put us in contact!

To Anne Crabb, a true historian of the heart: thank you for your friendship, and for the treasure trove of information you preserved and so reverently shared. Your firsthand knowledge helped bring these men to life. I'm so grateful to know you!

To Bonnie Boyle, Joe Coons, Barbara-Ann Foley, J.D. Leasure, Larry Mathews, Lynn Dolski, Sheila Howerter, Katie Simmons, and Anthony Belef, thank you for so generously sharing memories of your loved ones. Whether through photographs, stories, or small, treasured details, your contributions helped me glimpse the men behind the uniforms. Those insights brought depth, warmth, and truth to the pages of this book. I'm deeply grateful.

To Robert Lloyd, who witnessed the crash in Wales and held a steadfast reverence for the men lost that day, my gratitude forever. And to his son, John Lloyd, who so faithfully carries on that legacy—preserving and protecting the place where their journey ended, and ensuring they are never forgotten. Thank you from the bottom of our hearts.

My thanks to the archivists, curators, and historians who preserve the legacy of the Eighth Air Force—especially the 351st Bomb Group Association, the National Museum of the Mighty Eighth, the Imperial War Museum at Duxford, the Cambridge American Cemetery, and the volunteers who quietly keep memory alive.

And to the boys across the pond—those who flew, and those who never made it home—this is for you. May we remember not just your sacrifice, but your laughter, your longing, and the love you left behind.

SELECTED REFERENCES

This story rests on the shoulders of many—not only the brave souls who lived it, but the historians, memoirists, and memory-keepers who preserved their world. The following sources helped me listen more closely to the past. Through them, I was able to better understand and absorb rhythms of speech, routines of flight, textures of daily life, and the enduring courage of men at war. I am profoundly grateful.

A special thank you to Lt. Charles "Norm" Stevens, whose memoirs offered not only historical clarity but emotional resonance. His recollections of Polebrook and life aboard the B-17 became a lifeline in shaping this story. I'm deeply honored to have corresponded with him before his passing.

Ayres, Travis L. *The Bomber Boys: Heroes Who Flew the B-17s in World War II*. NAL Caliber, 2005.

Berardi, Joseph R., Sr. and Berardi, Virginia. *Memoirs of My War Years 1941–1945*. 48HrBooks, 2013.

Childers, Thomas. *Wings of Morning*. Perseus Books, 1995.

Harbour, Ken and Harris, Peter. *The 351st Bomb Group in WWII: The Duty to Remember*. Cross Roads, 2008.

Hutchinson, T/Sgt James Lee. *The Boys in the B-17: 8th Air Force Combat Stories of WWII*. AuthorHouse, 2011.

Kaplan, Philip and Smith, Rex Alan. *One Last Look: A*

Sentimental Journey to the Eighth Air Force Heavy Bomber Bases of World War II in England. Artabras, 1990.

Lande, D. A. *From Somewhere in England.* Motorbooks International, 1990.

McNab, Chris. *The Mighty 8th At War.* Metro Books, 2017.

Pearce, A. J. *Dear Mrs. Bird.* Picador, 2019.

Stevens, Charles N. *An Innocent at Polebrook: A Memoir of an 8th Air Force Bombardier.* 1stBooks, 2004.

Stevens, Charles N. *The Innocent Cadet: Becoming a World War II Bombardier.* AuthorHouse, 2008.

Wilson, Kevin. *Blood and Fears: How America's Bomber Boys of the 8th Air Force Saved World War II.* Pegasus, 2017.

The following are selected online sources that were accessed between 2020 and 2025 during the ongoing research phase of this project. While some links may have changed, they remain listed here in acknowledgment of their contribution to the shaping of this story.

"Anatomy of a Bombing Mission," by Annette Tison, 392nd Bomb Group Memorial Association, https://www.b24.net/MissionAnatomy.htm.

"Army Air Force WWII Codes," The Military Yearbook Project, https://militaryyearbookproject.org/references/old-mos-codes/wwii-era/army-air-force-wwii-codes/aaf-mos-codes-wwii-era.

"The B-17 Ball Turret Gunner," The Arrowhead Club, https://thearrowheadclub.com/2021/12/29/the-b-17-ball-turret-gunner/.

"B-17 Ditching Procedures," 303rd Bomb Group (Heavy) Historical Society, https://www.303rdbg.com/ditch.html. (This detailed account of emergency landing procedures provided essential clarity for shaping key scenes in the novel.)

"Biography and Memories of Wally Hoffman," Justin Museum of Military History, https://www.justinmuseum.com/famjustin/WHoffmanbio.html.

"First US Army Rehabilitation Centre: Recuperation and Training at 8th Convalescent Hospital, Stoneleigh Park, Kenilworth, Warwickshire, UK, 1943," Imperial War Museum, https://www.iwm.org.uk/collections/item/object/205200448.

"How Britain's abandoned Anderson shelters are being brought back to life," The Guardian, https://www.theguardian.com/world/2018/aug/21/how-britains-abandoned-anderson-shelters-are-being-brought-back-to-life.

"In God I Trust: The Story of WWII B-17 Ball Turret Gunner Frank Perez," World War 2 History – Short Stories, https://ww2history.org/war-in-europe/in-god-i-trust-the-story-of-wwii-b-17-ball-turret-gunner-frank-perez/.

"Military Records and Family Archives," Ancestry, https://www.ancestry.com. (Used to confirm service details, enlistment dates, and family connections for several crew members.)

The Newspaper Archives of Stars and Stripes, https://starsandstripes.newspaperarchive.com.

"Operation Manna-Chowhound: Deliverance from Above," The National WWII Museum, New Orleans, https://www.nationalww2museum.org/war/articles/operation-manna-chowhound.

"The Points Were All That Mattered: The US Army's Demobilization After World War II," The National WWII Museum, New Orleans, https://www.nationalww2museum.org/war/articles/points-system-us-armys-demobilization.

"Polebrook AAF 351st Bomb Group," YouTube, https://www.youtube.com/watch?v=EzIlDHjaPsE.

"The Rehabilitation Program European Theater of Operations APO #871," WW2 US Medical Research Centre, https://www.med-dept.com/articles/the-rehabilitation-program-european-theater-of-operations-apo-871/.

"The Sperry Ball Turret," RootsWeb, https://freepages.rootsweb.com/~josephkennedy/military/sperry_ball_turret.htm.

"The Troopship *Queen Mary*," by Mildred A. MacGregor, excerpt from *World War II Memories: An Army Nurse's True Account*, University of Michigan Press, 2008, https://www.press.umich.edu/pdf/9780472033317-ch1.pdf.

"The Use of Rest Homes in the Eighth Air Force for the Two Year Period November 1942 to November 1944," Headquarters Eighth Air Force, Office of the Surgeon, APO 634, World War 2 Collection, https://worldwar2collection.com/wp-content/uploads/2013/02/Rest_Homes_Documents.pdf.

The following are selected historical/museum resources. These visits offered deep context and emotional resonance that shaped the writing of this novel.

Imperial War Museum, Duxford, England. Personal visit, archival review, and exhibit exploration.

National Museum of the Mighty Eighth Air Force, Pooler, Georgia. Personal visit, archival review, and exhibit exploration. Of special note was a transcript of remarks by Ben F. Love (National Conference of Christians and Jews Dinner, April 12, 1988), which included an account of a May 10, 1945, mission to Linz, Austria for the repatriation of French POWs.

Personal site visits (2025). Travel to key locations during research related to the 351st Bomb Group and this story's setting, including the former Polebrook Airfield and memorial site; the Eagle in Cambridge; the Cambridge American Cemetery; and Ebrington Manor in Gloucestershire, a former flak house (viewed externally).

www.ingramcontent.com/pod-product-compliance
Lightning Source LLC
Chambersburg PA
CBHW020933310726
48980CB00007B/749/J

* 9 7 9 8 9 9 3 4 6 3 0 2 5 *